GOOD vs. EVIL

A War
of the
Spirits

D0710118

ENDORSEMENTS

"Once again Jack Simpson has 'sounded the alarm' to awaken an apathetic America from her moral and spiritual slumber. *Good vs. Evil* takes us to the realm of the 'why' but doesn't leave us there for it deals with the 'what' and the 'how' for our nation's survival. This book is must reading for anyone anywhere who longs to see the restoration of our traditional and moral values."

—**Dr. O. S. Hawkins,** Pastor, First Baptist Church, Dallas, TX

"I must say that I was captivated by your sense of urgency as you deal with the issue of the unseen war. We are at war in these final days and *Good vs. Evil* exposes the battle plans of the enemy as none I have seen. I congratulate you on this outstanding work."

—**Dr. Larry L. Thompson,** Pastor, First Baptist Church, Ft. Lauderdale, FL

"This hard-hitting description of the plight of America at the end of the Twentieth Century is calculated to arouse the most complacent among us. Christian layman Jack B. Simpson exposes society's most virulent sores, and he offers the only prescription capable of healing them."

—**Dr. D. James Kennedy,** Coral Ridge Ministries, Fort Lauderdale, FL

"Jack has assembled a fascinating amount of material from contemporary sources to illustrate the seriously troubled times in our nation. The material is provocative and insightful. He calls for Christians to, again, be salt and light."

—**Dr. John F. MacArthur, Jr.,** Pastor-Teacher, Sun Valley, CA

"It is amazing to me how sometimes a Christian layman is able to see the spiritual conflicts that beset our modern America even more clearly and dramatically than does the preacher. You will find this to be true in this dynamic book by Jack B. Simpson. In the increasing and tragic collapse of America before the fierce and unmitigated onslaught of the minions of Satan, we desperately need this awakening book. May God grant that it helps to open the eyes of all the Lord's people, and may God also grant that the Holy Spirit will use it to awaken His people to the desperate needs of this tragic hour."

—**Dr. W. A. Criswell,** Chancellor, Criswell College, Dallas, TX

"A no nonsense look at America's darkest dangers and her brightest hope. *Good vs. Evil* is an easy read on the hard facts of Satan's hold on the rock music industry. A valuable resource for students and pastors . . . a must read for parents."

—**Rev. Woody Cumbie,** Pastor, Northside Baptist Church, Indianapolis, IN

"In a day when there is a massive gray of what's right and wrong, Jack Simpson gives us a point of reference for Christian thinking."

—**Rev. Steven W. James,** Pastor, First Baptist Church, Tompkinsville, KY

GOOD vs. EVIL

A War
of the
Spirits

Jack B. Simpson

Restoration Press
Santa Rosa, California

Restoration Press
a division of Vision Books International
3360 Coffey Lane, Santa Rosa, CA 95403
707-542-1440   800-377-3431   Fax 707-542-1004

All Scripture quotations, unless noted otherwise, are from the *Holy Bible: New International Version.* Copyright 1973, 1978, 1984, International Bible Society. Used by permission of Zondervan Bible Publishers.

Printed in the United States of America
99 98 97 96 95   6 5 4 3 2 1

Library of Congress Catalog Card Number 95-61213

ISBN 1-56550-023-7

CONTENTS

CONTENTS

ACKNOWLEDGMENTS

Without the help of others, *GOOD vs. EVIL: A War of the Spirits* would not have become a reality. Encouragement is important to any writer. Also, having someone willing to carefully read and seriously comment on the "rough drafts" required to compose a chapter of meaningful text is critical. The following people, in their own unique way, were very helpful to me in composing this volume:

My Family—Winona, my wife of 38 years. Without her understanding and patience concerning the endless hours of reading and research required to produce this volume, it would have been impossible. Our two daughters, *Janet* and *Angela,* provided much needed encouragement. Angela was especially helpful in the research effort. Our two sons, *Richard* and *Randall,* gave me their views and observations concerning the evil of rock music and how it had adversely affected some of their acquaintances.

O. S. Hawkins—my best friend. He is also my mentor. O. S. was pastor at First Baptist Church in Fort Lauderdale until 1993. He took me under his spiritual wing and showed me what Christian love—agape love—was all about. His true friendship and guidance have changed my life dramatically over the past eight years, second only to my Lord and Savior, Jesus Christ. Words cannot express how much I am indebted to O. S. His great leadership, his magnificent preaching, his outstanding knowledge of the Bible, and his godly character are envied by ministers of all denominations. O. S. is currently pastor of the First Baptist Church in Dallas, Texas.

Maxine Schenks—composing this book would have been a hopeless endeavor without Maxine's help. She is the primary reason you are holding this book in your hand. She spent endless hours reading the manuscript and correcting my mistakes. The many multi-hour telephone conversations concerning the text as it related to the Bible were especially helpful. Maxine is a remarkable lady and a Christian of the highest order. She is a retired college professor and will always have a special place in my heart. The best way to describe Maxine is to say, "she is a saint."

Loretta Katterhenry—my wife's sister. She was my biggest encourager, always there to give me a boost when it was needed. She poured over every word of the manuscript and gave me valuable ideas. Thank you, Loretta, for being such a great supporter.

Wanda Todd—a very special friend. Wanda was O. S. Hawkins' personal secretary for many years. She is now executive secretary to Dr. Larry Thompson, Pastor, First Baptist Church, Fort Lauderdale, FL. Wanda has in-depth knowledge of the Bible and was helpful to me in Scripture selection. I deeply appreciate the many hours she spent reading my drafts. Her honest comments were also helpful.

Kenneth L. Sackett—my publisher. Although we were unknown to each other at the outset, we quickly became close friends. Ken's first comment after reading the manuscript was "this contains a great message and we must share it with the world." He is a true believer in Jesus Christ, and I learned a lot from working with him. It was Ken's wise counsel that enabled me to put the "finishing touches" on the manuscript. I truly believe that God brought us together to publish this book. I know that we will both give all glory to our Lord and Savior, Jesus Christ.

PREFACE

The seeds were sown for this volume in 1992 after the completion of my first book entitled *Sounding the ALARM: Moral Decay in the U.S.A.* Dr. O. S. Hawkins, my friend and mentor, encouraged me to continue exposing the problems within our society today. He shares my concerns that the deterioration of personal responsibility, the loss of moral perspective, and the weakening of our sense of purpose in life are problems no nation can survive.

The unseen spiritual realm that surrounds us is not understood by many people, Christians included. It is my prayer that this volume will reveal to the reader that each of us, whether we realize it or not, is indeed involved in a war of the spirits. Satan is constantly present, waiting for an opportunity to attack and destroy every person on earth. However, the power of the Holy Spirit that resides within the believer is the most powerful force in the universe. When we place our trust in Jesus Christ, Satan cannot win.

This volume addresses the evil of rock music. Satan uses this medium to adversely affect the spiritual and physical lives of many people. However, the Holy Spirit can help anyone to overcome these adversities. Only through Christ can we be victorious in our daily battle with Satan. This point is detailed throughout the volume.

America's physical resources and our current level of wealth are unprecedented in history. But the very soul of the nation is being challenged today as never before. The American character is being tested at the core of its very being. Beyond the physical challenges, many find they are confronted by weapons that are emotional, ideological, and spiritual in nature. In some ways, this nation has grown older and wiser, but we are still surprisingly immature, without much experience in soul-searching.

We have allowed a vain and rationalistic view of man to infiltrate our homes and schools and to rob us of faith in the great Creator who is the source of Truth. We have denied the reality of the soul, and our spirits are dying.

People in all walks of life feel overwhelmed by the physical and emotional problems of today. They are faced with unprecedented problems. How are they to respond? What is happening to American culture? In the pages to come we will take a hard look at each of these questions.

Many catastrophic events are reviewed from a biblical perspective, such as the Kobe earthquake, massive flooding, the poison-gas episode in Tokyo, and the Oklahoma City bombing. The book reveals a rising tide of cults, many of which are led by fraudulent Christians. The deadly AIDS virus is discussed (now we must be concerned about another virus—the deadly Ebola virus has resurfaced in Zaire). We will see why the book of Revelation holds a powerful message for the world population today. It appears God is becoming impatient with the increasing sinful nature of Man.

The volume also explores the relationship between America's Christian heritage and our future hopes. If the warnings of George Washington, Benjamin Franklin, and the other great leaders of American history are valid, we already have reason to be worried about the prospects for this nation. The failure of American character is already a matter for serious concern, but when combined with a rise of lawlessness, growing immorality, corruption, and abuse in every area of society—and when compounded by the willful destruction of moral standards and ethical values— we have to recognize that we are in a state of national emergency. We cannot afford to look the other way any longer. There is too much at risk. We must stare into the face of reality. We have to recognize that the face in the mirror is our own. The future of America depends on what you and I decide today!

Our nation faces a crisis of moral authority. Christians have the hope and the promise of ultimate victory. It is time to become committed and reclaim America for Christ.

FOREWORD

As a Christian book publisher, I have the opportunity to look over a lot of materials submitted by new Christian writers in hopes of finding a publisher. In the case of Jack Simpson's manuscript, I decided to read his work myself instead of passing it on to a manuscript reviewer. *GOOD vs. EVIL* was a manuscript I could not put down until I completed it. This manuscript has what it takes to stir up the Christian and non-Christian alike.

This controversial Christian manuscript is filled with facts that should arouse conservatives, fundamentalists, and pentacostals. It certainly did in my own company. Everyone agreed it was hard hitting and would cause the reader to react. Even the non-saved were asked to read the book. They remarked that this book sure makes you see things differently.

In *Webster's New World Thesaurus*, the second synonym for "react" is "catch the flame" and it also directs the reader to see "feel" for further synonyms. I suggest you look up the true meaning. The Hebrew word is vada (pronounced "yaw-dah").

As humans we can live in denial, stating that all of the things happening around us are just coincidence. That's what people did in Noah's time. God has always given his people warnings and chances to make changes (Abraham/Lot, Sodom and Gomorrah).

In the old times of the Bible, prophets foretold what God was to destine. It hasn't changed in this period. *GOOD vs. EVIL* will open the eyes of every reader. It may even cause division. After all, in today's world, "What's bad is good, and what's good is bad."

Where do you stand with Good vs. Evil? Many people are actually falling victims to this war that is taking place in the heavens and here on earth. Without even being aware of it, they are falling right into the traps of the enemy. Young people by the thousands each week are lured into the excitement of the darkness. The enemy has penetrated the lines of moral America, turning its people into a blind race that is caught up in self-indulgence, self-love, and no respect for mankind. Values are at the place where most people don't care if they hurt anyone else.

The enemy Evil has crept into living rooms, bedrooms, schools, churches, government, boardrooms, media. There is no escaping Evil's purpose, "To Destroy all God has Ordained."

There is an escape from evil and its deadly grip. It is understanding how Good fights evil by exposing evil.

We welcome you to comment on this book both good and otherwise. Please feel free to address your comments to:

Restoration Press
c/o *Good vs. Evil*
3360 Coffey Lane
Santa Rosa, CA 95403

Thank you,

Kenneth L. Sackett, Sr.
Publisher

GOOD vs. EVIL: A War of the Spirits

SPIRITUAL
WARFARE

There have always been wars. All through recorded history we have read about warfare. One nation against another, one tribe against another, one ruler against another, the list is endless. Even today there are wars of all sorts and sizes raging around the world. You only need to check the evening news to get an update on the daily events relevant to the war of your concern. At this very moment, many people are being physically injured, maimed or killed, and property damage of substantial magnitude is occurring as a result of these wars.

However, this volume is dedicated to another war. It is called SPIRITUAL WAR and every one of us is involved in this battle. It is the most serious war in which we will ever be engaged because individually we will succeed or fail, and the outcome has eternal consequences.

The tragedy is that most people do not have any idea that they are involved in any kind of war. They do not even realize that there is an enemy or that there is anything going on, except what they see.

To many, seeing is believing, but that is not what the Bible teaches us. There are some things that cannot be seen but are very real.

The spiritual warfare that we all are involved in is a real war. The Bible teaches us to "Be self-controlled and alert. Your enemy the devil prowls around like a roaring

3

lion looking for someone to devour. Resist him, standing firm in the faith, because you know that your brothers throughout the world are undergoing the same kind of sufferings" (1 Peter 5:8–9).

Spiritual warfare involves everybody. The Bible says our enemy is not just Satan but a whole confederacy of evil spirits that make up the spirit world. "For our struggle is not against flesh and blood, but against the rulers, against the authorities, against the powers of this dark world, and against the spiritual forces of evil in the heavenly realms" (Ephesians 6:12).

When you are in spiritual warfare, the enemy is all around you. **Someone who says "I only believe that which I can see" is already in big trouble.** Our worst enemy sometimes is that which we cannot see. This enemy of ours does have certain limitations. Neither the devil nor any of his angels are omniscient or omnipotent. Those limitations will ultimately bring him and his troops down to the bottomless pit of hell where they will burn for eternity.

Satan is working day and night in his attempt to destroy the kingdom of God and that is why he epitomizes himself in rulers of nations to bring about war. They become demonically controlled and all they think about is power and jurisdiction. His reason for falling as an angel was because he wanted the same power that God Himself has. Satan believed that there can be two Gods. That's the kind of enemy we have.

Satan has four objectives. The first one is to cause us to doubt the Word of God. When a person begins to doubt the Word of God he opens himself up to problems. Satan deceived Eve in the Garden of Eden by urging her to question the Word of God.

Satan's second objective is to distract us from spiritual things by focusing on things that are material, or sensual, or not spiritual. He keeps us so busy that we don't have time for spiritual things. Our free will gets us into trouble.

Satan's third objective is to disable us in the Lord's service. He leads us to a point of sinful temptation and then constantly harasses us about our worthiness, and finally we just give in.

Satan's fourth objective is to destroy us physically. He lures us into alcohol and drugs which result in all sorts of damage. He tries to destroy us in every possible way.

Satan cannot destroy a child of God. However, he can put us in such a handicapped position that we become absolutely worthless. His primary strategy is deception, bringing us to believe something that is not true.

How can you be deceived if you have Christ in your heart? Well, the Bible teaches us to test the spirits. "Test everything. Hold on to the good. Avoid every kind of evil" (1 Thessalonians 5:21–22).

Human beings are very gullible, and counterfeiting is a profitable occupation for many deceivers. But spiritual counterfeits are the most dangerous of all and at times the most difficult to detect.

There are also counterfeit Christians who are "false brothers" (2 Corinthians 11:26), as well as the "false teachers" (2 Peter 2:1–2), and "false apostles" (2 Corinthians 11:13). They preach "peace, peace, when there is no peace" (Jeremiah 6:14), and some will "perform great signs and miracles to deceive even the elect—if that were possible" (Matthew 24:24).

Satan himself is the greatest counterfeiter, for he "deceived the whole world" (Revelation 12:9) in his attempt to become a counterfeit God. Thus the Bible warns, "Dear friends, do not believe every spirit, but test the spirits to see whether they are from God, because many false prophets have gone out into the world. This is how you can recognize the Spirit of God: Every spirit that acknowledges that Jesus Christ has come in the flesh is from God, but every spirit that does not acknowledge Jesus is not from God. This is the spirit of the antichrist, which you have heard is coming and even now is already in the world.

"You, dear children, are from God and have overcome them, because the One who is in you is greater than the one who is in the world. They are from the world and therefore speak from the viewpoint of the world, and the world listens to them. . . . This is how we recognize the Spirit of truth and the spirit of falsehood" (1 John 4:1–6).

There is a spirit world out there that is not of God. Every wicked thing that comes through your mind does not come from your heart. Satan harasses us to make us think we aren't worthy. If you are a child of God you have the power to reject these thoughts. Compare what you hear to the Word of God, and if it doesn't match up to the whole Scripture, then don't believe it. **The Scripture is one message from the beginning to the end.**

How does Satan deceive us? The Bible is very clear when it says: "Do not be deceived: God cannot be mocked. A man reaps what he sows. The one who sows to please his sinful nature, from that nature will reap destruction; the one who sows to please the Spirit, from the Spirit will reap eternal life" (Galatians 6:7–8). Here the Word of God is instructing us not to be deceived into thinking that we can sin against God and not suffer the consequences. Satan's deception is for us to not look beyond the temptation. Just take what you want and don't look beyond that. However, God clearly says that we will reap what we sow.

There is a spirit world out there that is not of God

What is Satan's next deception? He will try to deceive us into thinking our evil temptation is God's work! The Bible says: "When tempted, no one should say, 'God is tempting me.' For God cannot be tempted by evil, nor does He tempt anyone; but each one is tempted when, by his own evil desire, he is dragged away and enticed. Then, after desire has conceived, it gives birth to sin; and sin, when it is full-grown, gives birth to death" (James 1:13–15).

More than likely if you are blaming temptation on God it is because you are yielding to it. If you lust after something it will ultimately turn to sin unless it is checked. The

Scripture says, "Do not be misled: 'Bad company corrupts good character'" (1 Corinthians 15:33). We need to be bold and brave and separated. Before we become a part of anything we should ask, "What is this and where will it lead me? Do I want to become what they are?" Every habit begins with a single act.

If you think that the world's wisdom is the way to live, then you are deceived. Most of the world's ways are an antithesis to the Word of God. The Word teaches us, "Do not deceive yourselves. If any one of you thinks he is wise by the standards of this age, he should become a 'fool' so that he may become wise. For the wisdom of this world is foolishness in God's sight. It is written: 'He catches the wise in their craftiness'" (1 Corinthians 3:18–19).

Why do bad things look so good? Many people have always been fascinated by things that are off limits. Things they shouldn't do often look better than the things they should do. Bad things look good because they offer us a quick fix to painful feelings.

One reason forbidden things look so good to us is because evil spiritual forces in the universe have the power to give them a glitter that attracts. **Satan is evil and he tries to make evil look good.** He will use any means he can to bring us under his power. When we are devoted to someone or something other than God, we are involved in idolatry. When we turn from God to idols, He doesn't stand in our way. Instead, He hands us over to our lustful cravings. He allows us to become consumed with our passions. He not only lets us have what we want, but He allows us to stuff ourselves with it until we realize how helpless we are without Him. God allows Satan to try to prove his point. The Bible says, "There will be trouble and distress for every human being who does evil . . ." (Romans 2:9).

There are many people who claim they are Christians but live according to the world's standards. False Christians are doing the same as Satan, saying there can be more than one God! However, in the Bible we are commanded not to conform ourselves to the values and the philosophies of this world. No one should be deceived—the values a person adopts will either bless his life or curse it. Jesus Christ is always present and He is recording our every action.

Jesus also said that each of us will finally be accountable to Him alone and that He will hold us responsible for what we did with the life He gave us. We cannot escape the day of judgment before Jesus Christ.

Genuine *demonic* power is acknowledged in the Scriptures. We are instructed to take a strong stand against Satan and ". . . against the powers of this dark world and against the spiritual forces of evil in the heavenly realms" (Ephesians 6:12).

Satan's deception is for us not to look beyond the temptation

In addition to the Bible, history and personal experience demonstrate that there is a Satan. He is a finite spirit being, a creature of pure energy not hindered by a physical body. Around him are gathered millions of other 'energy beings' (demons) who can kill, mutilate or possess the bodies and minds of human beings. This vast horde of extra-dimensional energy-beings is the force behind Satan and his kingdom. They represent him in the spiritual warfare that we are talking about in this volume.

In many cases, Scripture explicitly cites Satan or his demons as the reality behind idolatry and false religion. Moses tells us in Deuteronomy 32:16, "They made Him jealous with their foreign gods and angered Him with their detestable idols."

As we have seen, the Scripture speaks of the reality of a personal devil and myriads of demons who have "great power" and who should be regarded as cunning enemies of all men. One of the devil's key tactics is to masquerade as "an angel of light" or as a servant of righteousness.

Yes, we must test the spirits according to the Word of God. "Beloved, do not believe every spirit, but test the spirits to see whether they are from God." The Bible tells us to "Be joyful always; pray continually; give thanks in all circumstances, for this is God's will for you and me in Christ Jesus.

"Do not put out the Spirit's fire; do not treat prophecies with contempt. Test everything. Hold on to the good. Avoid every kind of evil.

"May God Himself, the God of peace, sanctify you through and through. May your whole spirit, soul and body be kept blameless at the coming of our Lord Jesus Christ." (1 Thessalonians 5:16–23).

Good will always win over evil if the above instructions from the Holy Scriptures are followed. And each of us can be victorious in our daily encounter with Satan in this war of the spirits.

GOD
AND
SATAN
CHAPTER TWO
THE TWO
KINGDOMS

The Bible tells us there are two "kingdoms" on earth—Satan's kingdom and God's kingdom. The Bible also teaches us a great deal about Satan (the devil) and his kingdom. Further, the Bible asserts that Satan has a kingdom that is hostile to Christ's kingdom. Each of these "kingdoms" will be evaluated and discussed throughout this volume. It will be made clear that every person on Planet Earth, whether they realize it or not, belongs to one of these kingdoms. **THERE ARE NO EXCEPTIONS!**

So, let's open the Holy Bible, the inerrant Word of God, and see what the Scriptures teach us about Satan or the devil.

The devil is seen to be an apostate (false, disloyal) angel who fell from heaven. ". . . I saw Satan fall like lightning from heaven" (Luke 10:18). "And the angels who did not keep their positions of authority but abandoned their own home—these he [God] has kept in darkness, bound with everlasting chains for judgment on the great Day" (Jude 6). "The great dragon was hurled down—that ancient serpent called the devil or Satan, who leads the whole world astray. He was hurled to the earth, and his angels with him" (Revelation 12:9).

When we come to know the Lord Jesus Christ, we move from one authority to another and from one kingdom to another. We move out of the kingdom of the devil into the kingdom of God. This is when A WAR OF THE SPIRITS begins. We enter warfare when we become children of God because our allegiance changes. We have become a threat to the kingdom of Satan. Therefore, we become his enemy instead of his pawn. The greater our determination to be God's instruments or soldiers, the greater our threat is to the kingdom of Satan.

The Lord Jesus gives us His plan in Acts 26:18 with these instructions: "to open their eyes and turn them from darkness to light, and from the power of Satan to God, so that they may receive forgiveness of sins and a place among those who are sanctified by faith in me [God]."

The devil seems to be very successful in his warfare against Christians. Satan has had his ultimate coup by getting people out of the Scriptures. He has pulled them away from a personal, intimate relationship with God that is found only through studying His Word. Everything dealing with victory in warfare is based on our relationship to Christ—we are in Christ and He is in us—and our relationship to the Word of God. Everything about the protective armor of God needed in our warfare against Satan is clearly outlined in the Bible.

Many Christians are not doers. They often say: "I don't want to study spiritual warfare because I don't want to be at war with the enemy." However, the Bible says, "Do not merely listen to the Word, and so deceive yourselves. **Do what it says"** (James 1:22). (Emphasis added.)

Another tactic of the enemy besides getting us away from the Bible is fear. That is why Paul told Timothy in 2 Timothy 1:7 that God has not given us the spirit of fear, but He's given us power in Christ. He's given us love, which is our security; and He's given us a sound mind. We can never exhaust God's resources. He has an eternal grip on our lives. No need is too great for His omnipotence (power), His omniscience (knowledge), His omnipresence (presence).

The reason people are frightened of spiritual warfare is that they are blinded and really don't understand what warfare is about. They are ignorant of the truth. They think they can bury their heads in the sand and not be troubled with spiritual warfare. Instead, they are real targets for the devil. When he charges in, they don't know it's him because they have their heads buried in the proverbial sand. As long as Satan can keep us ignorant of his schemes, we won't deal with them as spiritual warfare and, therefore, we won't have the victory.

Probably all of us, at one time or another, have felt like we've been defeated in our Christian lives. This usually occurs when we are not walking by the Holy Spirit.

The Scripture teaches that a Christian is commanded to walk by the Spirit. It is not an option but is an imperative command: "So I say, live by the Spirit, and you will not gratify the desires of the sinful nature" (Galatians 5:16). The emphasis of this message is that God empowers us for the life that He's called us to live.

Basically, the Christian has three enemies: the world, the flesh, and the devil. Satan uses the world and the flesh to try to prove to God that saved people do not love Him and that Grace is null and void, therefore, he is their master and their god. The devil is very powerful. His purpose is to lure us into his kingdom and destroy us. Yes, Satan rules the earth, but know this, it is a temporary position.

This world system in which you and I live, until our Lord Jesus Christ returns, is a society without God! The first two enemies mentioned above are external, and there is not a great deal that we can do to change them. However, we are instructed in the Bible: ". . . do not grieve the Holy Spirit of God, with whom you were sealed for the day of redemption" (Ephesians 4:30).

The devil seems to be very successful in his warfare against Christians

As long as we keep our desires in the sphere of God's will, everything works fine. When we begin to desire those things that are outside of God's permissive will, we get into trouble. Because our human side is still there we have the potential to sin against God at any given moment. That's why the Holy Spirit of God came to live within us. So that when we are tested, tempted, or tried, we have the privilege of relying upon the indwelling presence of the Holy Spirit to enable us to say no to sin and yes to God.

"For it is by grace you have been saved, through faith—and this not from yourselves, it is the gift of God—not by works, so that no one can boast" (Ephesians 2:8–9). When we receive the Lord Jesus Christ as our personal Savior, that's the work of grace. It is not something that we've earned but is a gift from God. Sure, before we were saved Satan's power had a grip on us; but when we received Christ that grip was broken and the presence and the power of the Holy Spirit came into our lives.

"For the sinful nature desires what is contrary to the Spirit, and the Spirit what is contrary to the sinful nature. They are in conflict with each other, so that you do not do what you want" (Galatians 5:17).

"The acts of the sinful nature are obvious: sexual immorality, impurity and debauchery; idolatry and witch-craft; hatred, discord, jealousy, fits of rage, selfish ambition, dissensions, factions and envy; drunkenness, orgies, and the like. I warn you, as I did before, that those who live like this will not inherit the kingdom of God" (Galatians 5:19–21). Sometimes Satan will accuse us as well as God of break-ing these points, jealousy and drunkenness, for example.

Satan will launch his most vicious attack where we drop our guard. That is why God said walk by the Spirit and you will not yield to the flesh and you won't give in to those strong desires when they come and seem to be irresistible.

"But the fruit of the Spirit is love, joy, peace, patience, kindness, goodness, faithfulness, gentleness and self-con-trol. Against such things there is no law. Those who belong to Christ Jesus have crucified the sinful nature with its passions and desires" (Galatians 5:22–23). This is what we are capable of when the Holy Spirit of God is in control.

We must walk by the Spirit in our daily lives as we

continually make decisions. We must rely upon the Holy Spirit to enable us to walk obediently before God. If we walk by the Spirit, we will not fulfill the lust of the flesh. This will allow us to live a life that is pleasing and honorable and victorious in our battle against the kingdom of Satan.

Today, as never before, the world is blind because it sees the ungodly acts of Christians and they do not seem to repent. Satan has many ways in which he blinds us.

First, the lost are blinded. One of Satan's tactics is to blind the unbelievers so they can't see the gospel.

"And even if our gospel is veiled, it is veiled to those who are perishing. The god of this age has blinded the minds of unbelievers, so that they cannot see the light of the gospel of the glory of Christ, who is the image of God" (2 Corinthians 4:3–4).

Second, Satan blinds us by keeping us from the Word. He gives us false teachers, and he raises up a host of people disguising themselves as children of God. "But I am afraid that just as Eve was deceived by the serpent's cunning, your minds may somehow be led astray from your sincere and pure devotion to Christ" (2 Corinthians 11:3).

Satan deceived Eve by causing her to question the veracity of God's Word and God's love and care for her. Likewise, Satan will put thoughts in our minds of anything that could keep us from trusting God and walking in total submission to Him. He causes us, in a sense, to fear God in an unholy way while convincing us that we can run our own lives by being our own gods.

How does a person find the right balance with spiritual warfare? In her excellent book, *Lord, Is It Warfare? Teach Me To Stand,* Kay Arthur[1] centers on the book of Ephesians. However, she provides balance by masterfully covering Scripture from Genesis to Revelation. Many people tend to focus on Ephesians 6 where it talks about putting on the full armor of God, but they do not empha-

---

1 Kay Arthur. *Lord, Is It Warfare? Teach Me To Stand.* (Portland, OR: Multnomah, 1991).

size that Ephesians first establishes what their **position** is in Christ.

In establishing their position in Christ, Paul provides the balance to what he says at the end of Ephesians, which concerns spiritual warfare. As we analyze this war of the spirits, this battle of good versus evil, we too will be visiting the book of Ephesians as we study the whole Word of God in preparing our defense against the evil kingdom of Satan and his demons.

For example, in Psalm 121: 5, 7–8, the Bible says, "The Lord watches over you . . . The Lord will keep you from all harm—he will watch over your life; the Lord will watch over your coming and going both now and forevermore."

One of Satan's tactics is to blind the unbelievers so they can't see the gospel

One of the most precious doctrines in all of Scripture is that of the secure position of the believer in Christ Jesus. Nothing in all creation is "able to separate us from the love of God that is in Christ Jesus our Lord" (Romans 8:39).

Let's look at what the Bible teaches us in Ephesians, Chapter 5: "Be imitators of God, therefore, as dearly loved children and live a life of love, just as Christ loved us and gave himself up for us as a fragrant offering and sacrifice to God.

"But among you there must not be even a hint of sexual immorality, or of any kind of impurity, or of greed, because these are improper for God's holy people. Nor should there be obscenity, foolish talk or coarse joking, which are out of place, but rather thanksgiving. For of this you can be sure: No immoral, impure or greedy person—such a man is an idolater—has any inheritance in the kingdom of Christ and of God. Let no one deceive you with empty words, for because of such things God's wrath comes on those who are disobedient. Therefore, do not be partners with them.

"For you were once darkness, but now you are light in the Lord. Live as children of light" (Ephesians 5:1–8). As you can see from these verses, as Christians and being a part of the kingdom of God, we must be a proper and holy people in the eyes of God. And from this position in Christ we will be very effective soldiers for Him and surely be victorious in our battle against Satan and his troops.

We must not forget that basically the Christian has three enemies: **the world,** which wants us to conform to its corrupt ways; **the flesh,** which is weak and becomes vulnerable to lustful desires but is handled by our walking constantly in the Spirit of God; and **the devil,** who always tempts us, but whom we are to resist at all times.

Satan uses several avenues to harass us. His primary pathway is through our minds. This is where spiritual warfare is so subtle. We think an attack by demons will be obvious. We think of people screaming, falling on the floor, or foaming at the mouth because we see these examples in the gospels. The enemy, in a sense, uses the fear of the demonic to keep us from studying spiritual warfare. We think we are going to have all of these horrible experiences but he is far more indirect than that.

Our warfare is not against other people. The Bible teaches us that it's against principalities, against the powers of this dark world, and against the spiritual forces of evil in the heavenly realms. As Christians we have God-given protection to overcome these assaults through the Holy Spirit. All we have to do is put on the armor of God and be strong in the Lord and in His mighty power.

The armor the child of God is to put on is defined by Paul in the sixth chapter of Ephesians. We are to gird our loins with truth. Then there is the helmet of salvation. This protects our minds against Satan's accusations. We are also to take up the shield of faith and the sword of the Spirit which is God's Word.

Standing with our loins girded by truth and holding up the shield of faith, truth of the inerrant Word of God, we can defeat any assault that Satan and his multitude of evil spirits may launch.

Satan was defeated at the cross. This is what so many

people, Christians included, don't realize. In John 16:11, the Bible tells us that the ruler of this world, Satan and his kingdom, has been judged. The devil was defeated at Calvary because the blood of Jesus Christ took care of our sin. Sin is what gives Satan power in our lives. That is why he wants to entice us into sin, and that is why we have to put on the breastplate of righteousness which is our new position in Christ. It declares us totally accepted by God despite our erratic behavior.

Satan has very precise schemes orchestrated to frustrate believers in Christ. We can thwart his shrewd tactics and walk in victory by recognizing and understanding his ploys. The devil seeks to impede our spiritual progress by keeping us from prayer. He accomplishes this by propagating a doctrine of guilt. When we are overloaded with guilty feelings, we withdraw from God. This is Satan's cruel hoax. Our guilt, all of it, was placed on Christ at Calvary. We are completely accepted by God.

Satan's other primary stratagem is to foil our walk with Christ by causing us to doubt God's promises. This human weakness that we have is not outside God's power. It is not outside His wisdom. It is not outside His love. Evil may seem to reign, but God overrules evil for His purposes.

Born into sin, man suffers from the emotional and spiritual wreckage of life apart from God, driven by wayward desires and instincts, walking in the darkness of his own counsel. The spiritual conflict, the war of the spirits, hinges upon faith. Do we really believe God will do what He says? Will He honor His Word? Can we rely on the Scriptures without reservation and expect God to fulfill His pledges? Absolutely. God's word came directly from Him. It is His unalterable Word to us.

In this secular society in which we live today too many people are trying to find "themselves" rather than Jesus Christ. They do not realize that true peace and happiness can only be found in a personal and intimate relationship with God through Jesus Christ.

Sin gives Satan power. That is the way he gained power

over Eve. When she sinned she moved into Satan's world. Our escape from the kingdom of Satan is the forgiveness of sin through the shed blood of Jesus Christ. "Since the children have flesh and blood, He too shared in their humanity so that by His death He might destroy him who holds the power of death, that is, the devil" (Hebrews 2:14).

Satan hates the cross because what seemed to be his ultimate moment of triumph was his ultimate moment of defeat. Christ's blood was shed there for our sins, allowing us to overcome Satan by the blood of the Lamb and by the word of our testimony.

What is our testimony? Our testimony is 1 John 4:4: "Ye are of God, little children, and have overcome them: because greater is He that is in you, than he that is in the world" (KJV). Our testimony is Ephesians 1:20–23 in that we are seated with Christ in heavenly places above all principalities and powers and spiritual wickedness in high places. All of the devil's authority is subject to Christ; Satan has been put under His feet.

Since we are one with Christ, the power of Satan is underneath us. We are safe in Christ. In Christ we have authority over the enemy and his kingdom. Satan does not have the power of death over us any longer because we belong to the kingdom of Jesus Christ.

Christians face many problems. Most of us do not realize Satan's tactics. We don't understand the subtlety of spiritual warfare. We forget that he is the accuser, and he targets our minds. We fail to recognize whether a thought or suggestion is of God or a lie from Satan.

There are only two options: Perfection—God. Imperfection—Satan.

There are only two followings: God's following—small. Satan's following—large (read Matthew 7:13–14).

Ultimately there are two kingdoms and two types of people: those in God's kingdom who have been redeemed by God and those in Satan's kingdom who are trying to redeem themselves. The kingdom of God holds to one supreme commandment, "Love the Lord your God with all your heart and with all your soul and with all your mind and with all your strength" (Mark 12:30). The kingdom of Satan can be reduced to one essential law—"Do what thou wilt."

People who follow Satan simply deny the love and authority of God. They follow the sinful ways of the world. Always seeking love, peace and contentment but never finding it (read Ephesians 2:2–3).

GOOD vs. EVIL, a war of the spirits, is an issue that every individual must deal with. It is a daily battle and it will be won only by daily choices of obedience to God. We must all remember that any spirit other than the Holy Spirit of Jesus Christ is an EVIL SPIRIT!

SATANISM
CHAPTER THREE
IN AMERICA

Satanism is a fast growing teenage subculture phenomenon, and not just among metalhead underachievers. Intelligent, upper-middle-class honor students and covert adults in every professional vocation are involved. Concurrently, self-styled and self-generated Satanic cults are becoming more brazenly obvious in their recruitment of youth.

Whether Satan exists is a matter of belief. But we are certain that Satanism exists. To some people it is a religion, and to others it's the practice of evil in the devil's name. It exists and it's surely flourishing.

It is teenagers who are most likely to fall under the spell of this mixture of dark and violent emotions called Satanism. And in some cases they are driven to committing extremely bad deeds.

Satanism is more than a hodgepodge of mysticism and fantasy, more than an annual Halloween party. It is a violent impulse that preys on the emotionally vulnerable, especially teenagers, who are often lonely and feel rejected.

Satanism attracts the angry, the frustrated, and the powerless. They often descend into secret lives—possessed by an obsessive fascination with sex, drugs, alcohol, heavy metal rock music, and the supernatural.

Often Satanism seems to be a personal psychodrama, a kind of license for strange, sometimes violent behavior. Sometimes it is just half-baked mumbo-jumbo and scrawled symbols. But other times it goes deeper and is far more deadly.

Satanism goes far beyond teenage obsession. We've seen that Satanism can be linked to dope and pornography, child abuse, and murder. It has led seemingly normal teenagers into monstrous behavior. Some merely preach mysticism. Others, however, practice the horrifying kinds of evil. Although occult practices are as ancient as man, Satanism is a fast-growing subculture movement in the teenage community. Unlike the temporarily mimicked dress style of rock idols, Satanism among the young is here to stay. But where will it lead? I predict this will become the most hideous and horrendous reality for educators, parents, and teens themselves to deal with in this decade as we enter the twenty-first century.

How many of these kids are recruited, some of their personal stories, and how we can protect our own children from falling prey is carefully and meticulously set forth by expert law enforcement personnel. Jerry Simandl, a veteran specialist of the Chicago Police Department's Gang Crime Unit, reports that there are four distinct levels of the Satanic movement in America. They are:

1. THE TEENAGE DABBLERS. These are young people who have preoccupation with the occult through involvement with fantasy role-playing games, suggestive heavy metal music, drugs, seances (attempts to communicate with the spirits of the dead), and a quest for power. The teenage dabbler faithfully studies the *Satanic Bible* and has made it one of the best-selling paperbacks in America for the past twenty years. According to Avon Books of New York, as of February 1992, **the *Satanic Bible* is in its twenty-seventh printing with over 700,000 copies sold!** He or she is usually above average in intelligence and generally a loner. Occasionally there may be a small sect of friends (i.e., a coven). The dabbler practices chants, incantations, and reads many occult books, including *Satanic Rituals* and *The Complete Witch,* by Anton LaVey, among many others.

2. SELF-STYLED SATANIC GROUPS OR COVENS. Teens are recruited through free drugs and sex parties where they

are told only a select few may enter a special room. During the party the person is photographed or videotaped in a "compromising" situation. Then, if invited into the special room, candidates are gradually told about a contract with Satan. If they hesitate to join, they are told the photo or videotape will be used against them.

Who are the recruiters? Stereo-typical normal adults employed in every vocation in a community, but in reality, undercover Satanists. Sounds fantastic, doesn't it? And if it weren't so frequently reported and verified, we wouldn't be apt to believe it.

3. PUBLIC RELIGIOUS SATANISTS. Whether theatrical or truly intellectual adherents, these people attend the "First Satan Church," etc. (Michael Aquino and Anton LaVey are two prominent people in this category). Their number is surely growing. There are hundreds of comparable religious Satanic groups in cities everywhere. Since they are incorporated as nonprofit, religious organizations they enjoy a tax-exempt status similar to a church or synagogue. The United States military even recognizes the Church of Satan. The most damaging contribution of this group is that their writings sell in the millions.

Debra Winger's gripping portrayal of the devastating shock she experienced upon learning of the intricate organization and high level members of the Ku Klux Klan in the movie "Betrayed," mirrors what could take our breath away if we only knew the full scope of this Satanic group.

The United States military even recognizes the Church of Satan

4. THE HARDCORE SATANIC CULTS. This group has always been with us. They are internationally located throughout the world. Perhaps more organized than the Mafia, they are known to kill, abduct and brainwash in great secrecy.

Dr. Al Carlisle of the Utah State Prison System has estimated that between forty and sixty thousand human beings are unmercifully killed through ritual homicides in the United States each year. This statistic is based upon estimating the number of Satanists at the level where they commit ritual human sacrifices times the frequency with which such sacrifices would be made during a Satanic calendar year. Dr. Carlisle estimated that in the Las Vegas metropolitan area alone, over six hundred people meet their deaths during Satanic ceremonies each year!

As you can see from the above report, the new category of "ritualistic oriented" crime is quickly establishing itself in police bureaus everywhere. The buzz word is "power."

During the past 30 years America has experienced a significant increase in Satanism

Of the various hazards that people face in a lifetime, from a broken leg to a car accident, some of the most serious dangers arise from enemies that are invisible—bacteria, viruses, etc. The AIDS epidemic has recently given everyone a new appreciation for the power of invisible enemies. We rarely see these invisible invaders; we see only their effects, the ruin they leave in their wake. A virus "tricks" the cell into believing that it is a "good" entity, so the cell lets down its defenses and "accepts" the invader. Only when it is inside, is the virus discovered to be a Trojan Horse, an invading parasite which begins the process of destroying its host.

The Satanic revival in our land is a spiritual AIDS, an AIDS of the soul. In many ways Satanic activity is similar to an unperceived virus operating within the human organism: It may exist for some period without producing symptoms, or it may kill quickly. Whichever it does, it means certain death for those terminally infected and an uncertain and precarious existence for those who have the virus within them but are currently without symptoms. **Apart from treatment, Satanism will kill spiritually just as effectively as AIDS will kill physically.** The only difference is that there is a cure for Satanic involvement: repentance and faith in Jesus Christ. Only Christ holds the key that will free you from the bondage of Satan and his demons.Throughout the past 30 years America has experienced a significant revival of Satanism. C. A. Burland, a science and history writer with the British Museum for 40 years acknowledges that "at no time in the history of civilization has Satanism and its various forms been so widely practiced as today."[1] Noted theologian Dr. Merrill Unger (Ph.D., Johns Hopkins University), the author of four books on the occult, asserts that, "The scope and power of modern occultism staggers the imagination."[2]

In his *The Second Coming: Satanism in America,* acclaimed novelist Arthur Lyons discloses, ". . . Satanic cults are presently flourishing in possibly every major city in the United States and Europe. . . . The United States probably harbors the fastest growing and most highly-organized body of Satanists in the world."[3]

Some startling details of this growing Satanic network are revealed in award-winning investigative reporter Maury Terry's book, *The Ultimate Evil.* Terry warns us: "There is compelling evidence of the existence of a nationwide network of Satanic cults, some aligned more closely than others. Some are purveying narcotics; others have branched into child pornography and violent sadomasochistic crime, including murder. I am concerned that the toll of innocent victims will steadily mount unless law enforcement officials recognize the threat and face it."[4]

---

1 C. A. Burland. *Beyond Science.* (New York: Grossett and Dunlap, 1972), p. 9.

2 Merrill F. Unger. *Demons in the World Today.* (Wheaton, IL: Tyndale House, 1972), p. 18.

3 Arthur Lyons. *The Second Coming: Satanism in America.* (New York: Dodd, Mead, 1970), pp. 3, 5.

4 Maury Terry. *The Ultimate Evil: An Investigation into America's Most Dangerous Satanic Cult.* (Garden City, NY: Dolphin/Doubleday, 1987), p. 511.

Unfortunately, Satanism, witchcraft, santeria, voodoo, and other "hard-core" forms of the occult are only the proverbial tip of the iceberg. If we were to consider the mediums, clairvoyants, psychics, channelers, spiritists, diviners, mystics, gurus, shamans, psychical researchers, yogis, psychic and holistic healers, etc., only then would we have a better grasp of the actual size of the modern revival of the occult.

UFO, near-death and past-life experiences, astral travel, astrology, mysticism, energy channeling, Yoga, psychic healing, Ouija boards, tarot cards, contact with the dead, and a thousand other occult practices dot the modern American landscape. As stated earlier, the Bible explicitly cites Satan and his demons as the reality behind these false religions.

The Bible also points out the reality of a personal devil and myriads (incalculable, infinite) of demons who have "great power" and who should be regarded as cunning enemies of all men. Folks, this is REALLY SPIRITUAL WARFARE and it should be taken seriously.

Not surprisingly, Gallup, Roper, and Greely polls have shown that tens of millions of people are interested in occult subjects or have had occult experiences.[5]

For example, a University of Chicago national opinion poll revealed that 67 percent of Americans "now profess a belief in the supernatural," and that 42 percent "believe that they have been in contact with someone who died."[6] Even Jim Jones, who engineered the slaughter of over 900 people in Jonestown, Guyana also "believed that he was guided by a supernatural spirit."[7]

---

5 Numerous polls have been conducted over the last two decades; contact the Gallup, Roper, and the University of Chicago's National Opinion Research Council organizations, respectively.

6 This was a national poll conducted by the University of Chicago's National Opinion Research Council; see the report in Andrew Greely, "Mysticism Goes Mainstream," *American Health*, January–February 1987.

7 Cited in *Christianity Today*, December 15, 1978, p. 38.

Also, the ABC News program "20/20" on May 16, 1985, ran a segment titled "The Devil Worshipers." It alleged that Satanism was "being practiced all across the country" with perverse and "hideous acts that defy belief" including "suicide, murders, and the ritualistic slaughter of children and animals."[8]

Rose Hall Warnke, wife of former Satanist high priest Mike Warnke, has written a sequel to his gruesome *The Satan Seller* titled *The Great Pretender*. In it she claims the following:

1. Documentation for 75 murders committed by Satanists in 1984.
2. The necessity for human sacrifice to move up in the ranks.
3. Cannibalism: "They tear out part of the heart and take it in their hands. Then, they tear a part off and eat it, just like an animal would do."
4. Numerous death threats from Satanists.
5. Infiltration of the church, e.g.: There is a professor of a college in a mountain state who has a Christian radio show where you can call in and get Christian counseling. But, in reality, he's a high priest in the Satanist church . . . Satanists go to Christian churches and sit there just like they belong. They go to keep their eyes on things.[9]

The Warnkes' ministry warning against Satanism receives some 50,000 letters and telephone calls each month. Yet many people, including Christians, refuse to accept that there has even been a revival of Satanism. However, Maury Terry warns in *The Ultimate Evil* that now, today, America is being victimized "at will" by killer Satanic cults.[10]

---

8 "The Devil Worshippers," transcript from "20/20," May 16, 1985.

9 Rose Hall Warnke. *The Great Pretender*. (Lancaster, PA: Starburst Publishers, 1985), pp. 14, 17–18, 121, 123.

10 Terry, *The Ultimate Evil*, p. 512.

The consuming, continuing drive of the Satanist is to gain greater power. Parents, educators, and teenagers themselves need to know what is happening on the high school campus and the university campus concerning Satanism and Satanic activity.

The occult, like a deadly cancer, will eventually lead to death. Our youth must be warned about the many dangers associated with these practices.

Another buzz word used frequently by teenagers today is "cool." "Cool" used to be leather jackets or hip talk or athletic prowess. It used to be fancy hair styles or "in" fashions. And I try very hard not to get upset about what children decide is fashionable or "in."

However, there is something very different now. Many teenagers today consider that it's "cool" to be cruel, stupid and headed nowhere.[11] Cool has an ugly, often vicious edge. There are no boundaries or lines anymore. Anything goes and cool is being defined in bold, Satanic, shocking terms.

Suddenly it's cool to be ignorant, and violent, and commit sadistic or criminal acts. It's also cool to show no respect, no compassion, and to be quite blatantly headed nowhere. These conditions allow Satan to operate freely in the minds of our youth.

Some of that is because we aren't paying attention to who is deciding what is cool. We've left the job of definition up to people who can't care about our children because they don't even care about themselves. We've let gang leaders, drug dealers, pimps, hustlers, and thugs create the criteria by which our children gauge what is appropriate, expected and worth emulating. We are allowing Satanism to flourish through these misfits as they set the immoral standards that our youth are encouraged to follow.

We who have—or should have—the most impact in the lives of the youth have turned the responsibility of defining "cool" over to the brain-dead and the slime merchants.

---

11 Don Williamson, *Seattle Times*, March 6, 1992.

It is because we have underestimated the value of cool. Defining cool is too crucial to be left to people who don't have enough sense to learn to read, or write, or figure their way out of a paper bag.

Parents, educators, civic and fraternal organizations, businesses, churches—all the various components of the community—have to begin changing what it means when a youngster says something or someone is cool. It needs to become cool to get good grades, treat people with respect and decency, obey the law and to look out for the well-being of the young, the old, or the physically and mentally different.

However, change is hard to make when we pay athletes more than teachers. Or when we put murderers on the front page and don't even mention the coming together of five hundred young people to talk about being a part of the decision-making process in their community.

Young people don't control television, newspapers, movies, magazines and billboards. Adults do that. Adults who exploit youngsters to make a buck any way they can. Adults who never consider the impact of the images on impressionable minds. We have created images so powerful that some young people will kill for sports jackets, tennis shoes, and cheap gold chains. Do you still question that Satanism is on the rise?

Many teenagers today consider that it's "cool" to be cruel, stupid, and headed nowhere

We should have the ability to make young girls and boys swoon over classmates who achieve excellent grades, earn citizenship awards, and maintain high moral standards. It is not an impossible task. It just requires a little practicing of what we preach and some consistent attention to what's going on in the lives of our children.

However, we should not lay the entire blame on the bureaucratic shoulders of government or law. Why? The Bible no longer dominates our culture because its convictions no longer form the moral foundation for our people.

A question that troubles many true Christians today is why most highly educated leaders in science and other fields—even theologians—seem to find it so difficult to believe the Bible and the gospel of Jesus Christ. The answer is found in the words of Ephesians 4:17–19. They are "separated from the life of God" because of self-induced ignorance. It is not that they can't understand, but that they won't understand!

It is this growing rejection of Jesus Christ and His Word that has spiritually blinded so many and caused the tidal wave of sin that is destroying America today. **When we stray from the teachings of the Bible, our actions will soon be influenced by Satan.**

A recent *USA Today* poll stated that only 11 percent of Americans read the Bible daily. More than half read it less than once a month or not at all. Also, the Barna Research Group showed that only 18 percent of evangelical Christians read the Scriptures daily and that almost one in four professing Christians never read God's Word.

GOOD vs. EVIL. Remember, "The only thing necessary for the triumph of evil is that good men do nothing" (Edmund Burke).

KIDS &

CHAPTER FOUR

MUSIC
LYRICS

It's 1995—do you know what kind of music your children are listening to? I can't believe the stuff kids are listening to these days!

Nowadays, with incredibly varied amounts of increasingly controversial music available to the young consumer, it's harder than ever for parents to keep track of what their kids are hearing. In the past six years, the record industry, under pressure from parents groups, has tried to address the problem by putting warning stickers on certain albums. But these stickers, which read "Parental Advisory—Explicit Lyrics," have proven woefully inadequate as a way to distinguish among albums with widely disparate artistic merit.

Under this nebulous system, Prince's "Graffiti Bridge" is just as potentially "damaging" to young minds as 2 Live Crew's "As Nasty as They Wanna Be," which is ridiculous. Prince's album is a work of considerable substance about sex, spirituality and temptation; the 2 Live Crew's album is just one long foul-mouthed stupid joke, which expresses gross hatred for women.

The warning labels refer only to lyrics and give parents little idea of the total picture. So the only way for a parent to really grasp what is going on here is to listen to the albums that their children bring home. If nothing else, being well-versed or at least familiar with, let's say, that new album just released by THE GETO BOYS could certainly open up some interesting topics for dinner-table conversation. Of course, trying to find a non-curse word may present a problem.

As a parent's guide to rock music, here's a quick primer (rock music in detail will be covered later) on recent popular albums and what parents should listen for:

GUNS N' ROSES, "Use Your Illusion I & II." This brazen hard-rock band is overly obnoxious on songs such as "Back Off [expletive]," in which singer Axl Rose declares war on women. The popular Gunners sing compellingly about topics such as rebelling against authority of any kind and worn-out relationships.

ICE CUBE, "Death Certificate." The Molotov cocktail of rap albums. To understand "Death Certificate," one must first understand the history of blacks in America and, more specifically, the environment of racism, police harassment and gang violence out of which Ice Cube emerged. His nearly pathological hatred for Jews, Asians, gays, and women makes this among the most disturbing albums ever released.

MICHAEL JACKSON, "Dangerous." It is easy to forget that this guy makes records, considering it's his videos and his bizarre lifestyle that catch all the attention. As for music, "Give In to Me" sounds like a date-rape fantasy.

SKID ROW, "Slave to the Grind." Anger is demonstrated on Skid Row's second hard hitting metal album. The Skids have a rebellious attitude and a nasty reputation for cursing and throwing things in concert.

NED'S ATOMIC DUSTBIN, "God Fodder." The most controversial thing about these Brits is their hot-selling concert T-shirts, which have a giant profanity printed across the back. Ned's serve up quirky dance rock with clever, alienated lyrics.

MADONNA, "The Immaculate Collection." Madonna's greatest hits package reminds us that much of the controversy about this performer is visual rather than aural. Not so much what you hear but what you see. And what we see is extreme vulgarity.

OZZY OSBOURNE, "No More Tears." In the past, Ozzy was mesmerized with the occult and frequently referred to Satanism and suicide. Here, however, he concentrates on emotions.

N.W.A. (it stands for Niggers With Attitudes), "Efil4zaggin." These hard-core, mean rappers hit a new low for self-loathing by endlessly repeating a vile epithet usually directed at a black person. This would be tragic if it weren't so cynical. This group is wretchedly bad, morally debased, depraved, foul, despicable, filthy, and just plain SICK!

MOTLEY CRÜE, "Decade of Decadence." The Crüe's music doesn't really do justice to the band's notorious reputation for their drug abuse and sexual excess. Mostly the band sings about girls and having a good time.

METALLICA, "Metallica." Metallica's sounds are loud and nasty. Some of its songs are often sensitive expressions of adolescent fear and anxiety. Its words and music don't paint a rose-colored picture of life.

PRINCE AND THE NEW POWER GENERATION, "Diamonds and Pearls." It was a Prince song, "Darling Nicki," that opened the Pandora's box of record labeling. When Tipper Gore, the wife of U. S. Sen. Albert Gore (now Vice President of the United States), discovered that the song referred to masturbation, she and her Parents Music Resource Center lobby group began forcing the record industry to put warning stickers on albums with explicit lyrics. "Diamonds and Pearls" does contain its share of sexual innuendo.

NIRVANA, "Nevermind." This hot, hot Seattle trio explores themes from teen apathy to rape, but the lyrics aren't clearly discernible because the music is so raucous and hardhitting. If future songs are released, they will need to be carefully scrutinized.

ANZIG, "Lucifuge." The lyrics are obsessed with religion, death, doom, and other lighthearted topics. Then again, you would only know that by studying the lyric sheet, because the words are swallowed up by the loud, distorted music.

THE GETO BOYS, "We Can't Be Stopped." Contains more curse words per line than even a 2 Live Crew album, and the horribly violent treatment of women is carried to the extreme of human imagination.

DEATH METAL ROUNDUP. Although no death-metal releases have made the top of the charts, plenty of kids are bringing these albums home. Cover art is invariably bloody and repulsive.

Although every death-metal group sings of violence and death, some clearly have something to say while others are just trying to out-gore one another. Cannibal Corpse is useless gore, almost to the point of being ridiculous and stupid. The band Death limits the kill-o-rama on its new album, "Human," to discuss social issues. Sepultura, the most popular of the death groups, sings about living through poverty, and Slayer sings about the devil. Deicide are Satanists and proud of it, right down to the inverted cross branded into the bassist's forehead. Parents should be very alert as they evaluate each band on its own merits. [1]

Gangsta rappers, rock bands and their lead performers receive an inordinate amount of publicity. However, too many of them are coming to hard ends. They are living lifestyles that are representative of their reckless lyrics. Singer Easy-E, whose pioneering "gangsta" rap group N.W.A. brought the rawness of the inner-city to white suburbia, died recently (April 1995) of AIDS. [2]

Grammy-award-winning producer-rapper Dr. Dre is in a halfway house and rapper-actor Tupac Shakur is in jail, while reigning superstar Snoop Doggy Dogg faces life in prison on conspiracy-murder charges. Yet these and other gangster rappers who extol the virtues of bullets, bitches and 40-ounce beers, of "getting paid" and pocketing "mad loot," have been idolized as urban heroes. [3]

---

1 Brenda Herrmann, *Chicago Tribune*, February 22, 1992.

2 *Sun-Sentinel*, April 4, 1995.

3 *Newsweek*, April 10, 1995, p. 74.

The ghetto-centric lifestyles projected in their lyrics and videos, and their "hard," take-no-prisoners ethos, have become standards for millions of bravado, pants-sagging Americans, both black and white. Will any of these followers, mostly young men, change their attitudes about money, sex and violence now that gangster rap appears to be doing a drive-by on itself? The troubles of Easy-E and the others should be taken as a "wake-up" call to the youth of America.

In a jailhouse interview with *Vibe* magazine, Shakur repudiates his famous embrace of the "thug life" (words tattooed across his torso), calling it "just ignorance." A week before Easy-E died, his lawyer read a letter in which the rapper emphasized that anyone could get AIDS, that it "doesn't discriminate."[4]

Of course, rap is not just an attitude; it is a billion-dollar business. Will the weight of recent negative headlines bury gangster sales along with the gangsters? Probably never. Tupac's newest album, "Me Against the World," which was released the first week of April 1995 while he was in jail, debuted at No. 1.

These performers are idolized by a large and growing number of America's troubled teenagers. Our nation's youth is being brain-washed by the despicable lyrics of modern day rock music.

The Recording Industry Association of America said that rock 'n' roll accounted for one-third of ALL music bought in the United States in 1992. That is down from nearly one-half four years ago, according to a recent article released by the Associated Press.[5]

The burgeoning popularity of country music and urban contemporary, which combines rap and soul, boosted the industry to a record $9 billion in sales during 1992. Country music doubled its share of the market in two

---

4 Ibid.

5 David Bauder, the Associated Press, April 28, 1993.

years. It accounted for 17 percent of music sales in 1992.[6]

Although rock doesn't dominate as it once did, statistics show it still makes roughly the same money. It accounted for about $3 billion in business last year and $3 billion in 1988. In 1992, easy listening music made up 11 percent of the sales, classical and jazz 4 percent each and gospel music 2 percent.

According to the U. S. Census Bureau, there are 24 million teenagers in America, representing 7 percent of our nation's population. As many as 50 percent of teens live in single-parent homes headed by working mothers (*Newsweek*, 1990). Some seven of ten teenagers have had sex by the age of 18. The Center for Disease Control reports one in four sexually active teens will contract a venereal disease before finishing high school (*People*, 11-5-90). The suicide rate among teens has soared in recent years, and it's predicted that this rise will continue.

The record industry uses MTV to reach and influence the minds of our children

The Madonnas, the 2 Live Crews, and the Motley Crües of this world are leading kids down a one-way street to hell and getting rich in the process.

According to *Forbes* (9-26-94), here are the estimated 1993–1994 combined gross income figures for the following:

> Rolling Stones .....$53 million
> Michael Jackson ..$39 million
> Eddie Murphy .....$30 million
> Aerosmith ....$36 million
> Grateful Dead ......$35 million
> Guns N' Roses .....$32 million

---

6 Ibid.

Teenagers see these people as wealthy, glamorous and powerful. Is it any wonder that they try to emulate them? Children don't see these people for what they really are. In many cases these individuals suffer from unhappiness, loneliness, drug abuse, sex abuse, and alcohol abuse; and they are, generally speaking, misfits who cannot function in a normal society. A recent example is Kurt Cobain, who committed suicide in April 1994. Apparently their mission is to drag the rest of the world down to their level of moral failure and they know the best way of accomplishing that task is to capture the minds of our children.

The record industry uses MTV to reach and influence the minds of our children. At a very young age, the MTV generation is bombarded with vivid images of sex and death and the invincibility of heroes. Popular culture very easily beats out parental influence; and by the time children reach adolescence, many parents have already lost control, child experts say.

Madonna, who has no formal musical training, is now among the most powerful women in the entertainment industry. Her new $65,000,000 deal with media giant Time Warner, Inc., signed recently, is among the most lucrative offered to any performer, male or female. Said to be a notch more profitable than Michael Jackson's recent megadeal with Sony, the new pact will offer Madonna the opportunity to create anything she wants. That means movies, music, books, TV shows, merchandise, concert tours and videos for herself—and other artists she will shepherd. This will not be viewed as good news by many parents.

When Madonna went to New York in the late 1970's to seek her fortune and fame, she was simply a desperate young woman. She was broke, she was hungry and she didn't know a soul. Her early days in New York were spent making alternative films, and posing nude for photographers. Lacking any musical training, she taught herself to play barely passable drums, guitar and keyboards. She latched on to various musicians, disc jock-

37

eys and club owners and made her presence known.[7]

Her rise and incredible staying power in a most fickle industry have been nothing short of phenomenal. There simply has never been another woman like her in pop music, or perhaps all pop culture. And her influence on our society will be increased as a result of this new deal with Time Warner. Let's face it, $65 million will buy plenty of exposure for Madonna. She may even become richer at the expense of our children.

Is it any wonder that today's children have conduct disorder? In this conflict between GOOD and EVIL, this war of the spirits, the spirits of Satan and his demons have gained a powerful stronghold in the medium of rock music. **Many of these rock performers should be viewed as "the devil in the flesh."**

7 Deborah Wilker, *Sun-Sentinel*, April 26, 1992.

RAP
MUSIC
CHAPTER FIVE
& PROFANITY

Rap singers are not just entertainers; they are heroes and teachers to the young, and it is important to pay attention to what they teach. Elizabeth Leiba reported in the *Sun-Sentinel:*

> *"I got my twelve gauge sawed off.*
> *I got my headlights turned off.*
> *I'm 'bout to bust some shots off.*
> *I'm 'bout to dust some cops off.*"
> — 'Cop Killer,' Ice-T

Rapper Ice-T's song about killing police has indeed touched off a national controversy and several major record store chains have yanked Ice-T's album 'Body Count' from their shelves because it contains the song 'Cop Killer.'"[1]

The governor of Alabama called for a ban—and various law enforcement and religious organizations across the country are also voicing protests against the violence toward police officers that the album advocates. However, not everybody has reacted negatively. One store manager says all the attention may have boosted sales.

Time Warner Records, owner of Ice-T's record label, said the album's release is not a matter of profits but a matter

---

1 Elizabeth Leiba, *Sun-Sentinel*, June 27, 1992.

of principle. The company said it stands by a commitment to free expression of ideas. In my opinion, anyone who believes this is intellectually incoherent. This record is about making money, plain and simple.

Rap was created by and for blacks in the 1970's.[2] The rap revolution, like other revolutions, started with noble intentions; but during the '80's it eventually crossed the line into heavy metal and fell into Satan's trap of drugs and crime that always result in human degradation and self destruction.

In 1989, the Compton, California, group N.W.A. (it stands for Niggas With Attitudes)[3] released its debut album, "Straight Outta Compton," an angry record that ushered in "gangsta" rap. Its alleged mission was to convey the "reality" of inner-city violence. It resulted in glorifying violence and perpetuating stereotypes. The album had songs like "F— Tha Police." Ice Cube, who was a member of N.W.A., has since gone solo. He starred in the movie *Boyz N the Hood.*

Also about this time, 2 Live Crew released its "As Nasty As They Want To Be" album, which included misogynistic songs like "Me So Horny," whose lyrics are so disgraceful, vile and degenerate that I will not print them in this volume.

Ice Cube has now become a big star and has a popular album with a song that calls for the murder of "a white Jew" in the music business. The lyrics, according to an article in *U.S. News and World Report,* follow: "get rid of that devil real simple, put a bullet in his temple."[4]

SISTER SOULJAH'S MESSAGE

By now, I'm sure everyone has heard all the flap surrounding the Bill Clinton, Jesse Jackson, and black rap singer Sister Souljah (Lisa Williamson) spectacle. And I'm sure everyone also has heard arguments for and against

---

2 Devin Pritchett, *The Wall Street Journal,* July 3, 1992.

3 John Leland, *Newsweek,* June 29, 1992, p. 48.

4 John Leo, *U.S. News & World Report,* June 29, 1992, p. 19.

what the rapper said in a Washington Post interview. So I'm going to skip all of that and get right to the point.

By saying that gangs should take a week and kill white people instead of black people, Sister Souljah has told America's children that it's OK to commit murder. The trouble with Sister Souljah's message is that children take it literally. And more specifically, she told black children that it's OK to kill people—period.[5]

Oh sure, the part about "if you're a gang member and you would normally be killing somebody" may soften the harshness of such words, and focuses on the reality of what gangs do. But in truth, that clause is nothing more than a symbolic copout. If Sister Souljah really meant for black gangs to stop killing each other, she could have said so without telling them to kill somebody else—in this case, white people.

It would have been better if she had said that directly to the gangs. But she said it to *The Washington Post;* in other words, she said it to the world![6] Because Sister Souljah's a rapper, her words have considerable appeal to children.

I'm talking about children, 10 and under, who take most, if not all, of what they hear literally. Today's pre-teens have a great deal of difficulty separating fact from fantasy. And everything, particularly the words of a rapper, is very real to them.

Many children, especially those in their early teens, are far more concerned with the latest fad than anything else. It is very disturbing that a rapper like Sister Souljah would encourage gangs to kill anyone, black or white.

How does a fair-minded American respond to Sister Souljah's words? Well, Bill Clinton condemns these words as racist and gets attacked in turn by Jesse Jackson. Jackson says Sister Souljah "represents the feelings and hopes of a whole generation of people." He asserts Mr. Clinton has

---

5 Woodrow Wilkins, *Delta Democrat Times,* June 30, 1992.

6 Ibid.

a character flaw for speaking out and demands an apology.

Would he be saying this if it had been a white who had spoken so viciously about blacks? No. He would have gone ballistic. How sad that Jackson, a man of enormous talent, should descend to demagoguery—in effect, condoning black racism, which is just as evil as white racism. His excuse that Sister Souljah was "misunderstood" is unusually lame. Her remarks and lyrics are perfectly clear. Misunderstanding them would be a remarkable feat.

Fighting bigots, both black and white, is not a political issue, it is a moral obligation. Many of our leaders today have forgotten that America was founded on the principals of the Bible and the religion of Christianity. The founding fathers looked to the Bible for guidance as they prepared the "bill of rights." It commands humility, piety, and benevolence. It acknowledges equal rights in every person whether a brother or a sister. This is genuine Christianity!

God is color-blind and He offers to each of us the free gift of eternal salvation. Jesus Christ is the only cure for our problems. The Bible says, "There is only one Lawgiver and Judge, the one who is able to save and destroy. But you—who are you to judge your neighbor?" (James 4:12).

PERVASIVE PROFANITY

In schools across the U. S., worried educators report a rapidly rising tide of profanity among the very young. Nobody seems to have measured the phenomenon yet. But a growing number of principals report that vulgarities once heard mainly in the barroom and the barracks are now being tossed around in classrooms as early as kindergarten.

When Dennis Reed, a Tampa, Florida, elementary-school principal, calls on local parents, he confronts them with a long list of dirty words. In the comfort of his hosts' living rooms, Mr. Reed calmly unrolls a poster on which he has written four-letter obscenities—and five-letter and twelve-letter ones, too. As parents' eyes widen, he informs them that the words came straight from the mouths of babes— their own children who are his students. "That's where the shock came, when you saw what words were actually used," says one mother of three.

Although the problem isn't nearly as serious as adolescent gun use or teen pregnancy, school officials worry that it signifies a disrespect for authority, a growing tolerance for public rudeness and a lack of moral development among young children.

Children's use of profanity may reflect the extreme stress—marital, career and financial—experienced by many parents. "It's real difficult to have that close sense of family and good parenting when you're dealing with all these other issues," says a family psychotherapist.[7]

Many frustrated school principals blame the media, especially cable television, video rentals and hit movies that feed our children a steady diet of crude language.

Forget, for the moment, about all the violence in the *Rambo* movies and the kinky sex in *Basic Instinct.* Much of the sex, mayhem and even rough language that rattle across the wide screen with mind-numbing frequency today is hardly shocking in a pop culture that routinely exploits human dignity for commercial ends.[8]

The truth is, if you flirt with sin, it will end up destroying you

But what continues to disturb many people—in a nation where four in five believe the Bible is the actual or inspired word of God, according to Gallup polls—are the increasingly frequent profane references to the deity in movies and on television.

People are particularly upset with the use of profanity. They feel that God is holy and separate. He is their Lord and their Savior. The Bible teaches us to avoid profanity.

7 Gustav Niebuhr, *The Wall Street Journal*, July 8, 1992.

8 David Briggs, The Associated Press, July 12, 1992.

The Third Commandment warns us against the misuse of His name and the Bible continues to warn us when it says, " . . . If anyone curses his God, he will be held responsible" (Leviticus 24:15).

Hollywood thinks Americans like to hear profanity. However, in a 1993 Associated Press-Media General poll, eight in ten respondents said most new films have too much profanity. I think, by and large, it's a general antagonism, a rather deep-seated, almost reflexive antagonism to Christianity by Hollywood producers. I also suspect there are darker forces at work in the decision to add profane references to God into these shows. Satan utilizes all avenues!

POLLS CAN BE MISLEADING!

If we are to believe the two poll reports referenced above where 80 percent of the people say they believe the Bible to be the actual word of God and they dislike the use of profanity, then I must ask a serious question:

Why, in our society, do we flood our minds with things against God, pornography, liberalism, evil, filthy talk, and dirty sex? Sin, pornography, homosexuality, and sex dominate our movies, television, and other media. Moral standards have all but disappeared. Censorship is now considered gauche and unsophisticated. Phone companies and utility commissions have allowed dial-a-porn, obscenity, and sexually-oriented materials to invade telephones and televisions. Now you can dial a number and hear all sorts of filth and perversion—and YOU pay for it!

At a leading religious convention recently attended by many pastors and religious leaders, the management of the hosting hotel reported 75 percent of the rooms occupied by "Bible-believing pastors" turned on X-rated movies. No other group who had used the hotel—lawyers, politicians, educators, etc.—had used the pay-for-sex channels as much as these pastors. Disgusting! Sad! Sickening! Are they really Bible believers? No wonder so many churches are in trouble today.

Let's be realistic! Sexual temptation is not limited to

the world. Studies have shown that over seventy percent of born-again Christians have had sex outside of marriage. Sin is creeping into the minds and hearts of many good people, including Bible-believing Christians. Their minds are being filled, every day, with the immorality and garbage around us. The more we ignore its presence the uglier it grows.

People say, "Oh, a little bit of this and a little bit of that isn't going to hurt me. I'm a strong Christian. I don't have to worry." The truth is, if you flirt with sin, it will end up destroying you. Like the old saying, you can't lay down with the pigs without getting up dirty: little sins grow into big sins that will consume you and destroy your life.

Many Christians, sometimes innocently, start out watching R-rated movies, then X-rated movies. They gradually progress from soft-core to hard-core pornography until they become addicted, trapped by sexual perversions of all kinds. Satan uses pornography very effectively!

Pastors need to promote "revival" among Christian people. No, it is not old fashioned! Jesus said, "The eye is the lamp of the body. If your eyes are good, your whole body will be full of light. But if your eyes are bad, your whole body will be full of darkness. If the light within you is darkness, how great is that darkness! Either he will hate the one and love the other, or he will be devoted to the one and despise the other . . ." (Matthew 6:22–24).

Yes, we are involved in a war of the spirits and Satan will use any and all weapons at his disposal to lure us into committing sinful acts.

Christians are Satan's favorite targets. Once they stray from the Bible, losing the power of the Holy Spirit, they become easy prey for him and his evil spirits.

THE LOST GENERATION

CHAPTER SIX

Middle-class America, watch out: Some of your children are out of control. Values have changed and today's youth are bored with the suburbs and driven by impulse. They are disappearing from home for days, walking out of school at will and turning families upside down.

It's youthful rebellion, with a '90's edge. Materialism, violence and broken homes have all converged to mold a generation with fewer limits. Today's youth indeed lives dangerously as family values and habits change. "There was a big fire underneath me that just kept me moving," says one teenager. "I was sneaking out at all hours of the night, not coming home for days, weeks, using alcohol a lot."[1]

Today's children have been taught to speak their minds—and are doing it. Simultaneously, societal changes have forced them to grow up faster than earlier generations. Many children today live in constant fear. It is a very explosive combination. There is a certain impulsiveness to it all, a sense of "live once, so live wild."

"The mail is rife with horror stories about out-of-control kids," says Ann Landers, the advice columnist. "The old family structure is collapsing. The woman is sometimes working two jobs, the husband isn't around, the kids are home alone, and they get into trouble."

1 Karen Samples, *Sun-Sentinel*, April 19, 1992.

Many young people will excel in school, obey their parents, and think about the future. However, behavior problems have become so severe with others that parents are now tossing about fancy terms for their children's misconduct. Today they have conduct disorder, adolescent adjustment reaction, or opposition-defiant disorder.

At a very young age, the MTV generation is bombarded with vivid images of sex and death and the invincibility of heroes. Popular culture easily beats out parental influence, and by the time children reach adolescence, many parents have already lost control, child experts say. "When a six-year-old comes back and asks 'what's oral sex, mommy?' And an eight-year-old asks how many times you 'do it' in a week, and an eleven-year-old asks whether you have orgasms, I would say the world has changed a little bit," says Ron Taffel, a New York family counselor and author of *Parenting by Heart*.[2]

Parents of the '90's are dealing with fallout from what Landers calls the "pal syndrome." That's the warm, fuzzy idea that parents should always be friends with their children. Beginning in the '60's, Baby Boomers were encouraged to reject the authoritarian methods of their own parents and adopt a more psychological approach to child rearing. "We all raised our children with Dr. Spock ethics—sit down, have a conversation, children are entitled to an explanation for what you're doing," says one parent. "It didn't work."

Frustrated, many parents are turning their adolescents over to psychiatric programs that promise to straighten them out. From 1984 to 1988, the number of private, for-profit psychiatric hospitals in the country jumped from 220 to 444, said U. S. Behavioral Health Inc., a California firm that manages health care costs. About one-third of the youngsters (patients) in these hospitals have problems such as conduct disorder.

---

2 Ibid.

The children of this "lost generation" are the first to grow up in the shadow of AIDS. They are more likely to be slain or commit suicide than die of cancer. About 25 percent of them carry a weapon at least once every 30 days, for self-protection or for use in a fight, a 1993 study says. Gunfire is the most frequent cause of death for black males ages 15 to 19; and after traffic accidents, the second greatest killer of all teens, according to a national study by the *Journal of the American Medical Association*.[3] The study paints "a grotesque picture of a society steeped in violence, especially by firearms, with such ubiquity and prevalence as to be seemingly accepted as inevitable," said JAMA's editor, Dr. George Lundberg.

Guns are the murder weapons favored by teens, the study found, and the number of young black males killed today by gunfire is increasing fastest in major metropolitan areas of the country. In the period from 1979 to 1989, the number of shooting deaths for all Americans 15 to 19 increased 61 percent, while the number of homicides with other weapons fell 29 percent.[4] We have gangs in the streets today because there are no fathers in the homes.

The American family has been radically transformed over the past three decades. Simply put, the traditional, two-parent family is under siege. It is being displaced by the single-parent household. The percentage of white children living with one parent has almost tripled, to 19.2 percent during the past three decades, and it has more than doubled among blacks, to 54.8 percent. About half of all marriages now end in divorce. Out-of-wedlock births have rocketed in recent years. Consider this: A majority of children born today will spend at least some of their youth in a single-parent household.

Why has the family structure changed so dramatically? Many reasons. The simplicities of laws for obtaining a

---

3 *Journal of the American Medical Association*, June 10, 1992.

4 Christopher Farrell, *Business Week*, June 29, 1992, p. 90.

divorce and a debilitating urban drug culture that tear apart many families are two examples. The devil's mastery is quite obvious as we look at the enormous changes that have taken place during the past three decades.

As Christians, we are firmly engaged in spiritual warfare with Satan and his demons. What the adversary seeks is an opening from which he can build a spiritual stronghold and influence our thoughts and actions for evil. One can be giving demonic forces unnecessary inroads into his life by participating in questionable activities—watching movies overloaded with sensuality or trepidation, reading filthy materials laced with raucous references to carnal lifestyle, or listening to music with lyrics promoting lewdness and rebellion.

A fundamental reason for the spread of pornography and violence in the media is the pervasive moral permissiveness of our current society, which is rooted in the search for personal gratification at any cost. Associated with this is a moral emptiness, which makes personal pleasure the only happiness human beings can attain, and a sense of fatalism: if we're all going to die tomorrow, we might as well enjoy ourselves today. This permissive attitude, of course, plays right into Satan's hand. He loves it.

The American Broadcasting Company (ABC) is one of the worst perpetrators of immorality and violence on "network" television today (MTV is cable). In the 1990–91 Fall-Winter season, it had three prime-time shows featuring homosexual characters. "Heatbeat," with its lesbian lovers, was one of its feature programs. In "Hooperman," the main character was a homosexual cop who was constantly being enticed by his female partner to have sex with her.

ABC is using more and more family shows to promote prostitution, drunkenness, and women having babies through illicit sex. However, you can hardly find a program on any of the networks today that doesn't contain a constant stream of profanity.

Movies today are, in general, even filthier than television programs. They contain more profanity, violence, and blatant sex than television; yet many of them are ultimately shown on television. The level of profanity in many of these movies is staggering. For example, characters in the 122-minute movie, *Midnight Run*, used the F-word 125 times. That's more than one F-word a minute. Other filthy words were used 45 times for a total of 168 uses of profanity. Since then, the movie has been shown on television, and the TV movie and video guide of 1989 calls it "a socko action comedy." Since when did profanity become a laughing matter?

Vulgarity in movies, TV, and videos has progressed beyond anyone's wildest dreams. It is now beyond the level of any decent or moral person's standards. Many people have quit going to the movies because they are repulsed by the violence, sex, and profanity they see. We have too few morally wholesome and family oriented movies to choose from today. It seems writers and producers are incapable of creating movies of sound moral character anymore. They must think using violence, sex and profanity in a film will make the proverbial silk purse out of a sow's ear. That, of course, will not happen.

The American family has been radically transformed over the past three decades

A few years ago, for example, no one would have dared make a movie like *The Last Temptation of Christ*. The outcry against such a movie would have been unbelievable, and I doubt that many would have gone to see it. In fact, it probably would not have been shown in this country. Yet the film was made and publicly shown, and some who called themselves Christians defended it. I believe "The Last Temptation" is the most degrading attack so far on the Person who has done more good for this planet than anyone else, our Lord Jesus Christ. The film is sacrilegious, blasphemous, and anti-Christian. It makes Jesus out to be a man who had sex with Mary Magdalene, who was lustful and indecisive, and who desperately resisted God. It infers that

51

Jesus was unsure about His message and mission. This is pure Satan-inspired hogwash!

The only reason anyone would dare to produce a film like this is because of the complacency of Christians. They should have made their voices heard long ago. It's time we stood up for our Christian rights. Every group in America seems to be protected by the rights movement and the ACLU except Christians.

Can you imagine the public outcry that would occur if someone made a movie similar to "The Last Temptation" about the revered civil rights leader, Martin Luther King, Jr.? Even if the movie was completely true and factual, it would be branded as prejudicial, racist, and slanderous. The debasing of Christian beliefs is not only permitted but promoted by the liberals, the secular humanists, and the ACLU (these groups will be covered in more detail later).

I am not trying to be legalistic here. But anything that usurps Christ's role as Lord in your life, competing for your devotion and time, can likewise become fodder for demonic activity. You see, this lost generation that we are praying for, and deeply concerned about, has become rebellious and disobedient to God. Partial obedience is not obedience. It is rebellion that turns to selfish desires while ignoring the wishes of those in authority over us. At first glance this rebellion may appear insignificant, but don't be fooled. **The roots of rebellion grow quickly and run deep.**

Ultimately, all rebellion circumvents God's control even though its aim is usually directed at human authority. It quenches our fellowship with God and derails His blessings. We may think our rebellion is justifiable, but God never blesses anything that contradicts His will. He is holy and righteous and will not condone sinful behavior. Rebellion is always at enmity with God.

As parents, we face a serious challenge of enormous proportion. We cannot meet this challenge without being filled with the Holy Spirit. We need to be praying to God that He will give us strength, courage, and wisdom as we go to battle against Satan to save this lost generation. The devil and his evil spirits must be purged from their hearts, minds, and souls and replaced with the Holy Spirit. This freedom from Satan can be theirs immediately! All they have to do is ask Jesus Christ to be their personal Savior. It's that easy. It's not too late.

The Bible says, "Have two goals; wisdom—that is, knowing and doing right—and common sense. Don't let them slip away, for they fill you with living energy, and bring you honor and respect" (Proverbs 3:21–22 TLB).

God's way is not the way of rebellion but the way of obedience. It is not the way of pride but of humility. The Bible says, "Humble yourselves, therefore, under God's mighty hand, that He may lift you up in due time. Cast all your anxiety on Him because He cares for you" (1 Peter, 5:6–7).

This passage of Scripture is my prayer for THE LOST GENERATION!

BIBLE
ILLITERATES

As we evaluate GOOD vs. EVIL, a war of the spirits, let's look at how knowledgeable Americans are concerning the HOLY BIBLE. This book that everyone seems to know and talk about.

To say that every family owns a Bible, yet no one reads it would surely be an exaggeration. However, it would not necessarily be a gross overstatement either. More than 90 percent of U. S. households own a Bible, but only a small percentage get around to reading it. Let's take a look at what is going on in the world of the Bible today. What are people saying about the Good Book and its numerous translations?

In New York City, on the twelfth floor at Bible House, home to the venerable American Bible Society and its historic collection of leather-bound Scriptures, a flashy new videotape is playing. It is about exorcism. As a female voice narrates the story, vivid images race across the big screen: a graveyard, a rusty fire escape, and a dark beach lighted by a bonfire. And through it all, a tormented youth writhes in madness, haunted by a weird, wraith-like figure. Finally, the youth is touched by a compassionate young man. He is healed; the wraith is vanquished. Background music surges as the narrator concludes a New Testament passage (Mark, Chapter 5) about Jesus casting out a nasty set of demons.

What is this? MTV?

No, it is a new translation of a Scripture, aimed at a

young, "post-literate" generation. To hear some religious folk talk, it may be the biggest thing to happen to the Good Book since Johann Gutenberg invented movable type.

"This is really cutting edge," declares Eugene B. Habecker, the energetic new president and chief executive officer of the 175-year-old society, which also has developed interactive software that relates the text to contemporary teenage issues. "It will revolutionize the way people study the Bible in the 21st century," Dr. Habecker says.[1]

For those of us who are Christians and eager to spread the Word—or just get it heard—the revolution is coming none too soon. America is becoming a nation of Bible illiterates, its citizens unable to find the time or inclination to read the world's best selling book, THE HOLY BIBLE!

To be sure, the Bible—in basic black leather, pastel paperback or white cowhide and coffee-table-size—still racks up impressive sales. It is hard to understand why so many Americans buy Bibles. Most of the Bibles bought are put away and rarely or never read. The Barna Research Group, a Glendale, California, pollster, recently found only one in 10 Americans claims to be a daily reader. Among people under 25, it was fewer than one in 30. This is a troubling trend indeed and it could adversely impact the future of American culture.

As the Bible gathers dust, even the faithful grow forgetful. About a year ago, pollster George Gallup found that while a majority said that yes, they believed the Bible to be God's word, only half could name any of the four gospels. (They are Matthew, Mark, Luke and John.) Mr. Gallup also noted that MANY people could not recall who preached the Sermon on the Mount. (It was Jesus.) Is this SAD? YES, VERY SAD!

Funny, isn't it? Americans seem to have time to read "supermarket tabloids," read the daily sports page, read the financial section, keep track of the stock market, keep up

---

1 R. Gustav Niebuhr, *The Wall Street Journal*, March 2, 1992, p. 1.

with the local gossip, and spend several hours each day watching "trash" on TV but can't find time to read the Bible. Who do they think they are kidding? We are not THAT stupid! Can you imagine the excuses that will be given by these people when they stand before the Lord on judgment day?

"America is one generation away from atheism," warns the Rev. Dwight "Ike" Reighard, a Fayetteville, Georgia, pastor of a 5,000-member Baptist church. He blames this trend partly on the fact that the Bible is not read much in public schools.

The problem is that even churchgoers are daunted by the thought of tackling the Bible's 800,000 words on their own. "I just have a difficult time understanding the text," is a common expression. Many adult Sunday school teachers say the lack of time keeps them from regular Scripture-reading. "You are probably more likely to pick up a magazine than the Bible,"[2] is a commonly heard statement. To remedy such complaints, publishers, pastors, Christian music stars and even entire denominations are heading into the breach in what amounts to a multi-media effort to win back readers.

The tried and true method is simplifying the text—there are now more than forty English versions available. Thomas Nelson, the country's largest independent Bible publisher, says sales shot way up last year when the company began publishing the New Revised Standard Version. One Florida publisher still uses the King James New Testament but puts key words and phrases in bold-face, promising this "reduces reading time by two-thirds." This is, of course, mostly a gimmick designed to encourage people to read the Bible

It's the '90's. In uncertain times like these, church leaders have often urged people to turn to the Bible for help and comfort. So far, so good. But which version of the Bible? The Bible shelf at the local book store is growing rapidly

---

2 Ibid.

and increasingly mirrors this troubled culture in which we live today. In all, about 7,000 editions are on the market.

For starters, there are editions for Catholics, mainline Protestants, evangelicals, feminists, fundamentalists, "Spirit-filled" charismatics and folks in other flocks. Then there are Bibles for single adults, working mothers, stressed-out fathers, co-dependent children or others in various stages of counseling or 12–step recovery programs. The catchy title for one popular edition says it all—"The Life Recovery Bible."

"The point is to try to meet needs. . . . We also need to admit that it's getting harder to get people to read anything today," said Ken Abraham, a Christian writer who specializes in youth work. "Some people think the Bible is too intimidating—so they don't read it. . . . So we're trying to create new versions that are easier for people to relate to and read. Does it work? It's hard to tell, sometimes. But it's better to try to do something good than to not try at all."[3]

So as the '90's began, Abraham signed on to help create one of the most talked about Bibles on the market—a New Testament for students called "The King and the Beast: Making Sense Out of Matthew and Revelation and All the Great Stuff in Between."

Polls indicate the vast majority of teens and young adults believe in God. Yet they rarely read the Bible. Some have asked if it's proper to try to create a "Bible for the Bart Simpson." Many of today's other specialized editions face similar criticisms. "Kids simply aren't reading their vanilla versions of the King James Bible," said Abraham, whose background includes time as a rock 'n' roll drummer. "We needed to put together something that honors the Bible, but uses the language of today. We also needed to help young readers apply the Bible to their issues."[4]

Thus, "The King and the Beast" uses the Contemporary English Version of the New Testament text, which puts

3 Scripps Howard News Service, January 16, 1993.

4 Ibid.

it at a 4th grade reading level. A similar Old Testament text is in the works. The margins of this new edition are lined with answers to basic questions about the chapters and verses on each page. A 122-page prologue sets the tone. There are snappy chapters with titles such as: "Would God Send Me To Hell?" "Why Am I So Depressed?" "I Know Someone Being Abused" and "God Is Not Opposed To Sex."

Suffice it to say that Bibles for young people in the 1950's didn't include 10-page chapters on the occult. "We didn't make all this up," stressed Abraham, "We went to young people and asked questions like, 'What are the issues that kids worry about at your school?' We asked them why they do not read the Bible. We asked how we could apply the Bible to subjects that really matter to them."[5]

At concerts, Christian rockers Eddie DeGarmo and Dana Key have passed out copies of John's gospel taken from the user-friendly New International Version Student Bible. They performed under banners urging their youthful audiences to "read the Book," says the group's spokesman, Robert Michaels.

America is becoming a nation of Bible illiterates

But reading the Bible—even when it is simplified—is still too heady for some. The First United Methodist Church in Houston has plans to build a biblical theater—a 300-seat rotunda with a large floor-sized map of the Holy Land onto which computer-guided lights will trace the path of the Israelites' wanderings in the Wilderness or spotlight the towns where Jesus preached. "People just don't want to read anymore," says the church's pastor, the Rev. William Hinson, "they want you to show them."

We already have, of course, the full-length movie *Jesus.*

---

5 Ibid.

It is a literal rendering of Luke's Gospel which its owner, Campus Crusade for Christ, wants to show to everyone in the world by the year 2000. A spokesman says 461 million people have viewed it so far.

For its part, the American Bible Society, which publishes the Scriptures in 66 languages (Amharic to Urdu), recently introduced the Contemporary English Version whose plain-vanilla language is shorn of anachronistic words and phrases. So, the King James Version's passage of the birth of Jesus—"And she brought forth her first-born son and wrapped him in swaddling clothes and laid him in a manger . . . —is now "[S]he gave birth to her first-born son. She dressed him in baby clothes and laid him in a feed box. . . ."[6]

Dr. Habecker, the society's president, says, "If the [biblical] writers were to come back today and give us the message—that's what it would read like." As for the video, he adds, "that's what it would look like."

A person cannot grow spiritually without reading and studying the Bible

The organization isn't planning anything as grand as committing the entire Bible to film. Just getting a portion of the fifth chapter of Mark's Gospel on video took almost three years, beginning with the teenage focus group that selected the exorcism story from a list put together by biblical scholars. Then the challenge was to update the passage. For instance, as recorded in the Scriptures, after the exorcised spirits leave the possessed man, they infest a herd of pigs who fling themselves into a lake and drown.

But "pigs just don't have the same meaning of 'unclean animals' today," says Dr. Thomas Boomershine, a professor at United Theological Seminary in Dayton, Ohio, and the

---

6 R. Gustav Niebuhr, *The Wall Street Journal*, March 2, 1992, p. 1.

project's chief academic consultant. "A lot of people would cry over the destruction of the pigs." The pigs were nixed. The team also wanted to keep the settings contemporary and urban avoiding Cecile B. DeMille type treatment that can lend an antique feeling to the Scriptures. So the Jesus figure is pictured as a clean-cut, young laborer; the possessed youth wears a baseball cap. "In some ways [Hollywood] has made Jesus unreal for some people," says Fern Lee Hagedorn, the project's manager. "We did not want to perpetuate that because then we would have lost the power of Jesus."

Recently, as she toured various cities where the video is being test-marketed, Ms. Hagedorn said the finished product seemed to be getting thumbs up. "In every instance, none of the teenagers took their eyes off the screen," she said, after emerging from a session in Boston.[7]

Among those who have seen it recently is Derek Rader, a 16-year-old attending a Parkersburg, West Virginia, high school, who describes himself as "pretty illiterate when it comes to the Bible." Did he like what he saw? It was "intriguing," he says, enough so to prompt him to look up the biblical chapter on which it is based. "I've started it a couple of times," he says, "but haven't got completely through it yet."

Today, most of the biblical illiteracy witnessed in this country is self-inflicted. **According to a recent poll, once out of high school, over sixty percent of adults never again read a book.** There is no rational justification for this behavior. There is no "reason," only flimsy "excuses." When it pertains to the Bible, we have indeed become an illiterate society, Christians included! The devil seeks to impede our spiritual progress by keeping us from the Scriptures. For most of us to say that we do not have any time for Scriptural reading is simply a LIE! The truth is we need to rearrange our priorities.

A person cannot grow spiritually without reading and

---

7 Ibid.

studying the Bible. We will all face Jesus Christ on judgment day and give an account of our lives. All good and evil deeds that we have committed will be revealed to us by Jesus. He has a record of every single second of our time spent on this earth.

America's founding fathers considered the Bible an essential part of their civilization. So much that, according to the journals of the Continental Congress, the first official act of that newly-constituted body was to authorize the printing of twenty thousand Bibles to be given to the American Indians.

Regarding the founding fathers of this country and the first Puritans to come to New England, Daniel Webster declared in 1843: "The Bible came with them. And it is not to be doubted, that to free and universal reading of the Bible, in that age, men were much indebted for right views of civil liberty. The Bible is a book of faith, and a book of doctrine, and a book of morals, and a book of religion of especial revelation from God; but it is also a book which teaches man his own individual responsibility, his own dignity, and his equality with his fellow-man."

It seems appropriate here to recall President Lincoln's Fast Day Proclamation: "We have grown in numbers, wealth and power as no other nation has ever grown. But we have forgotten God . . . and we have vainly imagined, in the deceitfulness of our hearts, that all these blessings were produced by some superior wisdom and virtue of our own. Intoxicated with unbroken success, we have become too self-sufficient to feel the necessity of redeeming and preserving grace, too proud to pray to the God that made us! It behooves us, then, to humble ourselves . . . to confess our national sins, and to pray for clemency and forgiveness."

Are you really so busy that you cannot spend a few minutes each day reading the HOLY BIBLE? I hope you see the importance of this question. Bible illiteracy is a severe handicap to anyone who must be engaged in a war of the spirits and we are all involved in this war!

CHRISTIAN
CHALLENGES

It appears that evil abounds in our nation today. Crime, alcohol and drug addiction are on the rise. Abortion, pornography and divorce tear both individuals and families apart. Growing debt, personal and collective, demonstrates our selfishness and lack of discipline. "To solve these urgent problems, we must discover what God wants us to do, and quickly resolve to do it."[1]

Can we blame these problems on the breakdown of the traditional family? On the advance of false teachings that leave no room for God? Or perhaps on the increasing moral and spiritual corruption in our country?

No, these are symptoms, the result of people turning away from God and trying to live without Him.[2] The solution begins with individuals seeking a relationship with God, because change in society begins with change in individuals. If we are going to succeed in turning EVIL into GOOD and win this war of the spirits, then we must begin telling others about Christ and his kingdom and it should be the priority of each Christian! We are commanded by our Savior to take an aggressive role in evangelizing our nation. And in a real sense, Christians will

---

1 Jack B. Simpson, *Sounding the ALARM: Moral Decay in the U.S.A.*
2 Ibid.

have to re-evangelize America as it sinks more deeply into sin.

Acts 1:8 records Christ as saying, "But you will receive power when the Holy Spirit comes on you; and you will be my witnesses in Jerusalem, in all Judea and Samaria, and to the ends of the earth." I am convinced that Jesus' words were for each person who believes in Him, not just the 11 disciples. And each Christian should be telling others the "good news" that God's love and forgiveness are available to anyone who accepts Jesus Christ as their personal Savior.

In Matthew 28:18–20, we have Jesus' authoritative command, ". . . All authority in heaven and on earth has been given to Me. Therefore go and make disciples of all nations, baptizing them in the name of the Father and of the Son and of the Holy Spirit, and teaching them to obey everything I have commanded you. And surely I will be with you always, to the very end of the age." What more could we need? We have the omnipresent, omnipotent power of Christ at our disposal as we engage in combat with the evil spirits of Satan.

We have at least four reasons to obey our Lord's command: First, to express our love and deep gratitude for all our Lord Jesus Christ has done for us. Second, because of the tragic fate awaiting those who die without receiving Jesus as Savior. Third, because of the great hunger for God throughout the world. And, fourth, to experience His special blessings. "Whomever has My commands and obeys them, he is the one who loves Me. He who loves Me will be loved by My Father, and I too will love him and show Myself to him" (John 14:21).

Most of us know the Lord's command to evangelize, and we want to follow it. What can we do to help evangelize our nation? I suggest the following five steps: First, depend totally upon the person and ministry of the Holy Spirit. As Jesus told his disciples in Acts 1:8, power to evangelize, and for that matter, to live the Christian life, comes from the indwelling power of the Holy Spirit. **Jesus alone holds the key to spiritual understanding.**

His power is available to all believers by faith, just as salvation is a gift from God that we receive by faith. God's word commands each believer to be filled with the Holy Spirit: "Do not get drunk on wine, which leads to debauchery. Instead, be filled with the Spirit" (Ephesians 5:18).

He also promises that if we ask anything according to His will, He hears us and answers our prayer; "This is the assurance we have in approaching God: that if we ask anything according to His will, He hears us. And if we know that He hears us, whatever we ask, we know that we have what we asked of Him" (1 John 5:14–15). So, any believer who willingly surrenders control of his life to the lordship of Christ, and turns from all known sin can, by faith, appropriate the power of the Holy Spirit. And, with His power, we can help evangelize our country and win the war of the spirits.

Second, pray. As much as we desire to see our friends and loved ones come to know Christ, God desires it even more. The more we focus on Christ and His greatness, the more we magnify the presence and power of God, the easier this task will be. He will answer our prayers, if we trust and obey Him and claim His promises by faith.

Third, seek spiritual training in discipleship and evangelism. No matter how zealous a person may be, his effectiveness will be severely hampered without proper training. Each Christian should learn a simple, clear Gospel presentation.

Fourth, develop a personal evangelism strategy that harmonizes with Christ's global plan. Ask God to help you develop one. Study His Word in a spirit of prayer, asking Him for insights into how you can help fulfill His Great Commission, ". . . The prayer of a righteous man is powerful and effective" (James 5:16).

As He answers your prayers, outline the thoughts He gives you. Plan how you can tell the people with whom you have contact each day about Christ. This group—family members, people with whom you work, neighbors and friends, fellow students, those who serve you in stores or restaurants—is your "Jerusalem." They are the ones Christ mentioned first in Acts 1:8.

Finally, take the initiative to tell others about Christ. Many Christians are not bold enough. It's not enough to be filled with the Holy Spirit, to pray, to be trained and to develop a plan for evangelism. We must take aggressive action in sharing Christ with others as we go about our task of changing EVIL to GOOD.

Millions of Americans are waiting to be introduced to our Savior. We must join those already helping to fulfill His Great Commission by telling those around us about Him. As Christians, we must accept this challenge to evangelize in the 1990's. In doing so, we will be providing the only solution to the problems that trouble our society, our nation, and our world.

There are also FAMILY CHALLENGES that concern Christians. The American family faces immense challenges in the coming decade, many of which strike at the very heart of what a family is and what a family does. The 1990's will see a growing clamor for redefining "family" as "domestic partnerships" so homosexuals and unmarried heterosexual couples can receive the same benefits as traditional families—especially in the areas of adoption rights, health insurance, federal income tax, and Social Security. We must meet these challenges head-on; otherwise Satan and his evil spirits will continue to flourish.

It appears that evil abounds in our nation today

Several cities, including Tacoma Park, Maryland, and Madison, Wisconsin, have already accepted such policies. Some reform efforts define "family" so broadly even Charles Manson's group would qualify.

Traditional definitions are further challenged by the emergence of in vitro fertilization, embryo freezing, surrogate motherhood and other reproductive technologies that throw into question what constitutes "motherhood," "father-hood" and "personhood."

Satan will use every tactic possible as he continues his assault on the traditional family unit. This will be one of our toughest battles in this war of the spirits.

Let's examine the broken family. In her extensive research, social scientist Judith Wallerstein found the children of divorce suffer years after the breakup. The resulting fallout affects our society in countless ways. And as illegitimacy rates climb, **"millions of children don't know what it means to have a father,"** writes Richard John Neuhaus. **"More poignantly, they don't know anyone who has a father."**

Even in homes with both parents present, serious obstacles to family well-being exist. They include economic pressures and careerism that prompt more couples to adopt a two-career life style. As a result, child rearing responsibilities are being transferred to daycare workers and educators.

A growing challenge for parents is finding ways to meet family financial needs without sacrificing significant time with their children. Some solutions: reducing the tax burden of families with children, particularly those living off a single income, and expanding opportunities for parents to work part-time, at home or under a flexible schedule.[3]

The family's demise has serious implications for society. Syndicated columnist William Raspberry noted recently that "so much of what has gone wrong in America, including the frightening growth of the poverty-stricken, crime-ridden and despairing black underclass, can be traced to the disintegration of the family structure." The reality of this family unit destruction cannot be ignored.

The family must be restored! The most significant consequence of the family disintegration may be the way we understand God and how He relates to man. It's no acci-

---

3 Ibid.

dent that God describes Himself as God the Father and God the Son, His followers as children, their relationships to each other as brothers and sisters, and His relationship to the church as bride and groom. Satan tries to undermine this understanding through attacks on the family and children. The battle at the base of these problems is spiritual rather than political or social. Remember, there has been an ongoing war of the spirits since Adam and Eve.

We still have hope, the picture isn't totally bleak—if we don't give in. Here's what we, as Christians, must do:

Get on our knees. Prayer is our first and most important action. As the psalmist wrote, "Unless the Lord builds the house, its builders labor in vain" (Psalms 127:1).

Pray for the restoration of the family. Pray for mothers and fathers, church leaders, and business and government leaders who are developing policy that affects the family.

Get involved. First, get involved socially in the lives of family members, neighbors and co-workers. Plan activities that bring the family closer together and help friends and neighbors do the same. Second, get involved politically. Work to elect pro-family officials who support pro-family legislation. Support the work of pro-family organizations. Write letters to elected officials. Vote. If we ignore government, we get government that ignorance allows.

As we Christians face the challenges of the 1990's and beyond, no family challenge is more urgent or important than the need for restoration. And nobody is more important in meeting that challenge than those who care deeply about the family.

We need to slow down and examine our lives! Today all life seems to be running at high speed. We rush to lunch; we rush back to work; we rush home only to rush to the store, to our sports, and to our evening's activities. We even rush through our vacations. This quick flight produces a life that yields less and less meaning. Lost in a world of rapid transit, instant foods, and quick-thinking computers, for thousands life has lost its joys. Life has become filled with a valid sense of emptiness, loneliness, and frustration. This is Satan's way of twisting the minds within a family, which ultimately causes problems.

Christ recognized this same restless, uncertain feeling troubling the people of His own day as they rushed about their daily business too exhausted to seek the real meaning and purpose of life. Softly He urged them, "Come to me, all you who are weary and burdened, and I will give you rest. Take My yoke upon you and learn from Me, for I am gentle and humble in heart, and you will find rest for your souls. For My yoke is easy and My burden is light" (Matthew 11:28–30). "For whoever finds Me finds life . . ." (Proverbs 8:35).

Here Jesus was talking about the kind of burden that comes as the result of our having done something that causes us to feel guilty. This could be a vast number of things in this rush, rush world in which we live, thus bringing the burden of sin or guilt upon ourselves. Also it could be sin or guilt which comes into our lives for which we are not responsible, but which brings a weight, a burden, into our lives.

A burden can become so weighty that it moves us to the point of despair. Our failure to deal with the burden brings us to the point where we really can't cope. We become immobilized emotionally and mentally, and we begin to suffer physically. This describes the needless growth of a burden from a small and seemingly insignificant issue or matter to a point of severe magnitude. This is Satan's way of bringing havoc into our lives which may result in serious damage to the family.

Millions of Americans are waiting to be introduced to our Savior

How do you lay down your burdens? How do you give them to Christ and truly leave them with Him? First, you must ask yourself if you believe Jesus Christ is able to handle your burden. Is He sufficient to deal with your troubles? Then you must believe that Jesus is willing to take this burden out of your life. Does God want you to be a happy, joyful Christian? Or, has He selected you to harass with burdens and heartaches and problems? This is not His plan, not at all.

Bringing a burden to Jesus should be a deliberate act on our part, if possible. And, what we bring to Him should be something definite. However, if we cannot state the nature of our burden, we need only to ask Him and He will show us the true nature of the issue. And we should be honest in all of this for it is dangerous business to trifle with God's great provision to release us from our burdens. When God shows us the nature of our problem, then we must immediately deal with the issue. So we should be definite, if possible, and we must be willing to be open and honest with God, to face whatever He requires of us.

Yes, we can be free from the burdens that Satan has placed upon us if we respond to Jesus' invitation: "Come to Me, all you who are weary and burdened, and I will give you rest" (Matthew 11:28). Jesus doesn't send us to others to get rest from our burdens. He calls us to Himself.[4]

From the moment we are conceived to the moment we draw our last breath, God knows all about us. We never come to God with the attitude of informing Him of anything. Instead, we can bring to Him our needs as an act of faith that He knows our burdens and how to deal with them.[5]

Faith is our expression of confidence in God. It is our way of saying to our heavenly Father that we trust Him with every aspect of our lives.

What a Savior! We have God's love to guide us, comfort us, sustain us, strengthen us, and keep us for every trial. For every day, forever!

---

4 Several sermons by Dr. Charles F. Stanley, In Touch Ministries, Atlanta, GA, were valuable to the writer in composing this chapter.

5 Jack B. Simpson, *Sounding the ALARM: Moral Decay in the U.S.A.*

SPIRITUAL
ADULTERY

Many Christians today are committing spiritual adultery. "Husbands, love your wives, just as Christ loved the Church, and gave Himself up for her" (Ephesians 5:25). Many times the Bible compares the husband-wife relationship to the relation between Jesus and the Church.

Christ considered the love and harmony between husband and wife so great that He compared it to His love for us. Of course, Christ loves the Church far more than husband and wife could even begin to love each other. But no greater love was there on earth with which Christ could compare His love than that of the union between man and woman.

The union of man and woman is strong. If the marriage is centered on Christ, it can endure all things. But there is one thing that will try a marriage more than any other and that is the sin of unfaithfulness of one mate against the other mate. That is the sin of adultery. It is the one thing that seems impossible to forgive and even harder to forget. Only through Christ can this sin truly be forgiven and forgotten.

From a legalistic point of view adultery would seem like a very simple thing to overlook. After all, no one is hurt. There is no physical damage. There is nothing physically taken from anyone. Still, this sin tears both sides of a marriage. The one who commits adultery is eaten up with guilt.

The other one feels defiled by a foreign entity being in union with the person who is theirs, and theirs alone.

Other things can be forgiven with ease, but in the case of adultery, only in the name of Jesus can all things truly be forgiven. It is probably the worst sin we could commit against our mate. In the same sense spiritual adultery is probably the worst sin we could commit against our God.

Spiritual adultery? What is that? I've never read anything about spiritual adultery in my Bible! Sure you have. Read Exodus 20:3–4, "You shall have no other gods before me. You shall not make for yourself an idol in the form of anything in heaven above or on the earth beneath or in the waters below." It's the first commandment. Is it the first because it just happens to be first? Maybe, but I seriously doubt it.

God is very clear here when He says we are not to have an "idol in the form of anything." Because God has no visible form, any idol intended to resemble Him would be a sinful misrepresentation of Him. "Do not worship any other god, for the Lord, whose name is Jealous, is a jealous God" (Exodus 34:14). God will not put up with rivalry or unfaithfulness. The "jealousy" of God demands exclusive devotion to Himself. No deity, real or imagined, is to rival the one true God in our hearts and lives. "For the Lord your God is a consuming fire, a jealous God" (Deuteronomy 4:24), and delivers to judgment all who oppose Him.

Just as a husband or wife is jealous when his or her mate commits adultery, so is our God jealous when we commit SPIRITUAL ADULTERY. Just as we grieve our mate by this act, so do we grieve God.

Spiritual adultery is putting something above God. We all know that much. But we need to dig a little deeper. Go back to the husband-wife relationship for a minute. When you commit adultery in the flesh, you don't necessarily put someone else before your mate. But, if only for a few minutes, you do put someone on the same level or in place of your mate and by the very act of adultery you allow someone else to take care of the needs that your mate has

vowed his or her life to fill. This is the very reason your mate will be so hurt by this act.

In the same respect, spiritual adultery is not only putting something above God, it is also putting something or someone in addition to, on the same level with, in opposition to, or in place of God. **For example, reading the horoscope out of the morning paper is spiritual adultery.** It is having a god in addition to your one God. You might say, "I really don't believe in it. I just read it for fun." This is probably very true. You don't really believe in it. But how do you think God feels when He sees you bringing a pagan god into your life?

"It's just for fun, God, I really don't believe in it." Go out and commit adultery in the flesh, then come home, smile at your mate and say, "Honey, I just committed adultery, but don't worry about it. I really didn't mean it. You know how it is, I just did it for fun." It will be a small consolation that you "just did it for fun." The fact remains that you defiled your body and the relationship that belongs to your spouse. No matter why it is done, your mate's heart will still be broken. That's just how God must feel.

Your mate might say in tears, "I'm a failure. I can't fulfill all of your needs. Am I not good enough to do that for you?" God might say, "What's wrong, my child? Why do you allow a pagan god to be a part of your life? Am I not a big enough God to fulfill ALL your needs?"

It's easy enough to picture how your mate might feel. Try to picture how God must feel when you cheat on Him. He sent His only Son, then He sent His Holy Spirit. He gives us power to tread on the devil. He gives us authority to use Jesus' name. And to top it all, He freely gives us love that we can't even begin to comprehend. And we respond to His love by starting our day by bowing to a pagan god, "just for fun."

We aren't the first generation to defile God with spiritual adultery. The Jews did it when they were just six weeks out of bondage. God had delivered them from the hand of their captors. He opened the Red Sea in their famous exodus from bondage. What a feeling that must have been to stand on the floor of the Red Sea and witness the power of the Living God literally holding back a wall of water, and then going into the desert and having their food fall from heaven like rain. Yet with these miraculous things still fresh in their minds, what did they do? They built a pagan god and bowed to their knees and worshiped it! How did God feel about their spiritual adultery? He came very close to destroying them all. This is how God felt.

Spiritual adultery is putting something above God

How does God feel when He is not first in your life? How does He feel about spiritual adultery? Read about the Israelites wandering in the wilderness 40 years. Read about Sodom and Gomorrah or the sins of mankind before the flood or even the Tower of Babel.

Saul was told (see 1 Samuel 28:5–19), while using witchcraft, that he would die because he did not obey the voice of the Lord. Whenever man walked away from God and turned to something else, he incurred the anger of God. God wants our fellowship. Yes, God is a Jealous God. Therefore, it behooves us to learn from the mistakes of others.

As children of God, we have no other choice and no other options are open to us. We are to serve Him and Him alone. We need not and should not dabble with horoscopes, mediums, fortune tellers, palm readers, hypnotism, drugs, charms, or any other type of divination.

Adultery, whether marital or spiritual, is a betrayal of a committed love. Those things that would tempt us to commit spiritual adultery will lose their appeal IF we put God first and allow Him to permeate every aspect of our lives and fulfill every need as it arises. "For we are members of His body, of His flesh, and of His bones" (Ephesians 5:30 KJV).

Have you ever considered how spiritual adultery will

affect us on judgment day? What does the Bible teach us about this? The apostle Paul wrote, "For we must all appear before the Judgment Seat of Christ, that each one may receive what is due him for the things done while in the body, whether good or bad" (2 Corinthians 5:10).

What are you doing that will count for eternity? This is a most important question that many Christians do not take seriously, yet they plan to spend eternity in heaven. Every opportunity to spread the Word of God that is squandered by believers will become costly when they appear before the Judgment Seat of Christ. What could have been a reward for them will be lost forever. How we live our Christian life is very important. Did you know that the Kingdom of God will not be the same for all believers?

Some believers will have rewards for their earthly faithfulness; others will not. "His master replied, 'Well done, good and faithful servant! You have been faithful with a few things; I will put you in charge of many things. Come and share your master's happiness!'" (Matthew 25:23).

Some believers will be entrusted with certain privileges; others will not. "'Well done, my good servant!' his master replied. 'Because you have been trustworthy in a very small matter, take charge of ten cities.'" (Luke 19:17).

Some believers will be rich in the Kingdom of God; others will not. "This is how it will be with anyone who stores up things for himself but is not rich toward God. Sell your possessions and give to the poor. Provide purses for yourselves that will not wear out, a treasure in heaven that will not be exhausted, where no thief comes near and no moth destroys" (Luke 12:21, 33).

Some will be given true riches; others will not. "So if you have not been trustworthy in handling worldly wealth, who will trust you with true riches?" (Luke 16:11).

Some will be giving heavenly treasures of their own; others will not. "And if you have not been trustworthy with someone else's property, who will give you property of your own?" (Luke 16:12).

Some will reign and rule with Christ; others will not.

"To him who overcomes, I will give the right to sit with me on my throne, just as I overcame and sat down with my Father on his throne" (Revelation 3:21).

As Dr. Charles Stanley, First Baptist Church, Atlanta, Georgia, states, "Privilege in the Kingdom of God is determined by one's faithfulness in this life. This truth may come as a shock. Maybe you have always thought that everyone would be equal in the Kingdom of God. It is true that there will be equality in terms of our inclusion in the Kingdom of God but not in our rank and privilege."[1]

Everything we do—the care we give our children, the time spent to care for our spouses, the motivation we have for going to church, the concern we have for the lost, the attempts we make to witness, the care we give to those with special needs, and even the quiet time we have with the Lord—is being watched and will be evaluated accordingly.

Every moment counts. No deed will go unnoticed. All of us must give an account. The Scripture says, "So then, each of us will give an account of himself to God" (Romans 14:12). No one will get by with anything. Every sinful deed will be examined. On the other side of the coin, we can rest assured that none of our good deeds will go unnoticed either. The Scripture continues, "Behold, I am coming soon! My reward is with me, and I will give to everyone according to what he has done" (Revelation 22:12).

Some of you who are not well-known and are not living in the spotlight now, but are faithfully serving our Lord, will someday be put in God's limelight when He Himself generously rewards you. The Scripture says, "So that your giving may be in secret. Then your Father, who sees what is done in secret, will reward you. So that it will not be obvious to men that you are fasting, but only to your Father, who is unseen; and your Father, who sees what is done in secret, will reward you" (Matthew 6:4, 18).

Further, the Bible says, "Each man's work will be shown

1 Dr. Charles F. Stanley, In Touch Ministries, Atlanta, GA.

for what it is." That is, what were our true motives for serving Christ? Our works will be tested in God's cleansing fire where "the fire will test the quality of each man's work. If what he has built survives, he will receive his reward. If it is burned up, he will suffer loss: he himself will be saved, but only as one escaping through the flames" (please read 1 Corinthians 3:13–15).

Adultery, whether marital or spiritual, is a betrayal of a committed love

After He has so graciously saved us, it's amazing that our Lord also chooses to reward us for serving Him. We didn't deserve His mercy to begin with, and yet He promises He will reward us for the most menial tasks done in service unto Him. Jesus said, "I tell you the truth, anyone who gives you a cup of water in my name because you belong to Christ will certainly not lose his reward" (Mark 9:41).

Christians don't do good works in order to be saved, but they do good works as a result of being saved. Once they have experienced His love, true Christians show their love for Christ by serving others and remaining obedient to Him.

The writer prays that the above illustration will be of value to the reader. We all need to evaluate our behavior. As you can see from what has been outlined here, the Scriptures clearly reveal to us that God is not only watching every move we make, He is recording them as well. We will be held accountable for each and every action we have taken when our day of judgment arrives.

This is why we must be very careful not to engage in spiritual adultery of any kind, regardless of how insignificant it may appear at the time. The horoscope was used in this chapter as an example because we can all relate to it and many people probably had never considered it as spiritual adultery.

However, as this chapter comes to a close, it is important that we look at one specific verse of Scripture to confirm that God does not approve of astrology and horoscope reading: "All the counsel you have received has only worn you out! Let your astrologers come forward, those stargazers who make predictions month by month, let them save you from what is coming upon you" (Isaiah 47:13). Reading God's Word would be an excellent substitute for anyone involved in horoscope reading.

Many other examples could have been used, but most spiritual adultery could be eliminated quickly if we would only think before we act. Satan works very hard and he has developed many clever schemes that will surely lead numerous complacent and compromising Christians into committing spiritual adultery.

Those Christians who are depending on the zodiac are not depending on Jesus Christ. There is only one true God of all creation (read Exodus 20:3).

Let us not forget, "For we must all appear before the Judgment Seat of Christ, that each one may receive what is due him for the things done while in the body, whether good or bad" (2 Corinthians 5:10).

This war of the spirits is serious business involving each and every one of us, and it's a daily battle.

CHAPTER TEN

WHAT IS
THE LORD'S
NAME?

The image of God as 'He' is losing its Sovereignty in many of America's churches as more and more worshipers challenge the language that describes Supreme Being as a male.

In the April 27, 1992, edition of the *Wall Street Journal*, staff reporter R. Gustav Niebuhr made the front page with a comprehensive look at the new translations that are sweeping many of the churches in America today.[1] This was a most informative article.

Let's examine how some particular people, churches, and universities are addressing God today.

The First Congregational Church located in Long Beach, California, looks every inch a bastion of religious tradition. Inside the imposing Italian Renaissance structure, graced with delicate rose windows, are mahogany pews and a grand old pipe organ.

Then the Sunday service starts. "May the God who mothers us all bear us on the breath of dawn, and make us to shine like the sun, and hold us in the palm of Her hand," intones Pastor Mary Ellen Kilsby.

Unorthodox? Some would say so. But no longer unique.

The ancient Western image of God the Father is coming under assault. Although still relatively unusual in most

---

1 R. Gustav Neibuhr, *The Wall Street Journal*, April 27, 1992, p. 1.

of America's 350,000 Christian churches, gospel like this is making inroads among church leaders, who have begun purging hymnals and liturgies of references to God as male, white as pure, black as evil and heaven as up.

CHANGING TEXTS

This year, a new translation of Catholic psalms used in worship that eliminates the word "He" as the pronoun for God will be circulated among Catholics for study.

The United Church of Christ, the liberal Protestant denomination to which First Congregational Church belongs, is revising its hymnal, and will "change some very treasured texts," says the Rev. James Crawford, pastor of Boston's Old South Church, who chairs the hymnal committee. Among those due for certain revision: the old Protestant favorite "Dear Lord and Father of Mankind." Folks, this is not a fabrication. These are the FACTS!

And soon, the staid United Methodist Church will ask delegates to a church-wide conference to approve a new Book of Worship, the text from which ministers design their services, that would allow congregations in certain instances to drop Father in favor of a genderless God. Although it remains largely traditional, the book also includes prayers in which the deity is addressed as "Father and Mother," "Bakerwoman God" and "Grandfather, Great Spirit."

For centuries, Christians have worshiped a deity that had explicitly masculine names. The Hebrew Scriptures, which form the Christian Old Testament, call God "He." In the Gospels, Jesus refers to God as Abba, an Aramaic word best translated as "Daddy." Culture has reinforced tradition: medieval artists and hymn writers portrayed God as a wise older king. Michelangelo painted the deity as a muscular, bearded giant. Hollywood cast actors who could speak basso profundo (deep bass).

SHE AND HE

Yet, these days, sweeping social shifts, primarily feminism, but also civil rights and environmentalism, have crashed against the ancient Christian picture of God and the creation. This scenario makes me very ill: But let us continue this investigation.

The ancient Western image of God the Father is coming under assault

"I don't think our conception of God will ever stand still again," says Joseph Hough, dean of Vanderbilt University's Divinity School in Nashville, Tennessee. In his public utterances, Dr. Hough alternately refers to the deity as She, then He. "I don't think anyone would want to defend the view that God values males more than females, but that's exactly what [traditional] language does," he says.[2]

The roots of the debate over what to call God are often traced to a book by Mary Daly called "Beyond God the Father," a critique of patriarchal religion that bluntly states, "If God is male, then the male is God." Dr. Hough also cites James Cone's 1969 book *Black Theology, Black Power,* which argues that the church must so identify with oppressed minorities that it becomes "theologically impossible" not to think of Christ as black.

Such books had an immediate impact on many seminaries, but only recently has their influence been felt in established churches, where church leaders have begun replacing the once-generic word "brethren" with "people."

THE FINAL WORD

For the orthodox, any question about God's name was settled once and for all more than 1,600 years ago at the Council of Nicea, where more than 300 bishops from across the Roman Empire convened to resolve a raging theological debate about what, essentially, God is. The group agreed to describe God as Father, Son and Holy Spirit, three inti-

---

2 Ibid.

mately connected "persons" within one "substance." The doctrine of the Trinity is important because, while it holds Christ to be fully and eternally divine, it also explains that Christians don't worship two or three separate gods.

These days, however, many pastors are choosing to baptize and marry in the name of a gender-neutral Trinity, the "Creator, Redeemer and Sustainer." And that is indeed causing great concern, especially among some traditional religious experts and academics, who believe such changes border on heresy.

"Once you deconstruct the Trinity . . . I think you've lost the Gospel," says Carl Braaten, professor of systematic theology at the Lutheran School of Theology in Chicago. "We're facing a battle in the future, and more and more people are going to get sucked into the vortex on the naming of God, how to pray to God."

The changes are troubling as well for many religious people who do not view themselves as particularly conservative. David Moss, an Episcopal priest in Atlanta and a psychotherapist, says the loss of a shared image of God—a central reference point in Western civilization—will lead to "confusion" among Christians and dissension among churches.

God's masculine names, he says, make up an almost indelible memory within Judeo-Christian culture. As evidence, he cites his offering communion at a home for elderly Alzheimer's and stroke victims. When he opens the service, the patients give little evidence of consciousness—until he begins the Lord's Prayer. "If I say, 'Our . . .' they say, 'Father.' It makes the hair on my arms stand up."

Yet a number of theologians warn that language shapes reality, and unless the church changes its imagery, it will effectively endorse gender and race bias. And by insisting on speaking of God as Father, they say, traditionalists risk deifying a mere word—committing the sin of idolatry.

We will analyze these "intellectual theologians" in considerable detail in the following chapter. It will be interesting to see how they "measure up" according to the teachings of the Bible.

ENDING JUSTICE

"As society becomes aware of the issue of injustice . . . the society's language has to change to mirror that," says Letty M. Russell, a professor of theology at Yale Divinity School. "The way to respect the original words is to re-translate them as our understanding of their meaning changes."

At First Congregational Church in Long Beach, the Rev. Kilsby says, "If there's no feminist imagery, then women weren't made in God's image." The Rev. Kilsby never speaks of a divine king or an almighty lord. "There's a certain tenderness and vulnerability about God," she says, which she tries to project by likening the deity to a shepherdess or a mother hen.[3]

Even Satan takes a different cast here. The church's associate minister, the Rev. Christopher Wilke, says he links evil with "shadows," not blackness, out of consideration for African-American friends. In a recent sermon, he says, "I didn't talk about the Prince of Darkness. I talked about the Prince of Evil."

The Rev. Kilsby's preaching has encouraged her congregation toward eclecticism. Gathering over coffee after the Sunday service, members talk about how they picture God: as a cloud, as a formless spirit, or as Mother Earth.

BIG BANG

Marjorie McMillan, a professional singer and voice teacher, remarks her former "very vivid" picture of a masculine God is now in transition. "I don't have this all-powerful male image in mind," she says.

And schoolteacher Karen Miller says that while she still believes in following Jesus' teaching, "I'm evolving into a sort of neo-pagan. I envision the universe as God and all in the universe as a part of God." Her husband, Tom, a history professor, long ago stopped saying Father in favor of Creator. His image of God? "It's like atoms," he says.

---

3 Ibid., p. 7.

Yet many people have been protesting the changes. A few months ago, 77 bishops, pastors and lay people associated with the United Methodist Church gathered in Memphis and issued the so-called Memphis Declaration. The group said inclusion of new language for God in the proposed book of worship would "alter the apostolic faith."

Many false prophets exist today in the churches and seminaries

One conservative Methodist group, the Good News Caucus, promises to argue to stop the changes in a word-by-word editing at the denomination's future conference. "It's not for us to decide what God's to be called. He's expressed that in Scripture," says the Rev. James Heidinger II, the group's executive secretary. Tampering with traditional biblical imagery, he adds, "leads to pantheism and goddess-worship."

Over the past year, opponents in the Episcopal Church and the United Church of Christ have issued their own declarations, branding changes in traditional languages about God as anything from a cultural fad to outright heresy.

If you don't believe that we are engaged in a war of the spirits, read on!

MEN AS GODS

Some proponents of change say they see in the opposition a backlash by men who fear their own authority is at stake. "They may feel the reverberations of the ax being laid to the tree, and they're up in the tree," says the Rev. Beryl Ingram-Ward, a Methodist minister in Tacoma, Washington.

Opposition comes from women as well. At the Lakewood, Ohio, Congregational Church, the Rev. Lyman Farrar says for years he's been quietly using the word God instead of male pronouns for the deity in prayers and sermons. But he encountered an "instant negative reaction" when he introduced a gender-neutral version of the doxology, a historic hymn of praise, a few months ago. As he stood shaking hands with congregants after the service, several women bluntly told him not to do it again.

"I can't understand why so many women are so upset by this," he says. Says Sue Bosworth, a member of the congregation, "I think we're in danger of losing the Trinity" when use of the name Father is diminished.

While this debate is just beginning in the pews, it has already reshaped religious vocabulary at many of the nation's prominent seminaries, particularly the Protestant seminaries, where women's enrollment has exploded. As their constituencies have changed, these institutions have found that previously standard terms—mankind, brethren, God the Father—seem antiquated, even politically charged.

INCLUSIVE LANGUAGE

Many seminaries today have guidelines recommending proper speech on campus. At Columbia Theological Seminary, a Presbyterian institution in Decatur, Georgia, the student handbook says that students, faculty and administrators, "are expected to use inclusive language" in the classroom, chapel and written work. Two years ago the faculty at Fuller Theological Seminary, an evangelical institution in Pasadena, California, recommended students speak of men and women, rather than man or mankind. (The seminary has retained traditional language for God.) But attempts to take such messages outside seminary walls have often met with anger and resistance.

In the mid 1980's, the National Council of Churches began publishing its multi-volume Inclusive Language Lectionary—Bible readings for Sunday services—which omitted male pronouns for God and re-translated Jesus' traditional title, "the Son of Man," as "the Human One." As the series went to press, the committee of scholars who put it together received anonymous death threats.

Committee Chairman, Burton Throckmorton, recalls registering under a false name when he went to speak to the council's board at a Hartford, Connecticut, hotel. Police patrolled the building with bomb-sniffing dogs. "It wasn't funny business," says Dr. Throckmorton, a retired professor of The New Testament at Bangor (Maine) Theological Seminary. "There are a lot of lunatics out there."

"BRING MANY NAMES"

Despite the hostility, the lectionary has sold some 80,000 copies, according to one of its publishers, Cleveland-based Pilgrim Press. And other, similar praise materials are now coming to market, including new hymns that indeed praise a distinctly nontraditional deity.

Brian Wren, an Oxford-educated poet who lives in Rome, Pennsylvania, is an author of many such hymns. One of his best-known is "Bring Many Names," whose verses invoke "strong Mother God," "warm Father God," "old, aching God" and "young, growing God." Dr. Wren gives seminars in which he encourages people to "brainstorm images of God." At one San Francisco gathering, ministers and church musicians came up with a long list of new names—"Beautiful Movement," "Straight-talking Lover," "Daredevil Gambler"—that he incorporated into a hymn.[4]

"The fact that Jesus called God Father doesn't mean he was teaching us to use that name for time and eternity," Dr. Wren says. "I think that at its best, the biblical tradition is that God cannot be contained in human language."

The Bible warns us about false prophets. The facts revealed here are obvious. Many false prophets exist today in our churches and seminaries. The Bible says, "For the time will come when men will not put up with sound doctrine. Instead, to suit their own desires, they will gather around them a great number of teachers to say what their itching ears want to hear" (2 Timothy 4:3).

---

4 Ibid.

THEOLOGICAL TEACHERS

ARE THEY REALLY INTELLECTUALS?

Did Jesus Christ really rise from the dead? Americans are overwhelmingly confident that He did. Surprisingly, however, many theological teachers are not.

"The gospel story is not journalistically descriptive," says one professor of theology. "It's a theological narrative in the afterglow of the death and resurrection of Christ."[1] This professor says that those who wrote the Bible believed Jesus rose in a "glorified" body with supernatural powers. Many modern theologians, however, deny the resurrection entirely. They say it was the "spirit of Christ" or the teachings of Jesus that were revived, not the man Himself.

In between the two lies another view held by some theologians: that Jesus rose in a changed form, best left unspecified. This group of theologians say "it's not necessary to say He has flesh and bones." Yet another group of theologians similarly believe that Jesus' body was changed after He rose. It is obvious that these theologians have radically departed from both Scripture and tradition. When scholars say it was not a physical body—that it didn't take up space and you could not touch it—they are playing fast and loose with the Scriptures.

The Bible teaches that even when the disciples saw the

---

1 James D. Davis, *Sun-Sentinel*, April 19, 1992, p. 1E.

resurrected Christ, "They were startled and frightened, thinking they saw a ghost" (Luke 24:37). But Christ urged them to "Look at My hands and My feet. It is I Myself! Touch Me and see; a ghost does not have flesh and bones as I have" (Luke 24:39). When the disciples finally became convinced of His bodily resurrection, they were quickly transformed into courageous evangelists.

The death, burial, and resurrection of Jesus Christ is the fundamental doctrine of Christianity. This is the doctrine that turned the world upside down in the first century, that lifted Christianity preeminently above Judaism, and the pagan religions of the Mediterranean world.

The resurrection of Jesus Christ is a historical fact, evidenced by the eyewitness accounts of the disciples and more than 500 people. It proves His deity (Romans 1:4). It is also the divine guarantee that each believer will live forever with God in heaven (John 11:25–26).

Many intellectual scholars and theological teachers poison the minds of the young students (preachers) that are graduating from the seminaries in this country. They are the future pastors of our churches. They are the future Sunday school teachers of our children. They are the future youth ministers that teach and influence our teenagers. Collectively, these intellectual theologians impact the spiritual lives of many people. One must ask the question, is this GOOD vs. EVIL: a war of the spirits?

When these professors of theology, these "intellectual giants," begin to question the Word of God they should no longer be viewed as intelligent or wise but should be considered as "agents of Satan." And their abilities to comprehend the Scriptures must be viewed with suspicion.

Just because an individual has earned a Ph.D. (doctorate) or similar degree from a prominent seminary or university does not necessarily conclude that this individual is an intellect. Many people have a tendency to assume that these people have superior knowledge and intelligence because of their academic credentials and achievements. However, somewhere along the pathway of life they forgot, or never knew, that all wisdom comes from God, not the seminary.

As many of our nations seminaries move further away from the light of the gospel, we must realize that Satan will surely use this opportunity to infiltrate our churches. As Christians, we must wake up and become aware of what is happening in this important arena of theology today. We cannot stand by idly and allow the inerrant Word of God, the Holy Bible, to be tampered with. These "smart" theologians will cause irreparable damage if they are allowed to proceed unbridled and unchallenged.

As lay people, we must never forget that we have the perfect instrument and the perfect teacher in the Scriptures which are God-breathed. Look at what they teach us: "If any of you lacks wisdom, he should ask God, who gives generously to all without finding fault, and it will be given to him." (James 1:5).

Any time we begin to rely on man, or should I say woman, to find solutions to our spiritual problems, we are surely in deep trouble. If scholars are allowed to change or modify the Bible so that it will neatly fulfill the social requirements and personal vogue of today, what area of the Bible will they target for change tomorrow? The Bible says, ". . . Don't you know that friendship with the world is hatred toward God? . . ." (James 4:4). God does not call on us to escape from the world as a place but to avoid worldliness as a system of belief.

As Christians and believers in the Lord Jesus Christ, we must not be deceived by these "blind intellectuals" that claim to know what God "really" meant to say when He gave us the Scriptures. The Bible says the following: "Do not deceive yourselves. If any one of you thinks he is wise by the standards of this age, he should become a 'fool' so that he may become wise. For the wisdom of this world is foolishness in God's sight. It is written: 'He catches the wise in their craftiness' and again, 'The Lord knows that the thoughts of the wise are futile'" (1 Corinthians 3:18-20).

The reanimation of a corpse is the unique claim of

Christianity among the world's religions. Believers cling to it as proof of Jesus' claim to be the Son of God. More than 80 percent of Americans today believe Jesus resurrected, according to pollster George Gallup, Jr.

"It's the heart of the gospel," says Dr. O. S. Hawkins, former pastor of First Baptist Church in Fort Lauderdale, Florida, a large church in South Florida with over 10,000 members. Dr. Hawkins continues, "If Jesus did not rise from the dead, he was not who he said he was. He said he was the great 'I Am,' not the great 'I Was.'"[2]

Yes, many theological teachers and preachers are truly intellectuals. **In my opinion, a few such individuals are: Dr. O. S. Hawkins, Dr. Charles F. Stanley, Dr. James Kennedy, Dr. John Ankerberg, Dr. R. C. Sproul and Kay Arthur.**

Concerning the resurrection, the Bible says, "Jesus said to her, 'I am the resurrection and the life. He who believes in Me will live, even though he dies'" (John 11:25). The Bible also says, "Regarding his Son, who as to His human nature was a descendant of David, and who through the Spirit of holiness was declared with power to be the Son of God by His resurrection from the dead: Jesus Christ our Lord" (Romans 1:3–4).

There are many professors of theology in our society today that are saying, "The way to respect the original words of the Bible is to re-translate them as our understanding of their meaning changes." What a shame. They are victims in this "war of the spirits." It is my prayer that these people will be touched by the Holy Spirit before it is too late.

They are indeed being manipulated by Satan and probably don't even realize it. The meaning of the inerrant Word of God never changes. It was true yesterday, it is true today, and, yes, it will also be true tomorrow.

Theological teachers: are they really intellectuals? Probably the best answer to this question is another question. Where did they obtain their knowledge and wisdom? If their

---

2 Dr. O. S. Hawkins, First Baptist Church, Fort Lauderdale, FL.

intellect came from God through studying His revealing Word, the Bible, and the truth contained therein, then they are to be considered true intellectuals. However, if they have only relied upon and obtained their knowledge through their professors of theology at the seminary, then their knowledge is questionable. They may possess no wisdom, since valid wisdom comes only from God.

Any minister who discovers that he was deceived by his theological professors should immediately pray to God and seek His wisdom, then spend some time studying the book of Revelation where it says, "I warn everyone who hears the words of the prophecy of this book: If ANYONE ADDS ANYTHING to them, God will add to him the plagues described in this book. And if ANYONE TAKES WORDS AWAY from this book of prophecy, God will take away from him his share in the tree of life and in the holy city, which are described in this book" (Revelation 22:18, 19, emphasis added).

Like the Bereans of Paul's day (Acts 17:11), Christians should check the veracity of all opinions against the only reliable standard of authority that God has placed in our hands: the Bible. This may mean a change in theology for some. This is not new. God had to change the views of Peter regarding his inclusion of the Gentiles into the household of faith (Acts 10:9–16). Paul confronted Peter "to his face" on a similar matter (Galatians 2:11–14). There are times when we all need to be knocked off our theological horses (Acts 9:4) to remind us that God is God, and "we are but dust" (Psalm 103:14).

The Psalmist David helps us to understand what God's Word is and what it does when he says, "The law of the Lord is perfect, reviving the soul; The testimony of the Lord is sure, making wise the simple; The precepts of the Lord are right, rejoicing the heart; The commandment of the Lord is pure, enlightening the eyes . . ." David goes on in Psalm 19 to say God's Word is "more desirable than gold, yes, than much fine gold; sweeter also than honey."

Another theological preacher and teacher who qual-

ifies as an intellectual, in the writer's opinion, is Dr. John MacArthur, Jr. Dr. MacArthur, who is the pastor of Grace Community Church in Sun Valley, California, is heard daily on "Grace To You," a half-hour radio broadcast ministry that reaches around the world.[3]

Dr. MacArthur has authored numerous books including the best-seller, *The Gospel According To Jesus*, and his most recent book, *Our Sufficiency In Christ*. In addition to his ministry, he is president of The Master's College, a fully accredited, four-year Christian college in California.

I recently had the opportunity to hear Dr. MacArthur speak at the First Baptist Church in Ft. Lauderdale, Florida. He gave a wonderful message regarding the inerrant Word of God and how simple it is for anyone to understand the Bible. However, they must be serious about learning how to apply the Scriptures in their daily lives.

Billy Graham is another individual who qualifies as an intellectual in most people's opinion. It is relevant here to point out that Dr. Graham did not attend seminary. His wisdom comes from God and his intellect from studying the inerrant Word of God. For many years, Dr. Graham's dynamic radio and television messages, books, and crusades on every continent have been reaching people in all walks of life. Literally millions of them have made decisions for Christ. Dr. Graham says, "Man has a problem and God has an answer in Christ." He gives his messages in simple, direct, and dynamic language that is taken straight from the Bible.

The power resident in the Word of God—both His spoken Word and His written Word, the Holy Scriptures—is so great that the Biblical writers almost exhaust their resources of language in trying to describe it. They used many and varied figures of speech to illustrate its wonders.

It is the Word of God that produces and maintains life. And it is our daily light. We are also admonished to "Take

---

3 John MacArthur, "Grace to You," Sun Valley, CA.

the helmet of salvation and the sword of the Spirit, which is the Word of God" (Ephesians 6:17).

"Is not My Word like fire, declares the Lord, and like a hammer that breaks a rock in pieces?" (Jeremiah 23:29).

"The Word of God is quick, and powerful, and sharper than any double-edged sword" (Hebrews 4:12).

As God-fearing Christians, the Bible is our foundation. And it should be the solid foundation on which our lives, our families, our churches and our communities are built.

Theological teachers that are really intellectuals will know and quickly cite the following Scripture, "For it is written: 'I will destroy the wisdom of the wise; the intelligence of the intelligent I will frustrate.' Where is the wise man? Where is the scholar? Where is the philosopher of this age? Has not God made foolish the wisdom of the world?" (1 Corinthians 1:19–20).

"Man has a problem and God has an answer in Christ."

Most modern evangelical Christians no longer doubt the reality of the sacrificial death and bodily resurrection of Jesus Christ. The evidence has become overwhelming, and these truths have become the glory and the power of the Gospel. Intellectualism should be replaced with simple childlike faith.

However, the fearful reluctance to take God's Word literally is still a great problem among some "Bible-believers." Whenever such a stand might become costly, many Christians eagerly accept non-literal ways of "interpreting" Scripture to fit their own preferences.

Yes, Jesus Christ, our Lord and Savior, did rise from the dead. He was a real person. He was flesh and bones. He walked. He talked. And there were witnesses to all of this. How do I know? Well, the Bible tells me so and these wonderful Scriptures are God-breathed!

THE
CHARACTER
OF A GODLY
PERSON

As we continue to analyze good versus evil and proceed with the examination of this rampaging war of the spirits, is there anything greater that can be said of a man than: "He is a godly person?"

Godly people are victorious in their everyday battle against Satan and his evil spirits. We certainly need godly people in the workplace who will provide examples of true Christianity and in the home who will incarnate the reality of the indwelling Christ. We need godly people in places of civil and spiritual leadership who display the wisdom and humility of a person under the lordship of Jesus Christ.

How would one define a godly person? There are many definitions. However, as we journey through the Bible—the inerrant Word of God—which is our most reliable source of information, perhaps the clearest and most appropriate is David's description which says: "Blessed is the man who does not walk in the counsel of the wicked or stand in the way of sinners or sit in the seat of mockers. But his delight is in the law of the Lord, and on His law he meditates day and night. He is like a tree planted by streams of water, which yields its fruit in season and whose leaf does not whither. Whatever he does prospers" (Psalm 1:1–3).

You see, the Scripture reveals to us here that a godly person is one who has a personal relationship with Jesus Christ. Nothing else will substitute. We are not talking about appearance or image but about a living vital relationship with the Savior. This is the bedrock for any attributes of godliness. Until a person is born again, he is alienated from God and cannot be like Him. He may be a good person, but he is not a godly person. He may be kind and he may be gracious, but he does not know God as his personal Deliverer from sin. But when he trusts in Christ for the forgiveness of sin, God's Spirit regenerates him and he is indwelt by God Himself and given the grace to grow in the true knowledge of God.

If you do not have an intimate, personal relationship with Jesus Christ and if He is but a vague ideal or childhood moral lesson, then you need to receive Him as your Savior. Acknowledge your sin—your independence from God. Admit you are lost—the end of which is hell, eternal separation from God. Ask for Christ to forgive you of your sins—which is why He died on the cross. And accept His gift of eternal life—unending fellowship with God on earth and in heaven.

Another characteristic of a godly man is that he orders his life after the counsel of the godly. He is not too proud or self-sufficient to seek advice. He is not too egotistical to admit he needs help and wisdom. A godly father who wants to rear his children well is wise enough to seek the counsel of other men who have experienced the perplexities and dilemmas of fathering.

A godly husband who wants his marriage to work should look to the wellspring of wisdom that can be stored in the hearts and minds of men who have enduring marriages. A godly businessman will indeed seek the instruction of other businessmen who adhere to the ethical practices of the Scriptures in their jobs, even in the face of secular pressure.

In each instance, advice is to be sought from other godly men who have a personal relationship with Jesus Christ and have demonstrated the reality of His presence. You should never make crucial decisions based on the counsel of the ungodly. They have no fear of God, and though their suggestions may seem successful initially the long-term results are empty and vain.

The Psalmist David helps us to understand what God's Word is and what it does when he says, "The law of the Lord is perfect, reviving the soul. The statutes of the Lord are trustworthy, making wise the simple" (Psalm 19:7). A godly man seeks to be wise. He understands he can find God's wisdom implanted in the hearts of other men committed to Christ who have weathered the storms and remained faithful to the sound principles of God's Word. That does not mean they are perfect but that their bent is toward God.

A godly man seeks companionship among other believers. He looks for opportunities to develop beneficial relationships with other Christians. This provides additional strength to the believers as they battle against the many evil spirits surrounding Satan and his troops. The writer of Proverbs understood the pivotal role of honest and sincere Christian fellowship: "Iron sharpens iron, so one man sharpens another" (Proverbs 27:17).

That does not mean a believer should refuse to associate with non-Christians. If that were the case, we would negate God's command to carry the good news of Christ's love to the unredeemed. But we are not to make such contacts the source of our close companionship. Our intimate friendships are to be centered with other like-minded followers of Christ. We relate, converse, and enjoy the friendship of all people, but our focus is primarily on cultivating relationships with Christians who will challenge us, reprove us when necessary, encourage us, pray with us, and help us grow in godliness.

A godly man is not passive about defending his faith

A godly man is not passive about defending his faith. He does not "sit in the seat of scoffers." That means he has the courage to say the right thing in the right way when others attack the name of Christ or His church. He has the boldness to state his position as a Christian and his love for the Lord, His church, and His people.

He does not seek confrontation in such instances, neither does he shrink away in fear. He says something in a gentle spirit that lets the scoffer know his devotion is the Person of Christ and His kingdom. The Bible says, "First of all, you must understand that in the last days scoffers will come, scoffing and following their own evil desires" (2 Peter 3:3). When we stand firm in the name of Jesus Christ, the devil and his evil spirits will retreat very quickly. Satan knows that he can't win any battle against Christ.

A godly man is excited about the Word of God. It is not dull or boring. He sincerely wants to know the ways of God and how to apply them to his daily tasks. He wants to share the Scriptures with his friends and family because he knows the vast power of God's Word. There may be seasons when his devotion wanes and when his reading of Scripture slacks. However, he is sensitive to the prodding of the Holy Spirit and quick to return his focus to the truth. He meditates on the Word of God consistently. And he lingers over the Scriptures so that God's truth can become a part of his life, not just his memory.

A godly man is excited about the Word of God

Meditating on God's Word is one of the most productive spiritual disciplines for godliness. It saturates our minds and hearts with His instruction, warning, rebuke, encouragement, and comfort. It is food for the soul, builds us up in the faith, and enhances our behavior and thinking in the light of God's transforming truths.

God commanded Joshua to make meditation on His Word the core of his daily routine. The Bible says, "Do not let this Book of the Law depart from your mouth; meditate on it day and night, so that you may be careful to do everything written in it. Then you will be prosperous and successful" (Joshua 1:8).

Success, prosperity, and the blessings of an obedient life were all linked to Joshua's absorption of God's Word. That means you can succeed at being a good husband, a good father, a good employee or employer by developing a consistent pattern of meditation on Scripture. The positive truth of God is implanted in your heart, providing a divine context for wise decision making and behavior.

If you want to become a good soldier for Christ and have the power of the Holy Spirit working for you in this war between the good and evil spirits, ask God to help you begin meditating on His Word. Take small sections or even a few verses at a time. Pray over them. Think about them. Be still and let God speak to your heart with His customized application. You will be amazed at how fresh and relevant the Scriptures become for your personal life.

Your faith will not be artificial or superficial but deeply imbedded in the Word of God. Your nourishment is from God and when, NOT IF, the storms strike and the devil and his evil spirits surface and appear to be attacking you on all fronts, you are prepared. You are grounded in God's goodness, aware of His sovereignty, sure of His love, and kept by His faithfulness. And yes, you will be victorious in your daily encounters with sin and overcome any evil temptation that Satan may try to instill in your personal life.

A godly man is also a fruitful man. His life is marked by character traits produced by the Holy Spirit. He has learned to wait on God for His timing so that his decisions are right ones, proving productive for himself and his loved ones. His life is fruitful because he invests it in the lives of others. He is willing to sacrifice his time and energy to serve others. He does not look for an immediate harvest, but has an eye on the future. He sees the godly potential in a rebellious teenage son or daughter or underachieving co-worker.

Most people have heard of Billy Graham. But how many are familiar with Mordecai Ham, the evangelist who led Dr. Graham to saving faith in Jesus Christ? Ham was faithful in investing his life for the good of others, and his commitment led to the salvation of a man who would later become the world's greatest evangelist.

Finally, a godly person is a content person. He trusts in Christ for all his provision. He gives his anxieties and burdens to the Lord and leaves them there. He is self-sufficient in the sufficiency of Christ. He knows he is complete in Jesus Christ, and he can accept the ups and downs of life with the knowledge that he can do all things through Christ who strengthens him (Philippians 4:13).

Perhaps these qualities describe your life today. Perhaps you can relate to some of these principles, but you may not be able to identify with others.

Anyone can become the godly person they desire by first humbling themselves before God. God looks to the one who is humble and contrite in spirit, not proud or boastful. All you need to do is come to God, admit your inadequacy, and ask Him to help you become conformed to the image of Christ. It is a process, but it is a process that can begin today and continue throughout your lifetime. You must be willing to acknowledge your failings and look to Jesus Christ for His all-sufficient help. Then humble yourself before others. Be a servant to your spouse and children, not a dictator. Praise the efforts of others. Do not exalt yourself. God promises to exalt those who are humble. In His timing, you will see His character traits reproduced in your life, helping you to become a godly person.

My friend, Satan is no match for a godly person. He fears God and will immediately flee from your presence on command. Victory will be yours each and every time you encounter Satan in this war of the spirits.[1]

---

1 Sermons by Dr. Charles F. Stanley and Dr. O. S. Hawkins were valuable to the writer in composing this chapter.

THE
TRUTH
CHAPTER THIRTEEN
ABOUT
TV

What is destroying America today is not the liberal breed of one-world politicians, or the IMF bankers, or the misguided educational elite, or the World Council of Churches because they are largely symptoms of a greater disorder. If there is any single institution to blame, it is TELEVISION!

Television is more than a medium; it has become a full-fledged institution, backed by BILLIONS of dollars each season. Its producers want us to sit in front of its glazed-over electronic screen, completely discard our good judgment and understanding, and sit in a spangled, zoned-out state ("couch potatoes," in current parlance) while we are instructed in the proper liberal tone and attitude by our present-day Plato and Aristotle—Dan Rather and Peter Jennings.

These television celebrities have more temporal power than the teachings of Aristotle and Plato have built up over the centuries. Producers use this tremendous TV power to their own taste as they select the menu from which the public is fed.

Television, in fact, has greater power over the lives of most Americans than any educational system or government or church. Children are particularly susceptible. They are mesmerized, hypnotized and tranquilized by TV. It is often the center of their world and when the set is turned off, they continue to tell stories about what they have seen.

It should be no wonder, then, that as adults they are not prepared for the front line of life; they simply have no tools with which to confront the reality of the world.

TELEVISION: THE CYCLOPS THAT EATS BOOKS

One of the most disturbing truths about TV is that it eats books. Statistics reveal nearly 60 percent of all adult Americans, once out of school, will never read another book.

Alvin Kernan, author of *The Death of Literature,* says that reading books "is ceasing to be the primary way of knowing something in our society." He also points out that bachelor's degrees in English literature have declined by 33 percent in the last 20 years and that in many universities the courses are largely reduced to remedial reading. Many American libraries are in crisis, with few patrons to support them.

Thousands of our teachers at the elementary, secondary and college levels can testify that their students' writing exhibits a tendency toward a superficiality that wasn't seen, say, ten or fifteen years ago. It shows up not only in the students' lack of analytical skills but in their poor command of grammar and rhetoric.

It's not unusual for a graduate student to ask the purpose of a semicolon. The mechanics of the English language have been tortured to pieces by TV. Visual, moving images — which are the venue of television — cannot be held in the net of careful language. They want to break out. They really have nothing to do with language. So language, grammar, and rhetoric have become fractured.

Recent surveys conducted by dozens of organizations also suggest that up to 45 percent of the American public is indeed functionally illiterate; that is, our citizens' reading and writing abilities, if they have any, are so seriously impaired as to render them, in that handy jargon of our times, "dysfunctional."

The problem isn't just in our schools or in the way reading is taught; **TV teaches people NOT to read.** It renders them incapable of engaging in an art that is now perceived as STRENUOUS because it is an active art, not a passive hypnotized state.

Passive as it is, television has invaded our culture so completely that you see its affects in every quarter, even in the literary world. For example, it shows up in supermarket paperbacks, from Stephen King to pulp fiction. In reality, these should be considered as forms of verbal television—literature that is so superficial that those who read it can revel in the same sensations they experience when they are watching TV.

What is more important, the growing influence of television has changed peoples habits and values and affected their assumptions about the world. The sort of reflective, critical and value-laden thinking encouraged by books has been rendered obsolete. In this context, we would do well to recall the Cyclops—the race of giants that, according to Greek myth, predated man. Here is a passage from the well known classicist Edith Hamilton's summary of the encounter between the mythic adventurer Odysseus and the Cyclops named Polyphemus, as Odysseus is on his way home from the Trojan Wars. Odysseus and his crew have found Polyphemus' cave:

> At last he came, hideous and huge, tall as a great mountain crag. Driving his flock before him he entered and closed the cave's mouth with a ponderous slab of stone. Then looking around he caught sight of the strangers, and cried out in a dreadful booming voice, "Who are you who enter unbidden the house of Polyphemus? Traders or thieving pirates?" They were terror-stricken at the sight and sound of him, but Odysseus made shift to answer, and firmly too: "Shipwrecked warriors from Troy are we, and your suppliants, under the protection of Zeus, the suppliants' god." But Polyphemus roared out that he cared not for Zeus. He was bigger than any god and feared none of them. With that, he stretched out his mighty arms

and in each great hand seized one of the men and dashed his brains out on the ground. Slowly he feasted off them to the last shred, and then, satisfied, stretched himself out across the cavern and slept. He was safe from attack. None but he could roll back the huge stone before the door, and if the horrified men had been able to summon courage and strength enough to kill him they would have been imprisoned there forever.[1]

To discover their fate, read Robert Fitzgerald's masterful translation of the book. What is particularly appropriate about this myth as it applies today is that, first, the Cyclops imprisons these men in darkness, and that, second, he beats their brains out before he devours them. It doesn't take much imagination to apply this to the affects of TV on us and our children.

Television has an affect on learning. Quite literally, TV affects the way people think. Our usual processes of thinking and discernment are semi-functional at best. While television appears to have the potential to provide useful information to viewers—and is celebrated for its educational function—the technology of television and the inherent nature of the viewing experience actually inhibit learning as we usually think of it. TV destroys the capacity of the viewer to attend. Also, by taking over a complex of direct and indirect neural pathways, TV decreases vigilance—the general state of arousal which prepares the organism (us) for action should its attention be drawn to a specific stimulus (something else of more importance).

How are our neural pathways taken over? We think we are looking at a picture or an image of something, but what we are actually seeing is thousands of dots of light blinking on and off in a strobe effect that is calculated to hap-

---

1 Hillsdale College, *Imprimis,* February 1992, Vol. 21, No. 2: "Reprinted by permission from *IMPRIMIS,* the monthly journal of Hillsdale College."

pen rapidly enough to keep us, the viewers, from recognizing the phenomenon. More than a decade ago, researchers pointed to instances of "TV epilepsy," in which those watching this strobe effect overextended their capacities. The *New England Journal of Medicine* recently honored this affliction with a medical classification: video game epilepsy.

SHADOWS ON THE SCREEN

Television also teaches that people aren't quite real; they are images, gray-and-white shadows or Technicolor little beings who move in a medium no thicker than a sliver of glass, created by this intense bombardment of electrons. Unfortunately, the tendency is to start thinking of them in the way children think when they see too many cartoons: that people are merely objects that can be zapped; or that can fall over a cliff and be smashed to smithereens and pick themselves up again. This contentless violence of cartoons has no basis in reality. Actual people aren't images but substantial, physical, corporeal beings with souls.

And, of course, the violence on television engenders violence; there have been too many studies substantiating this to suggest otherwise. One such study that has been going on for 30 years was started by the psychologist Leonard Eron. He began research on 875 eight-year-olds in New York state. Analyzing parental child rearing practices and aggressiveness in school, Eron discovered that the determining factor is the amount of TV parents permit their children to watch.

Eron's present partner in this extensive ongoing study, University of Illinois professor of psychology Rowell Huesmann, has written:

> When the research was started in 1960, television viewing was not a major focus. But in 1970's, in the ten-year follow-up, one of the best predictions we could find of aggressive behavior in a teenage boy was how much violence he watched as a child. In 1981, we found that the adults who had been convicted of the most serious crimes were those same

ones who had been the more aggressive teenagers, and who had watched the most television violence as children.

Where is this important report? Buried in an alumni publication of the University of Illinois.[2] In 1982, the National Institute of Mental Health published its own study: "Television and Behavior: Ten Years of Scientific Progress and Implications for the '80's." This report confirmed that there is "overwhelming" evidence that violence on TV leads to aggressive behavior in children and teenagers. Those findings were duly reported by most of the major media in the early '80's and then were forgotten.

Why do such reports sink into oblivion? Because the American audience does not want to face the reality of TV. They are too consumed by their love for it. Children need parental love and supervision. However, during the '80's many parents were more focused on their own personal endeavors and this has produced many problem children. Television has indeed become a powerful and productive playground for Satan and his angels.

TV: EATING OUT OUR SUBSTANCE

Television eats books. It eats academic skills. It eats positive character traits. It even eats family relationships. How many families do you know that spend the dinner hour in front of the TV, seldom communicating with one another? How many have a television on while they have breakfast or prepare for work or school?

And what about school? Some professors say of their students, "Well, you have to entertain them." Others recommend using TV and film clips instead of lecturing, "throwing in a commercial every ten minutes or so to keep them awake." This is not only a patronizing attitude, it is an abdication of responsibility: A teacher should teach. But TV eats the principles of people who are supposed to be responsi-

2 Ibid.

ble, transforming them into passive servants of the Cyclops.[3]

TV eats out our substance. This could be called the compromise of experience: with television, what we see, hear, touch, smell, feel and understand about the world has been processed for us. And, when we cannot distinguish with certainty the natural from the interpreted, or the artificial from the organic, then all theories of the ideal organization of life become equal. In other words, TV teaches that all lifestyles and all values are equal, and that there is no clearly defined right and wrong, a terrible misconception.

In his *Amusing Ourselves to Death*, one of the more brilliant recent books on the tyranny of television, the author Neal Postman wonders why nobody has pointed out that television possibly oversteps the injunction in the Ten Commandments against making graven images.

In the 1960's and 1970's, many of the traditional standards and mores of society came under heave assault; indeed, they were blown apart, largely with the help of television, which was just coming into its own. There was an air of unreality about many details of daily life. Even the "big" moral questions suffered distortion when they were reduced to TV images.

With television, what we see, hear, touch, smell, feel, and understand about the world has been processed for us

During the Vietnam conflict there was graphic violence—soldiers and civilians actually dying—on screen. One scene that shocked the nation was an execution in which the victim was shot in the head with a pistol on prime-time TV. People "tuned in" to the war every night, and their opinions were largely formed by what they viewed, as if the highly complex and controversial issues about the causes, conduct, and resolution of the war could be summed

3 Ibid., p. 3.

up in these superficial broadcasts, usually lasting only a few minutes.

You saw the same phenomena again in the recent war in the Gulf. With stirring background music and sophisticated computer graphics, each network's banner script read across the screen "WAR IN THE GULF," as if it were just another TV program. War is not a program. It is a dirty, bloody mess. People are being killed daily. Yet, television all but teaches that this carnage is merely another diversion, a form of blockbuster entertainment—the big show with all the international stars present. Satan must be delighted.

In the last years of his life, Malcolm Muggeridge, a pragmatic and caustic TV personality and print journalist who embraced religion in later life, warned: "From the first moment I was in the studio, I felt that it was far from being a good thing, I felt that television [would] ultimately be inimical to what I most appreciate, which is the expression of truth, expressing your reactions to life to see the time when literature will be quite a rarity because, more and more, the presentation of images is preoccupying."

Muggeridge concluded: "I don't think people are going to be preoccupied with ideas. I think they are going to live in a fantasy world where you don't need any ideas. The one thing that television can't do is express ideas . . . There is a danger in translating life into an image, and that is what television is doing. In doing it, it is falsifying life. Far from the camera's being an accurate recorder of what is going on, it is the exact opposite. It cannot convey reality nor does it even want to."

For the most part, secular TV has replaced the family as the cornerstone of American society. We must return to the Bible—the one supreme source of revelation of the meaning of life, the nature of God and spiritual nature and need of men. It is the only guide of life which really leads the spirit in the way of peace and salvation.

The chief mission of Satan is to narrow our focus to such a degree that we lose our focus on the things of God. Satan uses TV very effectively to accomplish that mission.

THE POWER

CHAPTER FOURTEEN
OF ROCK
MUSIC

Rock music today is a powerful worldwide force with hundreds of millions of fans. Few that have studied music will deny that it has the ability to influence and dramatically affect our lives.

Further demonstrations of the power of rock music are the two largest media events in history. The largest media event ever was the UN's worldwide broadcasting of John Lennon's record "Imagine," in honor of the anniversary of his death. The second largest event was rock's "Live Aid" concert for the starving people of Ethiopia. Notice that both media events featured rock music. In the writer's opinion, those major media "events" were staged primarily to promote and empower rock music.

No analysis of the spiritual realms would be complete without investigating the effects of music on human society. For example, how does this powerful tool of music influence our behavior? Is rock music conveying messages of sexual promiscuity? Let's look at how the industry itself, the musicians, view the power of music.

When it is to their disadvantage, in other words when the music has a negative message, they say "Well it's just music and it doesn't affect anybody." However, when the message is what they perceive as being positive suddenly music becomes the most powerful medium for social change that one can imagine. Whenever the issue of destructive

109

lyrics and lifestyles in music is raised the typical response from its fans is summed up in this statement by recording industry lobbyist Bruce Boreano: "It's only music. So what?"[1]

Let's go one step further and look at what the musicians think about the real power of music:

Paul Kanter—"Our music is intended to broaden the generation gap, to alienate children from their parents . . ."[2]

Boy George—"Music is supposed to be this sort of international language of the world. It's supposed to bring us together."[3]

Danny Madden—"don't know if music can change the world, but I do know music affects people and people can change the world. I believe in the power of the people."[4]

L. L. Cool J.—"gotta convince the kids, you know what I mean? 'Cause their folks have already been brainwashed— you can't catch them, so you gotta catch the young kids, you know what I mean?"[5]

David Crosby—"I figured the only thing to do was to swipe their kids. By saying that, I'm not talking about kidnapping. I'm just talking about changing their value systems, which removes them from their parents' world very effectively."[6]

Deee-Lite—"Music is an international language."[7]

---

1 *Billboard*, March 24, 1990. p 77.

2 John Ankerberg. *The Power of Rock Music*. (Chattanooga, TN: Ankerberg Theological Research Institute, 1991).

3 Ibid.

4 Ibid.

5 Ibid.

6 David Crosby interview, *Rolling Stone*, p. 410.

7 John Ankerberg, *Rock Music's Powerful Messages*.

Many musicians understand that they have become the prophets and the town criers of modern culture. Musicians are featured very prominently in every poll that has attempted to identify the heroes of the young people today. And their songs and lyrics carry a corresponding weight, becoming as one noted adolescent psychiatrist has said, ". . . one of the two most powerful influences on youth."

When it comes to instilling true knowledge, musicians admit to this power with great pride. Politically correct causes such as fighting drug abuse, gang violence, racial strife, pollution, world hunger and war have all been tackled by them in songs, music videos, and concert and stage performances.

Music truly has become a powerful universal language and people within the industry know this perhaps better than anyone. What happens when that power is turned in a less than noble direction? What happens, for instance, when the music that is marketed toward young people becomes obsessively sensuous? Could it possibly be a contributing factor in the explosion of sexual promiscuity that is ravaging the United States of America and many parts of the world today? This writer believes it does!

Rock music today is a powerful worldwide force with hundreds of millions of fans

Music is a very powerful tool that can be used for good or evil. And this power is something that the Scriptures told us about for thousands of years. As Christians with the Holy Spirit as our guide we need to carefully analyze the songs we hear. We must see if they line up with the standards of God's Word (see Proverbs, Chapter 4). We should realize that there is a great spirit war over moral values raging today throughout America. One of the biggest battles of this war will be fought in the arena of rock music. And Satan and the evil spirits rule this arena! Christians have been presented with a very serious challenge from the evil spirit of Satan. He will surely use the powerful medium of rock music to adversely influence the youth of this country.

However, we find our instructions are very clearly stated in the Bible. It says, "But among you there must not be even a hint of sexual immorality, or of any kind of impurity, or of greed, because these are improper for God's holy people. Nor should there be obscenity, foolish talk or coarse joking, which are out of place, but rather thanks-giving. For of this you can be sure: No immoral person—such a man is an idolater—has any inheritance in the kingdom of Christ and of God" (Ephesians 5:3–5).

Are there moral absolutes: Yes or no? To most who are reading this volume, the answer to that would seem quite clear: "Why, yes, of course there are moral absolutes. Just read the Bible. For thirty-five hundred years the world has lived by those moral absolutes which have been given to us by God."

Well, wait a moment. Let's listen to what another very prominent individual has to say: "Whether we ought to follow a moral principle or not would, I contend, always depend upon the situation . . . If we are, as I would want to reason, obliged in conscience sometimes to tell white lies, as we often call them, then in conscience we might be obliged sometimes to engage in white thefts and white fornications and white killings and white breaking of promises and the like." Those are the words of Professor Joseph Fletcher, Visiting Professor of Medical Ethics at the University of Virginia and professor emeritus, affiliated with Harvard University, the famed author of the book *Situation Ethics*.[8] Professor Fletcher believes that there are no moral absolutes and that the situation must determine how we are to live. As we continue to analyze the power of rock music, it appears that the "situation" is one of sex, drugs and vio-

8 From a sermon delivered by Dr. D. James Kennedy, Summer 1992.

lence. And the youth of America have become very much involved with these deplorable activities.

There are absolute moral laws (see Proverbs, Chapter 28). In the physical realm we have physical laws which are laws of action. Moral laws are laws for action. "Absolute" is defined by the *American Heritage Dictionary of the English Language* as: "Perfect in quality or nature; complete, not limited by exceptions or restrictions, unconditional, not to be doubted or questioned; positive, certain." Those are precisely the things most rock stars want to do away with. They are saying there is nothing that is perfect in quality or nature, that is complete, or that is not to be doubted or questioned. You only have to observe some of their sex- filled videos and read some of the vulgar lyrics to come to this conclusion!

Music is a very powerful tool that can be used for Good or Evil

Satan not only urges us to question and ignore God's Word, but he also tempts us with ideas and issues presented through rock music and rock videos that challenge and distort God's Word. They fan the lust of the flesh, the lust of the eyes, and the pride of life (1 John 2:15–16). Many of the "super" rock stars today are demented and spoiled people with little musical talent who are getting rich off people who are even more demented than they are. The affect of rock music on teens and pre-teens can no longer be ignored. We are told by psychologists that "during the teenage years the adolescent value system is being molded and fixed, perhaps for all time."[9]

Where would the rock music industry be without sex? Rock music today mainlines a graphic sexuality that is as pervasive as it is perverse. With music video programming

---

9 Jack B. Simpson, *Sounding the ALARM: Moral Decay in the U.S.A.*

in over 80 million homes the average teenager today spends 2–3 hours a day plugged into these images of unbridled sexuality. The amount almost doubles when you add in the time spent listening to music through other mediums than television. And it's not just our teenagers who are being programmed in this way.

As Debra Habner, Executive Director of the Sex Information and Education Council has stated, "Our preadolescent's level of sexual sophistication is high because of the world kids are living in and the tremendous access they have to that world."[10] And what are our kids getting in return for all this sophistication? Recent studies show that over 50 percent of all 15-year-olds have had sex. This is compared to 10 percent in the 1960's.

By the age of nineteen, over 75 percent of all young people in America will have lost their virginity. One in ten girls will get pregnant before they finish high school, a total of over one million each year.

Every 104 seconds, a teenage girl gets pregnant. Four out of five children of teenage mothers who drop out of school live in poverty. This is a national tragedy!

Thirty to forty percent of all the sexually active young people are infected with one or more sexually transmitted diseases. There are now over thirty varieties to choose from. Several are incurable and at least two are fatal.

A sociologist for the Center for Disease Control in Atlanta, Georgia, notes that this cyclone of sexual activity has come at a time when there has been an unprecedented volume of public health messages regarding the risk of sexual activity. "We do not give very clear, unidirectional messages to our children. We say 'just say no . . .' but in a lot of our popular mass media messages we're putting so much emphasis on sexuality."[11]

While there is no question that these messages are

10 *Newsweek*, Summer 1991, p. 62.

11 Center for Disease Control—M.M.W.R., January 4, 1991.

being communicated to young people through a variety of mediums, none is as popular as music and music videos. Against this backdrop of sexual indoctrination, the Bible admonishes young people to "Flee youthful lust and instead pursue righteousness, faith, love and peace, along with those who call upon the Lord from a pure heart" (2 Timothy 2:22).

Music is indeed the language of today's generation. Every day kids identify themselves by emulating their favorite rock stars. Their heroes influence their values, and their values influence who they are. Today's young people do not listen to rock 'n' roll music, they experience it. It is their identity.

Jesus Christ is the rock that does not roll

It is time Christians became active and let their voices be heard. This frightening trend can be changed. It must be changed or it will certainly bring about the destruction of this civilization that we have known. Young people need to be taught that Jesus Christ is the rock that does not roll!

God gave us the moral law in order that society might be regulated and that the evil inclinations of mankind might be restrained. Satan's mission is to destroy anyone who is foolish enough to believe his lies!

MTV
CHAPTER FIFTEEN
PROGRAMMING

MTV has been very outspoken in its defense of contemporary music, crying censorship to anyone with a traditional view on social issues.

This defense spawned the ambitious "Rock the Vote" initiative that sought to encourage MTV's youthful audience to take part in the political process. More often than not the specter of censorship was invoked in order to arouse and inspire voter registration. And, by the way, most of the musicians featured in these ads never made it to the polls themselves to vote.

Also, consider the video programming that MTV helped to pioneer. These 3–4 minute collages of visual and oral imagery routinely feature, among other things, sexual situations. A viewer that plugs into MTV will typically see hundreds of overtly sensual images per hour. What is their effect on the viewer? According to the music apologist nothing. But then the music video is converted into a 30-second commercial that more often than not is edited exactly like the video that preceded it.

What is the effect on the viewer? MTV charges thousands of dollars for that 30-second spot because of its proven ability to change the viewers' buying habits. And, according to Judy McGrath, creative director, MTV: Music Television, MTV reaches 15 million 18- to 24-year-olds in 56 million households in the United States. It is true that

MTV has unmatched access and influence when it comes to reaching the young adult market.

As we analyze good versus evil, a war of the spirits, it appears that Satan and his evil spirits have found a stronghold in the area of rock music. Many of the rock music video performances seen by viewers on MTV are in direct violation of the Word of God. To put it more bluntly, many of these rock stars appear to be idolizing and glorifying Satan.

Let's consider the words of one of the most loyal and dedicated apologists for the contemporary music industry, the late Frank Zappa: "Music is only music. It can't hurt anybody." However, in an article he wrote for *Life* magazine in 1968, Zappa confessed to music's extraordinary power over the human psyche saying, "The ways in which sound affects the human organism are myriad and subtle. The loud sounds and bright lights of today are tremendous indoctrination tools." In the writers opinion, when these tools are under the control and power of Satan they do immeasurable damage to the spiritual minds and health of the youth in America.

It's obvious that the music industry understands that music is a very powerful tool as long as it serves their purpose. We need to get beyond the hype, which comes primarily from the devil, and begin to look at things with the understanding given to us by God from Scripture.

We need to seriously observe what music we listen to and carefully examine how it lines up with the Word of God. The Bible says, "I will sing of your love and justice; to you, O Lord, I will sing praise" (Psalm 101:1).

God's standard for Christians is the same regardless of the type of music they listen to. God says we must flee from immorality. Every sin that a person commits is outside his body except sexual sin which is committed against his own body. The Scripture tells us not to be drunk with wine but instead be filled with the Holy Spirit. These laws of God are the same for everyone, whether you are young or old or whether you like rock and roll or country music.

Let's examine the lyrics of country-western songs and

music videos and see if God's standards are violated by the message being portrayed. The standard of offense is not what we feel, it's God's Word. The scantily clad women seen are similar to what you see on most other MTV programming. God clearly commands women to dress modestly as Christian men were commanded to honor and respect women.

God's standard for Christians is the same regardless of the type of music they listen to

Country music is a different genre of music than rock and is usually associated with motherhood, home, family, the flag and apple pie. Nevertheless, its ethics in the areas of substance abuse, treatment of women, sexual morality, and even Satanism, in some cases, are similar to those in rock music. When country music degrades womanhood and glorifies drunkenness, drugs, premarital sex and adultery, it contributes to the undermining of American society as thoroughly as rock music. Despite the more "wholesome" appearance, when country music adopts such themes, it erodes family and social stability.

According to *People* magazine, Conway Twitty, perhaps the most popular country artist of all time, reflected on his twenty-year career by confessing, "As a country artist, I'm not proud of a lot of things in my field. There is no doubt in my mind that we are contributing to the moral decline in America."[1] Conway Twitty died in 1993.

Would you agree that the following song titles characterize an attitude of sexual permissiveness?—"To All The Girls I've Loved Before," "I Cheated On A Good Woman's Love," "I'd Love To Lay You Down," "I Just Can't Stay Married To You," "Now I Lay Me Down To Cheat" and "I'm On Fire." These songs were surely inspired by Satan.

1 *People*, September 3, 1979.

Alcohol, the number one drug of use in America, is featured quite prominently in country-western music. Performers sing about going to the bottle, to the bars, and to the taverns as a means of dealing with personal heartache, which is one of the primary themes of country-western music. The message that alcohol is the key to having a good time is morally unconscionable.

Substance abuse is also a problem in country music. *Billboard* magazine of October 11, 1980, noted that "Drugs are turning up in country songs with surprising frequency, along with frank references to sex." Jimmy Buffet's "Why Don't We Get Drunk," (containing the stanza, "Why don't we get drunk and screw?"); Willie Nelson's "I Gotta Get Drunk," ("I Gotta Get Drunk, I Can't Stay Sober"); and other songs like "Bombed, Boozed, and Busted," "Caffeine, Nicotine, Benzedrine, and Wish Me Luck," "Quaaludes Again" and "Drinkin', Druggin', and Watchin' TV"—all reveal that many country songs are promoting substance abuse.[2]

One prominent researcher, Dr. James Scheafer, Ph.D., Director of the University of Minnesota's office of alcohol and other drug abuse programming, has discovered that country music can lead to alcoholism among listeners. He says, "There is definitely a correlation between high-risk country and western songs and drinking, especially those of Kenny Rogers, Waylon Jennings, and Hank Williams."[3] In a press release promoting one of his albums, Johnny Paycheck had this to say: "Yes, I do cocaine, but cocaine isn't a killer drug and neither is alcohol. Heroin is a problem and P.C.P. is a killer drug. Cocaine and alcohol are OK up-front drugs."[4]

In a *Close Up* magazine interview, Waylon Jennings

2 *Billboard*, October 11, 1980.

3 Jack B. Simpson, *Sounding the ALARM: Moral Decay in the U.S.A.*

4 Dr. Marty Tingelhoff, Documentation of Expose on Rock and Roll, Soul and Country Music, Living Words Spoken Ministries, 1987, p. 18.

said he did drugs for 21 years (he says he kicked the habit in 1984). **"I did more drugs than anyone you ever saw in your life. I was a slave to drugs," the country singer says.** "Everything I did from music to sex—everything—I was high."

Many famous rock stars have paid the ultimate price of death for their drug use. Among them are Brian Jones of the Rolling Stones; Sid Vicious of the Sex Pistols; Dennis Wilson of the Beach Boys; Jimi Hendrix; Jim Morrison of The Doors; Elvis Presley; Janis Joplin; Bon Scott of AC/DC; Frankie Lymon; Tim Harden; Phil Lynott of Thin Lizzie; David Ruffin, lead singer for the Temptations—and many others could be mentioned. But in spite of this, drugs still play a prominent role in rock music and this seems to have a harmful effect on those who listen.

For example, one study in Post Graduate Medicine, "Heavy Metal Music and Drug Use in Adolescents," discovered that almost 60 percent of chemically dependent adolescents named heavy metal as their first choice of music, suggesting that such music may promote drug use. It also concluded that "evidence shows that such music promotes and supports patterns of drug abuse, promiscuous sexual activity and violence."[5]

The Bible tells us
we are to let nothing control us
except the Holy Spirit

The affliction of modern drug abuse is simply unimaginable—and yet rock music and country music continue to glorify drug use. The Bible tells us we are to let nothing control us except the Holy Spirit. God desires that people be under His loving influence, rather than under the influence of a drug substance that will certainly harm them physically, socially or spiritually.

---

5 Dr. Paul King, "Heavy Metal Music and Drug Use in Adolescents," *Post Graduate Medicine*, April 1988, p. 82.

Although country music has a more wholesome image than rock music and both are conveying anti-biblical standards, we really have the some evil spirit in country-western music that we have in contemporary rock music. Therefore, country music is Satan country!

Now let's evaluate a particular group known as the "New Kids On The Block." They are a seemingly wholesome pop group, whose estimated gross revenues for 1990 were over $800 million. But this group of youngsters, many of them from supposedly good Christian homes, are sending mixed messages, not able to discern what's right from what's wrong. What messages are being poured through the pipeline of their obsession? They stand young and impressionable before an adult world so brimming with sexual tension that it's ready to explode. Let's look at some of their lyrics: "I get up in the morning and I see your face, girl." "You're lookin' so good, everything's in place." "Don't you know I could never leave your side, girl." "Won't you stay here with me and be my bride?"[6] Do you get the picture here? The singer has just awakened next to a girl with whom he spent the night. This is surely fornication and Biblically a sin.

Donney (of the New Kids) echoes this sexually permissive attitude in these words taken from the official $25 New Kids fan book: "Making love is so special . . . almost like the best feeling in the world." Then Donney says: "You shouldn't have sex with someone you don't care about. When you make love with someone you want to be with that person because they are special to you."

How will these MTV music video messages influence and shape the youth of America? Here is what we should be concerned about:

FIRST, the media of music, the lyrics, and the visual images—individually and especially in combination—have

---

6 New Kids on the Block, "Cover Girl" live broadcast—The Disney Channel.

had a profound influence on society and its individual members for both good and ill from the beginning of recorded history.

SECOND, certain music and music videos promote negative thought and behavior by suggesting, advocating, or encouraging violence; vandalism; rape; murder; drug abuse; suicide; human sacrifice; degradation of women, children, and human life; sadism; bestiality; masochism; and other perversions.

THIRD, such indecent and negative material too often targets youth in the very impressionable teen and pre-teen years.

And FOURTH, such material is almost universally available to anyone with sufficient money regardless of age.

Compare rock's endorsement of violence with God's standards. The Bible clearly teaches that we are not to glorify violence of any kind, whether it is sadomasochism or suicide. Rather, we are to live in peace and harmony with one another. We are admonished, "Let us therefore make every effort to do what leads to peace and mutual edification" (Romans 14:19).

Only through the power and the authority of the Holy Spirit will we be able to defeat Satan and his evil spirits

Rock music videos as presented on MTV programming are urging rebellion against the moral values and ideas on which our society is based. Rock music unites sex, drugs and the occult into a philosophy of life; one that is filled with evil spirits. No one can honestly deny that the profanity, vulgarity and violence in modern rock music violate the will of God for men!

We need to wake up and realize that we live in a society today in which many have lost their moral bearings.

Many have begun to call "evil" good. God is calling for us to reject the sin of this world and the evil spirits within this world system. He wants us to embrace Him with our whole hearts and clothe ourselves completely with His Holy Spirit. This will open our eyes and then we will see all the sin and corruption that surround us.

Only through the power and the authority of the Holy Spirit can Satan and his evil spirits be defeated.

ROCK
MUSIC
CHAPTER SIXTEEN
MOCKS
& RIDICULES
JESUS CHRIST

What ideas and moral values are rock musicians conveying in their songs about Satan and the occult? And what are they saying about Jesus Christ? Please allow the writer to set the stage for this chapter by sharing with you the lyrics from a Ronnie James Dio song "Heaven and Hell:" "There's a big black sheep lookin' up at me, said, 'I know where you ought to be.' He said, 'come with me and I'll give you desire, first you've got to burn, burn, burn, burn in fire.' Son of God repent your sins and pledge your soul to hell. Pray that Satan will forgive once your God has fell. Expect the death of those who pray to a God so long since passed. Your God is dead and now you die. Satan rules at last."

Now, assuming that these words got your attention and you would like to hear more, let's consider the results of surveys which show that the average teenager listens to rock music 4–6 hours every day. The *Journal of the American Medical Association* reports that between the 7th and 12th grade the average teenager listens to 10,500 hours of rock music, which is equivalent to the total number of hours he has spent in a classroom from kindergarten all the way through high school.

During adolescence teenagers are developing standards of behavior that they will use their entire lives. What are the values and ideas being communicated to our young people through the powerful medium of music? Is rock music just harmless entertainment, or are there different messages being presented to those who listen?

Let's examine the broad spectrum of entertainment including such entertainers as Prince, Madonna, John Lennon, and several groups. You may be surprised to learn that rock musicians and their music have a lot to say about Jesus Christ.

The unholy scriptures of the legally incorporated Church of Satan appear as lyrics in the songs of some rock artists. The *Satanic Bible* was written by the church's founder, Anton Szandor LaVey. LaVey is perhaps the most famous Satanist of this century. Along with establishing his own religion he has served as a consultant to Hollywood on movies that involve the occult, even playing the role of the devil in movies like *Rosemary's Baby*.[1] What does LaVey's *Satanic Bible* teach? And are these teachings found today in rock music?

During adolescence teenagers are developing standards of behavior that they will use their entire lives

Beginning with the person of Jesus Christ the *Satanic Bible* says, "I dip my forefinger in the watery blood of your impotent mad redeemer, and write over his thorn-torn brow: The true prince of evil—the king of slaves" (*Satanic Bible* 1:6).[2] The obvious hatred expressed here is understandable when we consider that Satan's legal control over mankind was total and invulnerable to any human effort at breaking it until Jesus died on the cross. On the cross His thorn-torn brow and pierced body provided the perfect blood sacrifice for our sins.

---

1 The John Ankerberg Show. "The Dangers of Rock Music" with Eric Holmberg, 1991.

2 Ibid.

Now, Satan's once invincible power is broken over anyone who believes in that blood. It's no wonder Satan hates it. Can we find this demonic doctrine in rock music? Yes. We most certainly can! Jesus has become the focus of more ridicule in rock music than any other personality. Every facet of His life and ministry is mocked and criticized.

One rock anthology is entitled "The Birth of the y" and features the hideous litany of Satan. Here history's most significant event, the incarnation of God, is questioned and made frivolous. In like manner, Nina Hagen's "Nun Sex Monk Rock" lampoons the "Madonna and Christ," along with songs about reincarnation, witchcraft and blaspheming the Holy Spirit she sings "And my little baby I tell you, God is your father."

Jefferson Airplane's song "The Son of Jesus" is filled with sacrilege, suggesting among other things that Jesus was involved in the occult, had bastard children by Mary Magdalene. It also suggests that God the Father was sexually attracted to Jesus' daughter.

This same blatant disrespect for the Messiah characterizes the life of John Lennon. One biographer records that Lennon early on in his career with the Beatles drew a cartoon of a crucified Jesus. At the foot of the cross was a pair of bedroom slippers.

Another biographer recounts that on Good Friday, the day that marks the crucifixion of Christ, Lennon made some nuns the target of his abuse. As they left the convent to attend worship services ". . . they were shocked to behold across the street a grotesque life-size effigy of Jesus on the cross, which John had fashioned and hung from his balcony.

As the sisters gazed in astonishment at this sacrilegious display, Lennon started pelting them with Durex condoms filled with water." To top it off he urinated on them while crying "raindrops from heaven."

In his song "God," Lennon records not only his indifference to Christ but demeans the Son of God by drawing a comparison between Jesus, JFK, Bob Dylan, Hindu mantras, and the Beatles. These examples taken together make it obvious that Lennon's infamous quote about Christ meant a lot more than just a commentary or the unnatural adjuration given the Beatles. Lennon said "Christianity will go" and "We're more popular than Jesus." He longed for the obliteration of Jesus as Messiah and Christianity as a faith.[3]

The group Ludichrist pictorially and musically echoes Lennon's sentiments with these lyrics, "Holy Bible, Jesus Christ, philosophy and way of life. The fear of God—the fear of God. Just a book, just a man, son of who? All those lies, Immaculate Deception."

This type of overt blasphemy is not unique. Virtually dozens of groups openly sing about wickedness that until recently could not be found outside of occult bookstores. For many, it's a matter of economics. Rebellion sells in rock music. And for the hardest types what could be more rebellious than to blaspheme God?

Another example is "Possessed" by the band Vernon who says, "I am possessed by all that is evil. The death of your God I demand. I . . . set at Lord Satan's right hand," and "I drink the vomit of the priest, make love to the dying whore, Satan is my master incarnate, hail, praise to my unholy host."

Also, Billy Idol attempts "to show what a human rip-off religion is."[4] Leon Russell has commented that "organized Christianity has done more harm than any other single force I can think of in the world" and suggests that the religion of rock and roll replace it.[5] In "Hymn 43" the band Jethro Tull conveyed this message, "If Jesus saves, then He better save Himself." Ozzy Osbourne says, "I'm not a born-again Christian. I'm a born-again Hitler."[6]

---

3 Eric Holmberg, "The Hells Bells Study Guide." (Gainsville, FL: Reel to Reel, 1990).

4 *Rock*, June 1984, p. 322.

5 *Rolling Stone*, December 2, 1979, p. 35.

6 *Creem Metal*, March 1986, p. 12.

Is it really surprising that rock music, which often incorporates drugs, sex, amoralism and rebellion into its lyrics, would also openly oppose God, His Son, and the gospel? Sheila Davis, professor of lyric writing at New York University, comments that we "better give serious attention to the content of pop songs and to evaluate not only what lyrics are saying to society but, more importantly, what they may be doing to it."[7]

As we continue our analysis of musicians, let's consider the music of Merciful Fate, a group that takes their Satanism seriously. On their song "The Oath," King Diamond sings "I deny Jesus Christ the Deceiver and I abjure the Christian Faith, holding in contempt all of its works." In the world of rock music even the most significant, loving, and sacrificial act of the Lord's life, like the last supper, is dragged through the mud.

This infidelity, known as universalism, has become extremely popular lately, particularly with the growth of "new age" religion. The problem here is that no matter how nice it sounds to say that all religions lead to God, Jesus said they do not. We have irrefutable evidence that Jesus totally denied that there is any way to God except through Himself. The Bible says, "Jesus answered, 'I am the way and the truth and the life. No one comes to the Father except through Me'" (John 14:6).

Jesus is the true Messiah of God, and that is why Satan tries so hard to convince man to the contrary!

Think about it. If universalism is true, then not only is Jesus a liar for saying it was a false and demonic doctrine, He is also the stupidest man who lived because He

---

7 *USA Today,* October 11, 1985, p. 10A.

voluntarily underwent the most excruciating and shameful death imaginable for no reason at all. In other words if there are other ways to God then Jesus did not have to die in our place. Jesus is the true Messiah of God, and that is why Satan tries so hard to convince man to the contrary!

Moving from the person to the primary symbol associated with Christ, the *Satanic Bible* says, "Behold the crucifix; what does it symbolize? Pallid incompetence hanging on a tree" (*Satanic Bible* 2:1).[8]

Again, this hatred on Satan's part is understandable. The cross is at the heart of the Christian faith. Apart from the crucifixion and subsequent resurrection of Jesus Christ, which is, by the way, one of the most logically proven events in history, ". . . our faith is futile, and we are still in our sins" (1 Corinthians 15:17).

As a symbol of its defeat and future obliteration, Satanic religion loathes the cross and constantly seeks to discredit it. To this end the rock artist Prince, the prince of the air, attempts to influence man in one of two directions. The most subtle of the two and hence the most prevalent is to give it superficial respect while at the same time associating the cross with the very sins that nailed Jesus to it.

For example, millions of young people today think nothing of wearing the cross while engaging in everything from sexual immorality to drug use, the sins for which the Lord was sacrificed on the cross. Satan surely enjoys the irony. This type of desecration is virtually rampant in rock, with crosses the most popular jewelry choice of the stars. **It seems as though the more perverted the artist the larger or more obsessive is their focus on the cross.**

Jesus said, "If you love Me, you will obey what I command" (John 14:15). Jesus commanded us to avoid temptation, to avoid tempting others, to direct all worship to God, to clothe oneself modestly, to obey God and not our physical desires, and to keep oneself sexually pure.

---

8 John Ankerberg, *Rock Music's Powerful Messages.*

Prince's Jesus bears virtually no resemblance to the historical and Biblical Christ. His is a demonic substitution that gives new relevance to the passage in the Bible which says, "The Spirit clearly says that in later times some will abandon the faith and follow deceiving spirits and things taught by demons. Such teachings come through hypocritical liars, whose consciences have been seared as with a hot iron" (1 Timothy 4:1–2).

There is no doubt that rock music has extensively attacked, ridiculed, and mocked Jesus Christ. Human nature is such that we only attack things that we are frightened of. Satan as a personality is very much like us in that he is attacking something that terrifies him. Why is Satan afraid of Jesus? Because the Scripture says that Jesus came to destroy Satan and in fact on the cross of Calvary did precisely that. As already stated, the cross is the altar upon which Jesus was sacrificed and it was His sacrifice that atoned for our sins.

Jesus Christ offers us hope, complete deliverance and salvation. The whole basis of our righteousness, our acceptance to God, is what we do with the person Jesus Christ. "The eyes of the Lord are toward the righteous, and His ears are open to their cry" (Psalm 34:15). We either ignore Him or mock Him, or else we receive Him as Savior and Lord. And if anyone is willing to receive Him and trust Him to deliver them, He will do precisely that.

Jesus Christ offers us hope, complete deliverance and salvation

Satan is no match for Christ. Satan-inspired rock stars who boast about their personal relationship with him are no match for Christ. Satan and the rock stars mentioned in this chapter should be singing "Born to Lose."

True Christians have Jesus Christ, the Holy Spirit, to guide them and protect them against the evil spirits of Satan. A believer indwelt with the Holy Spirit will be a majority in any battle that comes his way. Christians need to remember the words of Jesus: "The thief [Satan] does not come except to steal, and to kill, and to destroy. I have come that they may have life, and that they may have it more abundantly" (John 10:10 NKJV).

ROCK
MUSIC &

CHAPTER SEVENTEEN

SATANISM

The intrinsic selfishness of a person's heart coupled with Satanic philosophy will inevitably result in violence and death.

The *Satanic Bible* (3:4) says, "Are we not all predatory animals by instinct? If humans ceased wholly from preying upon each other, could they continue to exist?"

Preying upon one another is a major theme running through rock music, album art work, stage shows, videos, and lies associated with the rock music industry. The intent mostly is to shock, to grab one's attention, and to increase album sales. However, evidence continues to mount that there are powers beyond the industry's control for whom this obsession with death is not a joke.

Many rock artists have found this out the hard way from asphyxiating in their vomit to dying of heart failure in the bathroom. Their premature and often vulgar deaths point not only to the Prince of Death but to the perverse way he treats his subjects. And it's not just the artists who are affected by this evil spirit of violence and death. The rock and roll era has seen violent crime among young people increase by more that 10,000 percent. Concert violence has become epidemic. However, it is in the incredible arena of ritualistic violence, bizarre murders, and self-mutilation that the Satanic influence can be most clearly discerned.

The last few decades have seen the appearance of some

133

of the most twisted and violent acts imaginable. Primarily, the thing that links these senseless violent acts together is an obsession with rock music and its similarity to ancient Satanic ritual. These mindless acts of violence are not unique to this era. The Scriptures recall a time when God's prophet Elijah challenged Satan's prophet to a contest in the supernatural. In 1 Kings, Chapter 18, the Bible relates what the devil worshipers did in order to get Satan to move on their behalf. Most, if not all, modern punkers have no idea that their behavior is virtually identical to this ancient form of Satanism.

The spiritual realm is the higher reality. We are all profoundly affected by the Lord of whichever kingdom we are a part of, whether we are aware of it or not. This was covered in Chapter 2.

Another way people are answering the ads in rock music is through suicide. It is now the second biggest killer of young people in America. Surveys have found that as many as one in seven teenagers have tried to kill themselves. Again, there are other factors contributing to this tragedy but rock music has played a major part.

For example, let's look at some of the words from Metallica's song "Fade to Black." "Life it seems will fade away. Drifting further every day. Getting lost within myself. Nothing matters, no one else. I have lost the will to live. Simply nothing more to give. There is nothing more for me. I need the end to set me free."

Suicide is perhaps the ultimate Satanic deception. For a person to take his life, some basic truths have to be destroyed and replaced with lies. The most fundamental truth is that life has a transcendent purpose: to know and experience God. We've already seen how rock has either ignored or ridiculed this truth. The Satanic lie is that life is fundamentally pointless: at best, our existence is given meaning by the pleasures we enjoy.

However, the Bible reveals the truth. "This is what the Lord says: 'Cursed is the one who trusts in man, who depends on flesh for his strength and whose heart turns away from the Lord. He will be like a bush in the waste-lands; he will not see prosperity when it comes. He will dwell in the parched places of the desert, in a salt land where no one lives'" (Jeremiah 17:5–6).

Suicide is perhaps the ultimate Satanic deception

The Bible clearly warns us when it says, "But mark this: There will be terrible times in the last days. People will be lovers of themselves, lovers of money, boastful, proud, abusive, disobedient to their parents, ungrateful, unholy, treacherous, rash, conceited, lovers of pleasure rather than lovers of God" (2 Timothy 3:1–2 and 4).

The fact is, life is full of trials for everybody. Maturity and greatness come from triumphing over them. Satan's deception is that if life is found in pleasure, then the absence of pleasure is to be avoided at all costs. When the pain becomes too great, killing oneself can become the logical way out. The soul of this present generation is so bankrupt that the pain of such trivial things as poor grades, a broken love affair, a disdain for reality, trigger much of the current epidemic of suicide.

As Dr. Alan Rosenberg noted in his address to the American Society of Suicidology in 1988, "It was thought that the way to prevent suicide (among teens) was to treat depression . . . It is not the case with these kids. Rather than being clinically depressed, these young suicide vic-tims are impulsive, acting out fantasies." And where are the fantasies coming from? Enter again rock and roll! Observe the words contained in a song by The Healing Faith: "I'll put a bullet in the chamber, Put the chamber in my mouth, Six to one I'm going to make it, One in six I'll snuff it out."

Is it just a coincidence that in many suicides around the country the victims have been obsessed with rock music? And, is it a coincidence that often these very songs about death and suicide were the last thing they listened to before they took their lives? No. Anyone who follows the news carefully and looks for the facts knows better. As the coroner's report in the death of one individual stated, "Decedent committed suicide by shooting self in head with .22-caliber pistol while listening to devil music."

In "Suicide Solution" Ozzy Osbourne sings: "Where to hide? Suicide is the only way out. Don't you know what it's really about?"

Another self destructive and occult related activity that has been popularized by rock music is drug abuse. It is stating the obvious to say that drugs are everywhere in rock music, from the ravaged bodies of the stars to the lyrics of their songs. This results in many fans becoming drug addicts as they try to emulate their favorite rock idol.

However, teen idols are taking a licking. Kurt Cobain committed suicide, Michael Jackson is accused of molesting a young boy, tennis pro Jennifer Capriati was charged with drug possession, River Phoenix died of a drug overdose and rap singer Snoop Doggy Dogg faces murder charges. Jim Morrison's 1971 death is thought to have been brought on by drugs. Jimi Hendrix died in 1970 of a drug overdose.

When Nirvana lead singer Kurt Cobain committed suicide in April 1994, his mother started to worry that his widow, Courtney Love, might try to kill herself, too. "I was so worried about her wanting to join him that I stayed in her room," Wendy O'Connor says in *Entertainment Weekly*. Unfortunately, some of Cobain's fans around the world followed his example and committed suicide. One such case was here in Fort Lauderdale, complete with a suicide note referencing Cobain's death.

The Beastie Boys' best selling album "License to Kill," contains over 90 references to drug and alcohol abuse. What is not so well known, however, is that drugs have a connection with the spiritual realm. Mind-altering substances are viewed by sorcerers and others involved in the occult as a gateway or a guide into the spirit world.[1]

1 John Ankerberg & John Weldon. *The Facts on Spirit Guides*. (Eugene, OR: Harvest House, 1988).

The reason God hates the misuse of drugs and connects it with the judgment of hell is because their use is a form of sorcery. The primary attraction of drugs is "getting high." This is undeniably a spiritual experience, one that opens the user up to the spirit world.

The Beatles song "Tomorrow Never Knows" says, "Turn off your mind, relax and float downstream. It is not dying—it is not dying. Lay down all thoughts—surrender to the void. It is shining—it is shining."

Rock musician and ex-Beatle George Harrison explains the origins of his Krishna-consciousness: "When I was younger, with the after effects of the LSD that opened something up inside of me in 1966, . . . a flood of other thoughts came into my head which led me to the yogis."[2]

Likewise, a rock magazine described The Cure's Robert Smith's creative process as follows: "He often comes up with his most macabre ideas for songs in the nightmares he experiences while sleeping off alcoholic binges. The entire album 'The Head Door' was written under those conditions."

A national newspaper described the uncanny fascination rock musicians inspire in their many devoted fans, "For many of the camp followers, the Grateful Dead are a religion and their lyrics a Bible . . . it is generally accepted that the Dead are tapped into some profound LSD-inspired truth. Not surprisingly, some hallucinating 'Deadheads' have weaved weird and elaborate theories about God and the universe from strands of Grateful Dead lyrics."[3]

Perhaps the most inevitable and extensive by-product or fruit of Satanic philosophy is an obsession with sex. The *Satanic Bible* (3:5) says, "Is not lust and carnal desire a more truthful term to describe 'love'?"

Sex is what rock and roll is all about. Even the term "rock and roll" coined by Cleveland, Ohio, disc jockey Alan Fried is a euphemism for sex in the back seat of a car. The

---

2 Ibid.

3 Eric Holmberg, "The Hells Bells Study Guide."

sex heralded by the rock music industry is not the mature and unselfish kind mandated by Jesus Christ. It is indeed the Satanic alternative—impulsive, carnal, and ultimately destructive.

As Dr. Alan Bloom said in *The Closing of the American Mind*—"Rock music has one appeal—a barbaric appeal to sexual desire—not love, but sexual desire undeveloped and untutored. It acknowledges the first emanations of children's emerging sensuality and addresses them seriously, eliciting them and legitimizing them . . ."[4]

Dr. Bloom makes an important point here. Moral sanity is not anti-sex but anti-exploitation. Contrary to popular belief God is not against sex. It was His idea in the first place. He designed our bodies with the capacity to enjoy it. Sex is a vehicle for man's participation in one of life's greatest miracles, the creation of another human being. In short, sex is an enormously powerful act. However, it has the potential to be destructive as well.

Sex is what rock and roll is all about

That is why God has so rigorously commanded that this very special act be reserved for a very special relationship, a lifelong commitment between a man and a woman. The writer has heard Dr. O. S. Hawkins, former pastor of the 10,000 member First Baptist Church in Fort Lauderdale, Florida, preach on this special relationship often. He ends this important message to the teenagers and the young adults by saying, "No matter what the crowd says, purity and morality are still the bottom line."[5]

Sex is a subject that many pastors seem to shy away

---

4 Alan Bloom. *The Closing of the American Mind.* (NY: Simon and Schuster, 1987), pp. 72, 73.

5 Dr. O. S. Hawkins, The First Baptist Church, Fort Lauderdale, FL.

from, yet it is an issue that is extensively covered in the Scriptures. More preachers should follow the example set by Dr. Hawkins. As a result, the youth of this nation would be much better prepared to face the temptations of Satan and the immorality that permeates our society today.

Scripture clearly states, "Do not be deceived: God cannot be mocked. A man reaps what he sows. The one who sows to please his sinful nature, from that nature will reap destruction; the one who sows to please the Spirit, from the Spirit will reap eternal life" (Galatians 6:7–8).

Scripture teaches us that rebellion is the very heart of Satanic philosophy. And rebellion is one of rock and roll's greatest themes. Biblically, witchcraft is synonymous with Satanism and rebellion is its root. The *Satanic Bible* (1:3, 5) says, "For I stand forth to challenge the wisdom of the world, to interrogate 'the laws' of man and God! He who saith 'thou shalt' to me is my mortal foe." That quote is not honest but a lie. It is rebellion that is evil, blasphemous, sinful, hypocritical, and ultimately destructive.

We live in a world besieged by sin and darkness where people lack identity and hope. Satan is the master of the terrorist attack. Right now he is trying to steal your heart, your family, your children and your health.

Just as a bad tree cannot produce good fruit, so an industry (like rock and roll) which is rooted in rebellion against God and His Word can never bring forth that which is truly good. The Bible says, "Then they will go away to eternal punishment, but the righteous to eternal life" (Matthew 25:46).

ROCK
MUSIC'S
OBSESSION
WITH SATAN

There is evidence that rock and roll is a devil's music. Like an invisible cancer that inevitably leads to death, the Satanic seed in rock and roll music has culminated in a blatant obsession with the occult.

Cryptic allusions to the devil and the music of blues artist Robert Johnson a generation ago has given place to an open worship of Satan and hell. It now comes complete with the symbols, liturgies, rituals and messianic personalities that attend any religious order.

Beginning with the symbols associated with Satanic religion there is none more foundational than the pentagram, the 5-sided star that is central to occult ritual. Next to the desecrated cross there is also no other symbol more common to the rock music industry.

Another symbol that is integral to Satanic religion is the L-cronotto, a hand gesture that represents the devil himself.

Like the pentagram it, too, is virtually everywhere in rock music.

Yet another Satanic symbol, 666, is taken from the Bible. Revelation, Chapter 13, assigns that number to the beast, the antichrist forces that war against God (a war of the spirits). Not since Nero's Rome has the mark of the beast found such widespread expression. In addition to symbols, occult ritual and philosophy also abound in contemporary rock music. Many groups within the heavy metal genre have popularized blatant, no holds barred Satanism and witchcraft in their music, album covers, and stage shows. For example, the song "Beyond the Gates" by the group Possessed goes like this: "Lucifer, hear me, I pray to the altar. I hear the sounds of insanity. Master, I drink the unholy water. Save me the torment that beckons for me."[1]

While most rock groups readily admit being spiritual and being influenced by spirits, most do so with the insistence that it is ultimately Christian in its orientation. This is very significant because Scripture makes it clear, according to Dr. O. S. Hawkins, that "the purest manifestation of the Antichrist spirit always comes not from without but from within the context of Christianity."[2]

It's really no surprise that the Antichrist spirit has become so manifest in rock music. There is abundant evidence that rock and roll's lifeblood has in some part been drawn from a musical form whose sole purpose is to summon forth evil spirits and voodoo.

An interest in backwards phenomena is characteristic of Satanic religion. Earlier we noted within rock and roll two examples of backward recording, commonly known as "backmasking." Each has been of the same variety, where the artist or engineer has simply reversed a vocal tract and then mixed it in with the rest of the music. The backmask section does not make sense when played forwards and has a distinctive A-tonal sound.

Consider the beginning of "In Lead with Satan" from Venom's "Welcome to Hell" album. When played forwards it makes no sense. But when it is reversed we hear "Satan, raised in hell, I'm gonna burn your soul, crush your bones.

---

1 The John Ankerberg Show. "The Dangers of Rock Music" with Eric Holmberg, 1991.

2 From a sermon delivered by Dr. O. S. Hawkins at the First Baptist Church, Fort Lauderdale, FL.

I'm gonna make you bleed. You're gonna bleed for me."[3]

Now, let's consider the second type of backmasking. With this variety, the vocal track makes sense both ways. When you listen to the music forwards, you hear one message. When you listen to it reversed, however, you hear something entirely different.

It has been suggested by some that when we listen to music in its normal forwards mode, the subconscious mind can decipher the backwards message and mind control results. It becomes what is termed a subliminal cue. Really there isn't a shred of evidence supporting that hypothesis. You don't need backmasking to pollute the mind and heart of someone. The forward music is more than enough to take care of that.

The real question is not "can a listener subconsciously hear a backmask message?" But "How did it get there?" There are three possible explanations:

1. INTENTIONAL. For a backmask message to be intentional the vocalist would have to sing just the right way so that Satan's message would come through at the same time, and nobody is that smart.

2. ACCIDENTAL. No. Not only are the mathematical probabilities of this absurd but the fact that virtually every example of this type of backmasking conveys a message that is intrinsically demonic even further disproves this hypothesis. Really the only workable explanation is our third choice.

3. SPIRITUAL. Outside intelligent forces with supernatural power are occasionally able to play an artist much like we would play a musical instrument.

Let's examine a piece of the Electric Light Orchestra's "Eldorado" album. Here's a segment from the title song played forwards: "I'll sail away, on a voyage of no return to

---

3 The John Ankerberg Show, "The Dangers of Rock Music" with Eric
    Holmberg, 1991.

see, if eternal life is meant to be." Note that even forwards there's an element of anti-Christian thought here. Eternal life is definitely meant to be. The only question is where. Now here's that same segment played backwards: "He's the nasty one—Christ, you're infernal."[4]

Another example is by Queen from their song "Another One Bites the Dust," one of the most popular and enduring songs in rock's history. Taking the same section and playing it backwards we get "Start to smoke marijuana." Since drugs and sorcery are tied together, it is easy to see the Satanic motivation behind the command "Start to smoke marijuana."

Next we'll take a song from Cheap Trick's popular album "Dream Police." The significance of the album's title "Gonna Raise Hell" becomes apparent when we reverse this segment: "You know Satan holds the key to the lock." Theologically, this is quite interesting because keys are symbolic to authority, particularly over sin and its penalty, death and hell. The Bible reveals Jesus Christ and His awesome power to us in Revelation 1:18, "I am the Living One; I was dead, and behold I am alive for ever and ever! And I hold the keys of death and Hades." Satan's claim to hold the keys (cheap trick) in this song is significant not only because it's a lie and typical of his empty bravado but because it points out how desperately he wants to take ownership of people's lives.

There is also theological significance in our next example, the version of the song "Anthem" by the group Rush. When this section is played in reverse we hear "Oh Satan, you are the one who is shining. Walls of Satan, I know you are the one I love." One of the many translations for Lucifer is "the shining one."[5]

Finally, let's look at Led Zeppelin's classic "Stairway to Heaven." Played forward we hear: "Yes, there are two paths you can go by. But in the long run there's still time to change

---

4 Ibid.

5 Ibid.

the road you're on." When this section is played in reverse here is what we hear: "My sweet Satan, no other make a path. For it makes me sad, whose power is Satan."

As we have seen throughout this volume Satan is not sweet. He's a liar and the father of all lies.

Many of the big-time rock stars have been heavily involved in overt Satanism. Trying to describe his own "Inspiration" process, John Lennon said: "It's like being possessed: like a psychic or a medium." Of the Beatles, Yoko Ono, "They were like mediums. They weren't conscious of all they were saying, but it was coming through them." Marc Storace, with the heavy metal band Krokus, told *Circus* magazine: "You can't describe it except to say it's like a mysterious energy that comes from the metaphysical plane and into my body. It's almost like being a medium."[6]

Little Richard had similar experiences and identified Satan as the source of his inspiration: "I was directed and commanded by another power. The power of darkness . . . that a lot of people don't believe exists. The power of the devil, Satan."[7]

Many of the big-time rock stars have been heavily involved in overt Satanism

Mark David Chapman, the man who murdered John Lennon, appeared on a recent CNN "Larry King Live" program.[8] Chapman admitted that he was possessed by the evil spirits of the devil when he committed that cold-blooded act. He said, "a voice inside me kept saying 'do it,' 'do it,'" as he shot Lennon five times in the back. He was not scared. He didn't even try to escape. He waited for the police to arrive.

---

6 Dave Hunt, "Satanism, Rock and Rebellion" in *America: The Sorcerer's New Apprentice.*

7 Ibid.

8 CNN-TV, "Larry King Live," December 17, 1992.

He felt no remorse. He was totally under Satan's control.

If the reader hasn't tuned in yet, it is time to get serious. We are indeed involved in a very important spiritual war. We live in a spiritual realm that is filled with evil spirits that can control the minds of individuals as is being pointed out in this chapter. These are real people. Satan has won the spiritual war in their lives. He is using them like puppets, they respond to his every command. They are the people that we read about in the daily newspaper. They are the people we frequently see on television. For whatever reason, they chose not to seek the love and protection provided by the Holy Spirit of Jesus Christ.

Jim Morrison, of The Doors, called the spirits who at times possessed him "The Lords," and wrote a book of poetry about them. Folk rock artist Joni Mitchell's creativity came from her spirit guide "Art." So dependent was she upon "Art" that nothing could detain her when he "called."[9]

It appears that the prevalence of such "spirits" among top rock stars seems to go far beyond the realm of coincidence. Superstar Jimi Hendrix, called "rock's greatest guitarist," . . . "believed he was possessed by some spirit," according to Alan Douglas. Hendrix's former girlfriend, Fayne Pridgon, has said: "He used to always talk about some devil or something was in him, you know, and he didn't have any control over it, he didn't know what made him act the way he acted and what made him say the things he said, and songs . . . just came out of him . . ."[10]

Keith Richards of the Rolling Stones once noted in a Rolling Stone interview that the Stones' songs came spontaneously, just like inspiration "at a seance." He described the songs as arriving "en masse," as if the Stones as song writers were only a willing and open "medium."[11]

---

9 Dave Hunt, "Satanism, Rock and Rebellion" in *America: The Sorcerer's New Apprentice*, p. 240.

10 Ibid.

11 *Rock*, June 1984, p. 138.

For those of you who are not completely convinced that rock music's obsession with Satan is a real phenomenon, read on!

Increasing numbers of other musicians are showing an interest in witchcraft, and even Satanism. Among the "black metal" groups, names that seem to indicate at least some interest in the occult are "Covens," "Dark Angels," "Demon," "Infernal Majesty," "Possessed," "Satan," "Cloven Hoof," and others. Did you read the names carefully?

Ozzy Osbourne has said, "I never seem to know exactly what I'm gonna do next. I just like to do what the spirits make me do. That way, I always have someone or some-thing to blame"[12] Osbourne, an ex-lead singer for Black Sabbath, actually gave an altar call for Satan while playing in Canada. He confesses, "Sometimes I feel like a medium for some out-side force . . ." Black Sabbath has also made altar calls to Lucifer at some of their concerts.[13]

The group Iron Maiden, openly admits that they are dabbling in the occult, including witchcraft and Satanism.[14] At times they seem to enjoy their relationship with Satan so much that they invite others to join them. One Iron Maiden concert in Portland, Oregon, opened with the words "Welcome to Satan's sanctuary." In an interview with *Hit Parade,* Glenn Tipton of the group Judas Priest confessed that when he goes on stage, he goes crazy: "it's like some-one else takes over my body."[15]

In describing what a Van Halen concert is like, David Lee Roth commented, "I'm gonna abandon my spirit to them [emotions], which is actually what I attempt to do. You work yourself up into that state and you fall in supplication of the demon gods."[16] According to a *Rolling Stone* interview,

---

12 *Faces,* November 1983, p. 24.

13 Tingelhoff, op. cit., p. 21.

14 *Creem Metal,* September 1982.

15 *Hit Parade,* Fall 1984.

16 *Rock,* April 1984.

Peter Criss, the first and most famous drummer of the rock band KISS stated, "I believe in the devil as much as God. You can use either one to get things done."[17]

There is evidence that rock and roll is a devil's music. Like an invisible cancer that inevitably leads to death

Guitarist Mick Mars of Motley Crüe, in an interview with *Heavy Metal Times* magazine, described his band as "demonic, that's what we are."[18] Nikki Sixx, referring to their "Shout at the Devil" stage show commented, "We have skulls, pentagrams, and all kind of Satanic symbols on stage . . . have always flirted with the devil."[19]

Stevie Nicks of Fleetwood Mac has several times dedicated their concerts to the witches of the world. An album of the rock group Venom, entitled "Welcome to Hell," contains the following words on the back cover. "We are possessed by all that is evil. The death of your God we demand: we spit at the virgin you worship, and sit at the Lord Satan's left hand."[20]

It should be pointed out that many of the rock artists covered in this chapter feature skulls and pentagrams on their album covers to promote their evil desires and close association with Satan. The very names of some of the bands in the heavy metal division termed "death metal" suggest an emphasis on death and violence: "Mace," "Carnivore," "Rotten Corpse," "Destruction," Blessed Death," "Mal-

---

17 *Rolling Stone*, January 12, 1978.

18 *Heavy Metal Times*, May 1983.

19 *Circus*, January 31, 1984.

20 Tingelhoff, op. cit., p. 25.

ice," "Sacrifice," "Violence," "Coroner," "Overkill," etc.[21] Are you reading the names carefully?

Their concerts also feature skulls and pentagrams, as well as simulated slashings, stabbings, and decapitations. Some even drink blood or gnaw on a few grisly bones. Some groups incorporate occult imagery, Satanic rites or reference to magic . . . This is dark, angry music. It focuses on death and violence, and a love for blood and gore . . . In many cases, the bands project a message that there is no chance, no hope, and no future. All they can do is beat their fists in the empty air. Live fast and die young—go out in a blaze of glory.

In reality, however, these people do not go out in a blaze of glory. They must face Jesus Christ who will enter judgment for all the sins they committed while here on Planet Earth. What they perceived as going out in "a blaze of glory" will surely result in eternal punishment in "a blaze of fire" in hell! The Holy Bible says, ". . . a man is destined to die once, and after that to face judgment" (Hebrews 9:27).

As we look at the spiritual influence in rock music, one gets the impression that anything and everything goes, except genuine Christianity. What a shame! The devil will exploit any medium that he can to blind us to the reality of God's love for us and our desperate need for His saving power. We live in a society filled with sin and darkness where people lack identity and hope.

But there is hope. Jesus Christ is the answer! He is waiting for your call this very moment. No personal problem is too large and no circumstance or situation is too complicated for Christ to handle. The Bible says, "Call to me [God] and I will answer you and tell you great and unsearchable things you do not know" (Jeremiah 33:3).

Accepting Christ as their personal Savior is all that is required of anyone who wishes to be free from Satan and

---

21 Dave Hart, "Heavy Metal Madness," *Media Update*, July/August 1989, p. 5.

his evil spirits. It's very simple. Just ask Jesus to forgive you of your sins, ask Him to come into your life right now and be your Lord and Savior.

From this moment forward you are a new spiritual creature with the power of the Holy Spirit abiding within you, giving you the ability to say no to Satan's temptations. You now possess the love, the joy, the peace, and the eternal security that are found only through a personal relationship with Jesus Christ. Congratulations!

Warning! Satan's temptations will still be there. His biggest attack is yet to come. Satan is a poor loser. He hates to see people discover his lies and accept Jesus as Lord and Savior. Surround yourself with strong Christians. They will help you be delivered from the old lifestyle. You will be amazed at how beautiful and uncomplicated life can be when Jesus is the centerpiece of your life.

SATAN'S MESSAGE

CHAPTER NINETEEN

DO YOUR OWN THING

Before we exit the devil's playground, let's focus on probably the most popular message in rock music: man should do his own thing. You are the boss and you can do whatever you want. This philosophy is the most elementary presupposition of Satanic religion.

To begin with, as we have seen, many of the artists that we consider neutral are not really neutral at all when you look beneath the surface. Isn't the so-called neutral music, by the very reason of its subtlety, potentially more destructive than the overt wickedness found in hard-core rock and roll?

Consider the following fact of life. For something to be truth, it has to be completely true. Inject into it even the smallest falsehood and immediately that truth becomes a lie. It becomes a lethal weapon in the hands of whom the Scripture calls the father of all lies.

The Bible warns us about the children of the devil when it says, "You belong to your father, the devil, and you want to carry out your father's desire. He was a murderer from the beginning, not holding to the truth, for there is no truth in him. When he lies, he speaks his native language, for he is a liar and the father of lies" (John 8:44).

Satan's most effective deceptions are those that carry a degree of truth. That is why the middle of the road in music as well as many other areas of life can sometimes be the most dangerous place of all.

151

By way of analogy, take strychnine, one of the most powerful poisons in the world. In its raw state it is unattractive and extraordinarily bitter. If this poison is left in the room with young children, it's unlikely that they'll pay much attention to it. And even more unlikely that they could stand to eat enough for it to be fatal. If you were to take the same poison and sugarcoat it and add pretty colors to it, for example like M & M's, and then leave it with the children, virtually every one of them will eat the poison without hesitation.

If you were the devil which method would you find more reliable, the bitter poison or the sugarcoated candy? The great philosopher and writer C. S. Lewis noted: "Indeed, the safest road to hell is the gradual one—the gentle slope, soft underfoot, without sudden turnings, without milestones, without signposts."

For something to be truth, it has to be completely true

God surely cautions us throughout the Scriptures to seek first His kingdom and not let the world system wear us down. The Bible says, "Above all else, guard your heart, for it is the wellspring of life. Put away perversity from your mouth; keep corrupt talk far from your lips. Let your eyes look straight ahead, fix your gaze directly before you. Make level paths for your feet and take only ways that are firm. Do not swerve to the right or the left; keep your foot from evil" (Proverbs 4:23–27).

Nearly two-thousand years ago Jesus amplified this teaching when He said that our eyes should be single, completely focused on God (see Matthew 6:23). The bottom line for us is that if we really love God we will find ourselves naturally offended by things that mock His character, ignore His love, or pervert His truth.

Throughout the Bible we are taught that if anyone loves the fallen world's ways, the love of the Father is not in them. For everything that is in the world—the desires of sinful man, the lust of his eyes, and the boasting of what he has and does—comes not from the Father but from the world. The world and its desires pass away, but the man who does the will of God lives forever.

In essence, Satanism is simply each individual acknowledging no one else, not even Satan, as a higher authority. As our own god or goddess, each of us is free to do as we please. This philosophy is reduced to a single axiom found in the *Book of Satan* 4:3, "Say unto thine own heart, 'I am mine own redeemer.'"

This philosophy brings to mind a recent article in the Fort Lauderdale *Sun-Sentinel* concerning rock performer Michael Jackson and his Dangerous Tour of Europe that started in Munich, Germany. He carted two tons of clothes to Europe for this tour.

A brief look at the costumes shows why. Two of Jackson's 9-foot-tall-by-7-foot-wide, 40-pound outfits were lined with 35,000 fiber optics, or points of light, which were designed to create mesmerizing lighting effects. The costumes' designed by Dennis Tompkins and Michael Bush had to incorporate a computerized laser rig that controls the lighting. One coat Jackson wore required 3,000 volts of electricity to power its 36 strobe lights. It had to be flame-proofed and insulated, as well as have other exacting safety measures put in, to avoid injury. The 3,000 volts draw energy from a concealed belt harboring 15 batteries.

Describing the tour's 300 outfits as "Rock & Roll Renaissance-silhouetted street clothes," Bush said: "Michael wanted things that have never been done and have never been seen. We feel confident we've helped him accomplish that goal."

News releases like this should remind us of what the Bible says, "for Satan himself masquerades as an angel of light" (2 Corinthians 11:14). There is no question about it, there is a supernatural war of enormous proportions raging throughout the world today and battles are being fought this very moment.

We are all born with a sense that we are not complete. The rest of life becomes a quest for wholeness and fulfillment. We need a redeemer! Some will look for it in money, power, sex, or some object. Others will seek God.

Satanism simply states "that God is us."

Christianity acknowledges that all of us are stained with sin and are unable to save ourselves. We need a Messiah, a supernatural redeemer. The Word of God is clear when it says, "In reply Jesus declared, 'I tell you the truth, no one can see the kingdom of God unless he is born again'" (John 3:3). And, "The god of this age has blinded the minds of unbelievers, so that they cannot see the light of the gospel of the glory of Christ, who is the image of God" (2 Corinthians 4:4).

Many people today who call themselves Christians do not have any understanding of the term "born again" (John 3:7). He said it emphatically. The theological doctrine is called regeneration. The message of the entire Bible could be summed up in three words: **creation** (or generation), **degeneration,** and **regeneration** (born again). This is the message of the Bible from the beginning to the end. God made man perfect. Man fell into sin and must be recreated into the image of God by the power of God's spirit working through the gospel of Jesus Christ.

The Old Testament further describes regeneration in Ezekiel 36:26 as a giving of a new heart. "I will give you a new heart and put a new spirit in you; I will remove from you your heart of stone and give you a heart of flesh"—a heart designed to love our God. The subjects of regeneration are made alive from the dead. They become new creatures through God's workmanship. "Therefore, if anyone is in Christ, he is a new creation; the old has gone, the new has come!" (2 Corinthians 5:17). In other words, he has been born again. Religiosity, piety, morality will not suffice. Unless we have hearts which have been transformed to love God in truth with all our hearts and souls, we will not see God, we will not enter the kingdom of Heaven!

Good vs. Evil is a war of the spirits. Ultimately there are two kingdoms and two types of people: those in God's kingdom who have been redeemed by God and those in

Satan's kingdom who are trying to redeem themselves. The kingdom of God holds to one supreme commandment, "Love the Lord your God with all your heart and with all your soul and with all your mind and with all your strength" (Mark 12:30). The kingdom of Satan can be reduced to one essential message—"Do your own thing."

Our country has lost sight of its Christian heritage. What used to be wrong is now considered right. What once was considered evil is now considered good by society:

● Books like rock star Madonna's *Sex* are touted in the media as the latest best-seller. The liberal media sees nothing wrong in promoting pornographic material that glorifies sadism and homosexuality.

● An unprecedented increase in support for abortion. There are many people who really believe that it is acceptable to kill unborn babies.

● Reckless spending and rising personal, corporate, and national debt. This is the by-product of a pleasure-seeking "me" oriented society. And it is pulling the rug out from under families, institutions, and governments.

● Banning Christian literature, symbols, and activity from traditional places. The Supreme Court has refused to review a tragically misguided lower court ruling that banned the Bible from a public school classroom. That same ruling said it is perfectly acceptable for a public school teacher to have a book about Buddha on his desk, but not a Bible!

● Rising influence of perverse lifestyles and values in media. On television today you can see a full range of evil and unrighteousness, everything from cross-dressing, incest, homosexuality, adultery—all in the form of sin that the Scriptures say is part of a nation that turns away from God. Yes, we live in a "do your own thing" society today.

Over the last several decades, moral and ethical standards in America have sunk to alarming depths. We don't seem to realize that every television program, every newscast, every magazine, every novel, every motion picture is based on some ethical presupposition, derived from among a wide variety of ethical systems. Unfortunately, many Christians just do not want to learn about them. Consequently, they are totally incapable of dealing with this wave of immorality based on phony ethical foundations that is inundating our country. Everything that we do is based upon some ethical, moral consideration.

Barbra Streisand, according to an article in the *Sun-Sentinel*, is said to have signed a $60 million movie and record pact with Sony Corporation that would put her in the same mega-bucks bracket as Madonna, Prince and Michael Jackson. Streisand has received a lot of press lately concerning her "hate" attitude, especially toward Christian males. We have seen what mega-bucks did for Madonna. Will we see the same rage from Streisand?

Prince recently signed an unprecedented $100 million deal with Warner Bros. Records making him the highest-paid performer in pop music. It has been reported that he will receive $10 million per album—plus royalties.

Contrary to the deceptive stereotype, no black-magic or wild sex rituals are really necessary to be a follower of Satan and his angels. This is done simply by denying the love and authority of God and by living your life the way you want to. You can even be very religious, attend church regularly, tithe, do good works and deeds. But if it's a religion based upon your own terms you are still very comfortably fulfilling the dictates of Satan's most primary law—Do what you want to do.

The primary reason for our existence is to know and experience God. An act called worship. God offers His love and friendship to everyone. But He does not force Himself on anyone. His promises and His presence are only for those who seek Him and accept His free gift of salvation by faith in His Son, Jesus Christ.

GOD
OFFERS
OPPORTUNITY
CHAPTER TWENTY

One of the primary reasons so many people miss God's blessing is because they are looking to their own resources instead of His.

Opportunities can provide privileges in life that we never dreamed would come our way. There are opportunities to learn and to help others. Some opportunities pass our way only once. Others may come a second and third time.

God alone knows the opportunities He has divinely engineered for our lives. When they do come, it is a wise man or woman who takes advantage of them.

One of God's primary goals is to teach us to be sensitive to His leading so we can identify the opportunities He presents. With some opportunities, we know from the outset they came from God. However, others slip into our lives quietly, and many times the only way we discern their coming is by learning to "sit before the Lord" in total stillness. This "quiet" time with the Lord is very important if we are seriously trying to find God's will for our lives. The Bible says, "Be still and know that I am God" (Psalm 46:10).

We cease striving when we "know that [He is] God." We don't have to white-knuckle it through life because our sovereign God is in control. We don't have to bend beneath life's emotional load because our loving God invites us to cast our cares on Him. We don't have to manipulate our circumstances because our wise God has a good and kind plan. And we don't have to yield to our weakness because our omnipotent God strengthens us for every trial and temptation. This will allow us to relax and rest in the all-sufficiency of God's grace.

We must always be aware of the evil desires of Satan and his evil spirits. They will do anything within their power to distract us from God and the opportunities that He has in store for us. We cannot allow the immorality, the sin, the violence, the corruption and the wickedness of the world society in which we live today to disturb our fellowship with Jesus Christ.

Turmoil, unrest, and anxiety make it difficult to discern the nature and source of the opportunity. The Israelites faced a similar situation as they approached the Promised Land for the first time. Fear and confusion clouded their minds. Their faith gave way to human reason, causing them to question God's supernatural provision. In their failure to obey God and enter the land, they missed a divine opportunity.

However, the second approach to the Promised Land delivered different results. When you fail to take advantage of God's opportunity, it is wise to ask God to show you exactly where you missed His instruction. If the opportunity comes again, you can apply what you have learned to the situation and move ahead in faith.

Consider the following Scripture: "Therefore arise, cross this Jordan, you and all this people, to the land which I am giving to them, to the sons of Israel. Every place on which the sole of your foot treads, I have given it to you, just as I spoke to Moses" (Joshua 1:2–3 NAS).

You see, God's opportunities are always perfectly timed. He didn't bring the people back to the Promised Land until they were ready to take advantage of the opportunity.

God is never in a hurry, and He never offers an opportunity ahead of time. Every event that touches your life has a purpose.

Any hesitation, unbelief, or fear only causes you to miss God's richest blessings. The Israelites initially disobeyed

God because they were not familiar with the ways of God. They surely did not understand His personal love for them. Many times our disobedience is a result of ignorance and human reasoning.

You see, God's opportunities are always perfectly timed

When we see opportunities approaching, we must be especially sensitive to God's will. He may be telling us to wait rather than move right ahead, It is important to understand that there are times to move ahead, to be still, to make financial decisions, to witness, to speak, to be quiet, to help others, and to pray.

God's timing is perfect. He knows the events that must take place before the opportunity is revealed. When we jump ahead of His timing, we are headed for trouble. Many times the reason so many people get ahead of God is because they are afraid of missing the opportunity when it comes. But if you are living in close fellowship with the Lord, you won't miss it. God is always in a process of preparing us for the future. He never offers an opportunity when we are unprepared. He knows the challenges we will face today and the ones we will face tomorrow. Many people get angry at God because He does not operate within their time frame. But God constantly orchestrates life according to His plan—not according to ours.

People often insist they are ready for a job promotion, a marriage, a new friendship, the responsibility of having children, of owning a home, or buying a new car; however, God in His sovereignty knows they are not and tells them to wait. Yet, many people refuse to listen. Not only do they miss God's best, they also have to suffer the consequences of making a wrong decision.

There are no shortcuts with God. Most of us can remember being involved with something very important and we wanted to take a quicker route. But God was always there to remind us that we can't afford to take shortcuts.

He is in the process of preparing each of us for a certain task. In going through the preparation process, we learn to obey Him and seek His will above our own.

Since God knows our future perfectly and how today's ordinary events fit into His plan, we can rely on Him every moment. The timeless principles of the Bible help us make wise decisions from God's viewpoint. God always uses His Word to prepare us for His blessings. Memorizing and meditating on Scripture sharpens our minds and teaches us how to correctly apply His truth to our lives.

Life's many trials and afflictions are a part of that preparation. Yes, even failure prepares us for God's opportunities. Failure—we hate the sound of the word itself, much less enduring its distasteful consequences. We want triumph. We crave to be on top and struggle every day to maintain an upward spiral.

Yet at some point, in some way, to some degree, we all fail. We stumble in our moral life. We let others down. We make a mess of our finances. We drift far from our devotion to Christ. We easily fall into the pit of depression. However, mistakes and failures are very much a part of our preparation for service. If we trust God during those times, we will find that He will pave the way to opportunity.

We have a personal responsibility to Him to move forward in faith and claim His promises. Faith is never exercised by sitting around wishing God would do something. He gave the Israelites the opportunity, but it was their responsibility to step forward by faith and claim the land.

People who trust God are movers and achievers because they rely on God's power. They are also the ones who accomplish great things for the kingdom of God.

They work diligently but "according to His power, which mightily works within [them]" (Colossians 1:29). They plan wisely, but with the knowledge that God's will is preeminent (Proverbs 16:19). They pray fervently, but with the knowledge that God's response is always best.

When God offers us an opportunity and we refuse, there is always a severe penalty involved. The first time Israel approached the land, the people simply refused to take advantage of the opportunity. They spent forty years in the wilderness as a result of their wrong decision.

When God offers us an opportunity and we refuse, there is always a severe penalty involved

Many people, particularly late in life have said: "If only I had taken the chance God gave me. If only I had tried. If only I had lived my life for Him." Whenever we refuse to be obedient to God, we always suffer.

Many think they are too old for God to use, or they think they have missed His best opportunities for them because of their disobedience. However, the wonderful thing about Christ is that He works with anyone right where they are. Young or old, it makes no difference to God.

You may have missed opportunities in the past, but there are no losers in God's eyes. The moment you open your heart to Him, He takes your life and uses it regardless of your past. The opportunities you take advantage of today are indeed gateways to life's richest blessings.

Remember we are doing business with Almighty God who loves us. He accepts us unconditionally, and He understands us completely.

We are engaged in a war of the spirits. You don't fight a real war with toy guns, and you don't fight the devil and his vast army of demons with mere determination or resolve. Our defense against Satan is provided by God. If we are to succeed, we must take up His weapons.[1]

---

1 Sermons by Dr. Charles F. Stanley, In Touch Ministries, were valuable to the writer in composing this chapter.

CHAPTER TWENTY–ONE
OUR BASIC NEEDS

All of us have needs—singles, married people, moms or dads raising children alone, teens, retired couples, widows and widowers. Our needs vary according to the individual.

We all have basic needs for acceptance, love, security, belonging, and competence. Each individual has his own set of personal, financial, social, emotional, intellectual, and spiritual needs also.

God promises to meet our needs. A promise we can claim for every situation is Philippians 4:19, "And my God will meet ALL your needs according to His glorious riches." God wants to meet our needs. He sent His Son to meet our greatest need—the need for eternal salvation.

Christ did not stop with the gift of salvation. He designed His entire ministry to meet the needs of men and women. He knew their struggles and longed to identify with them.

God's desire to identify personally with us was so great that He allowed men to curse His Son, beat Him, reject Him, and finally crucify Him. Jesus Christ can personally identify with all our feelings because He also experienced physical and emotional pain.

Jesus had needs just like we have needs. We should never forget that while Jesus was the Son of God, He also had human needs. He hungered just as we hunger. He experienced a wide range of emotions in the garden of Gethsemane the night of His arrest. He cried over the death of His friend, Lazarus. He wept for Jerusalem and the sins of the people. Jesus had needs—needs only the Father could meet. He knows the depth of our needs because He, too, experienced feelings of loneliness, rejection, and isolation.

One reason God doesn't meet our needs immediately is that we bypass Him and try to meet them in our own way. When we do this, we dig a deeper hole for ourselves. God wants to meet our needs, but He wants to do it His way and in His timing.

However, when we confess our needs to Him, we are really confessing our dependence on Him. This is when God can work in our lives—when we are open and dependent on Him. He knows the hidden desires and motivations of our hearts, and He knows what it takes to accomplish His will in our lives.

Frequently, the reason we don't feel like our needs are being met is because we can't identify what the real need is. There are some basic needs that we have other than food, clothing, and shelter that God has created in us and God has provided for us.

These needs are absolutely essential for a good healthy emotional life and essential to our relationships with others, with God, and with ourselves. God wants us to be whole persons and to have balance in our lives. In order for that to happen He created three basic needs in the life of every person.

The sense of belonging is the first basic need. To be needed and loved is a desire that begins in the mother's womb. Every child needs to grow up in a household where he feels he is wanted. When a child does not get this at home, he will find someone or some group and attach himself to that person or that group to fulfill this sense of belonging.

In the early years it is essential to build the correct emotional health in a child. You cannot separate emotional and spiritual things. We are emotional and spiritual beings. Many people have needs that go unmet because of something they have not dealt with in their lives.

It is very important that we feel we belong. Many children do not feel as if they belong today because mom has her career and dad has his and both are rarely at home. It should be no surprise that kids get into so much trouble today.

When a person doesn't have that sense of belonging, he will find some substitute. A person who can't relate to other people will focus on material things in life. Things replace the relationships that the people don't know how to build. God makes it possible for us to have a sense of belonging.

For example, He gave us the idea of the family: a husband, wife, and children. In a close family everyone fits, they have a sense of being one unit. God has put all kinds of people with different spiritual gifts in the church so they can be of help to each another.

To make this sense of belonging complete, God has fashioned our relationship with Him so that we are born again. Through our faith in Jesus Christ our sins are forgiven and we become the children of God. We belong to the kingdom of God. We become reconciled with Him.

No matter what our circumstances are God, has made it possible for us to sense belonging. The Bible teaches, ". . . in all these things we are more than conquerors through Him who loved us. For I am convinced that neither death nor life, neither angels nor demons, neither the present nor the future, nor any powers, neither height nor depth, nor anything else in all creation, will be able to separate us from the love of God that is in Christ Jesus our Lord" (Romans 8:37–39).

If you are not saved, it doesn't matter what you belong to or how many friends you have because only God can fulfill that complete sense of belonging through a relationship with Him. No person will ever fill that gap in your life. The sense of belonging may partially be filled with friends and family but it will ultimately be fulfilled by God. We belong to Him and He belongs to us as the Heavenly Father.

A sense of worth is our second basic need. We should love ourselves in a wholesome fashion. Many people around us feel unworthy. The primary reason for this is the way they were treated by their parents. Many parents do not spend quality time with their children because they are so caught up in their own self-interest or because they lack the knowledge of what quality time is or the importance of quality time with the children.

We have a generation of kids growing up today that are very angry. They are creating a society that is not to our liking, not very pleasant, not very good, and not pleasing to our Lord. The parents are mainly responsible for this problem. When a person comes to the point in his life where he feels so unworthy, the next question is "why keep living?"

Frequently there are failures in our past that we can't quite overcome. The people who succeed in life are those who absolutely refuse to let past failures convince and persuade them that they are worthless.

Sin is another reason people feel unworthy. Sin strikes out at your sense of self esteem. This is why guilt can destroy our sense of worth and make it difficult for us to accept admiration from someone else or accept another person's love.

Sometimes it is the sin of other people that causes us to have that sense of unworthiness. Other people may say or do something to hurt our feelings. We should not place our sense of worth in another person's hands.

Christ did not stop with the gift of salvation

We may also build a false premise on the idea of performance. That is, if I perform well, you'll like me. When your self worth is based on your performance then you have to perform well at all times.

A second false premise is appearance. We base our self worth on our appearance and how others see us.

A third false premise is status. This is what gets people in debt. God never intended our sense of worth to be based on our appearance, performance or status. He said we were worth dying for. That is how worthy we are.

A sense of competence is the third basic need. God has given each of us a special gift. We should seek and find this gift in our life. The writer feels that we are to share this gift with others which will in turn glorify our Lord.

We can do anything God wants us to do. The Bible says, "Such confidence as this is ours through Christ before God. Not that we are competent to claim anything for ourselves but our competence comes from God. He has made us competent as ministers of a new covenant—not of the letter but of the Spirit; for the letter kills, but the Spirit gives life" (2 Corinthians 3:4–6).

In summary, as believers, our three basic needs are:

1. A sense of belonging—He is my Father. I know I belong.

2. A sense of worthiness—He said this is how much I think you're worth. I died for you.

3. A sense of competence—I'm sending the Holy Spirit to live within you and to equip you.

These three basic needs are not in anyone else's hands except God's and ours. The God who is the process for healing you will help you to accept what needs to be accepted about the past. We are to forgive, to forget and to go forward with Christ in control of our lives. You can be a whole person if you have a healthy sense of belonging, worthiness, and competence.

We are engaged in a war of the spirits. We must be prepared to engage in battle each day against Satan and his evil forces. The need to be emotionally and spiritually healthy is a prerequisite to becoming a successful, triumphant soldier for God.

Abraham Lincoln understood these basic needs during the Civil War. He often prayed to God during his struggle with the spiritual dimension of the battle which was tearing the nation apart because the battles had escalated to herculean proportions. Part of his 1862 meditation follows: "I am almost ready to say this is probably true: that God wills this contest, and wills that it shall not end yet. By His mere great power on the minds of the now contestants, He could have either saved or destroyed the Union without a human contest. Yet the contest began. And, having begun, He could give the final victory to either side any day. Yet the contest proceeds . . ."

Since we live in a sinful world, our struggle with the spiritual dimensions of the war between good and evil will proceed also. However, our personal victory over evil is assured because we have the Holy Spirit on our side.

All of our basic needs can be traced back to a need for self-worth. People want to feel they are worthy, loved, and accepted. The only true basis for our worth is found in Jesus Christ. When basic needs go unmet, people naturally attempt to meet those needs some way. Many times these ways are horribly destructive.

If you are trying to derive your worth from the world, people, and things, you are going to be disappointed. The world places tremendous expectations on us by telling us what to drive, where to live, who to be with, and where to work.

Jesus accepts us and loves us unconditionally. We are worthy in the eyes of God. If we weren't, He would not have died for us. It does not matter what the need is. Until you settle the issue of self-worth, you will continue to struggle with unmet needs.

No amount of money or success can satisfy your needs. Marriage will not be an eternal honeymoon, a new car isn't new for long, and even a dream home has a few nightmares. The only person who can completely meet your every need is Jesus Christ. People and things were never meant to meet your needs. Only God can meet all the needs you have in your heart. We would have no need for God if we could meet all our needs.

When you come to the conclusion that only God is your Need Meeter, then you will stop looking to others to make you happy or satisfied. When you give Jesus His rightful place in your life and allow Him to meet your needs, then you will begin to experience incredible peace. There will be a sense of belonging, worth, and competence like you have never known before. Loneliness, fear, doubt, resentment, and guilt will gradually subside. Surety and confidence will fill your heart.

Yes, Satan and his evil spirits will always be present. However, when you depend on the Holy Spirit to meet your basic needs, Satan will pose no threat to your contentment.

May the "joy of the Lord" be "your strength" in the days to come (Nehemiah 8:10) as you decide to place your total confidence in Jesus Christ.[1]

---

1 Sermons by Dr. Charles F. Stanley, In Touch Ministries, were valuable to the writer in composing this chapter.

CHAPTER TWENTY-TWO
THE WORDS JESUS SPOKE FROM THE CROSS

Seven times our Lord spoke from the cross of Calvary. Are you familiar with the words Jesus spoke from the cross?

Let's open the Bible and examine the last words our Lord and Savior spoke as He hung from a Roman cross outside the city gates and city walls of Jerusalem.

Three times our Lord spoke before that strange terrifying darkness enveloped the earth. Jesus was crucified at 9 a.m. At noon a horrifying darkness enveloped the earth that lasted until 3 p.m. He spoke once during that darkness and three times after the darkness in rapid succession.

The first words Jesus spoke from the cross were, "Father, forgive them, for they do not know what they are doing" (Luke 23:34). Note that His first words were a compassionate prayer for other people.

No one knows how many times Jesus must have repeated this silently as He was nailed to the cross. Here He was practicing what He had preached. He knew that they did not know the magnitude of what they were doing.

The first, the fourth and the seventh time Jesus spoke were prayers. At the beginning He prayed, in the middle He prayed and at the end He prayed.

The second time Jesus spoke was a comforting promise, "I tell you the truth, today you will be with Me in paradise" (Luke 23:43). Jesus was crucified between two thieves. One

171

of the criminals who hung there hurled insults at Jesus saying "if you are the Son of God, save yourself and us too." The other thief looking at his friend on the other side of Jesus said "we are getting what we deserve but this man in the center has done no wrong" and then he turned to Jesus and said "Jesus, remember me when you come into your kingdom." (Luke 23:42). Jesus turned His face toward this dying thief and said, "I tell you the truth, today you will be with Me in paradise."

This shows us very vividly that the most wicked and sinful person can find hope and faith and trust in Jesus Christ without a lot of sacramentalism. It is truly an instantaneous act of God. And here He demonstrates to us what it takes to be able to come into fellowship with God and to know God eternally through Jesus Christ.

In order for you to have this eternal relationship with Jesus there are three basic things you must do:

One, admit your own sin. All of us at one time or another have played outside the boundaries of God's laws. It's difficult for many of us to overcome our pride so that we might receive the free gift of eternal life.

Two, recognize the sinless deity of Jesus Christ. See Him for who He really is. He was not just a teacher but one who came clothing Himself in human flesh. Jesus had been tempted but was without sin so that He might really become the sin bearer for all mankind.

And three, open your heart and surrender your life to Jesus Christ. The Bible says, "That if you confess with your mouth, 'Jesus is Lord,' and you believe in your heart that God raised Him from the dead, you will be saved" (Romans 10:9).

The third time Jesus spoke from the cross there was a concerned pronouncement. He looked down and there was Mary, His mother, standing next to John, the disciple whom He loved. Then Jesus said to His mother, "'Dear woman, here is your son,' and to the disciple, 'Here is your mother'" (John 19:26–27).

Jesus wasn't talking about Himself here when He said

son, He was talking about John. He was telling Mary to take care of John and be a mother to him. And He was saying to John, you take care of my responsibility to my mother. Even on the cross He remembered individuals and He remembered to fulfill all of the law. From this time on, John took Mary into his home and cared for her.

Then a terrifying darkness enveloped the earth at noon. For three hours Jesus Christ hung on the cross and as the Bible says, "He who knew no sin became sin for us that we might become the righteousness of God in Him."

The fourth time Jesus spoke from the cross He completed a prophecy when He suddenly cried out in a loud voice from the silence and the darkness that covered the earth for three hours, "My God, my God, why have you forsaken me?" (Matthew 27:46).

These are sad words. What was happening here? How does the Bible explain this? Well, the Bible teaches that God is holy and He can't look on sin (Habakkuk 1:13). The Bible also teaches that we, like sheep, have all gone astray and God has laid on Christ the sins of us all (Isaiah 53:6).

The Bible continues in 2 Corinthians 5:21, "God made Him who had no sin to be sin for us, so that in Him we might become the righteousness of God." On the cross Jesus was becoming what we are (sinners) so that we could become what He is (righteousness). He was being forsaken as He bore that sin, taking God's punishment for us, so that we might never have to be forsaken.

The cross of our Lord Jesus Christ is right at the very heart of Christianity

Every sin you have ever committed, every possible sin that you could commit, Jesus took in His own body on the cross and suffered as though He had done it Himself.

Then it was over. Right before He died on the cross He spoke three other times in rapid succession. When Jesus spoke the fifth time He said, "I'm thirsty" (John 19:28). On the cross He had fought this battle for your soul and mine against Satan, against sin and He WON! Now He looks back at the completed task and only when all is finished did He think of Himself.

Jesus hung on the cross for six hours and after the darkness passed He said "I'm thirsty." Here we see the two sides of Jesus Christ. This is the great miracle we call the incarnation. The Bible says, "In the beginning was the Word, and the Word was with God, and the Word was God.

He was with God in the beginning" (John 1:1–2).

The Bible also says, "The Word became flesh and lived for a while among us. We have seen His glory, the glory of the one and only Son, who came from the Father, full of grace and truth" (John 1:14).

God came to earth and clothed Himself in human flesh as Jesus Christ, that unique God-man, not God and man. On the divine side He lived in Heaven. He created this whole expanse and this whole created order, and He made man. On the human side He came to earth. He was born of a virgin. He laughed. He cried. He knew emotion like we do. As God He walked on water and stilled the storm. He healed the sick. He even raised the dead. As a man He hungered, He got thirsty, He suffered, He was tempted. On the human side He stood at Lazarus' grave and wept. On the divine side He said Lazarus "come forth" and He brought him back to life. On the human side He was a servant and on the divine side He was a king.

Now on the cross we see these two sides of Jesus. On the divine side He says to the dying thief "Today you will be with Me in paradise." On the human side He says, "I'm thirsty."

Then came the sixth time He spoke from the cross and in a concluding proclamation, He shouted, "It is finished" (John 19:30). Everything had been accomplished. All the prophecies of His life and death were now fulfilled.

We don't have to add anything to what Jesus Christ did for us. What He had done for us on Calvary was sufficient.

All these other things such as baptism, good works, and good deeds are important in our obedience, but Jesus paid for our sin.

Then came the seventh and final time Jesus spoke from the cross. He began the first time with a prayer (Father, forgive them . . .), in the middle was a prayer (My God, . . .) and the last time was a prayer. He began, He immersed, and He finished this experience with prayer. The final words that Jesus spoke from the cross as He turned His face toward the Heavens were, "Father, into Your hands I commit My spirit" (Luke 23:46). IT WAS ALL OVER!

There were three men crucified that Friday. There were three crosses:

THE CROSS OF REJECTION: This man died in sin. He was a dying sinner. He died with sin in him. This is the cross of many today. Like the criminal, they sneer at the cross and hurl insults at Christ. To his many sins the criminal added the greatest sin of all: unbelief. Of such Jesus said: ". . . If you do not believe that I am the one I claim to be, you will indeed die in your sins" (John 8:24).

THE CROSS OF REDEMPTION: This man died for sin. He was a dying Savior. He died with sin upon him. This cross is the wonder of all time. The sins upon Jesus were the sins of the world. "For God so loved the world, that He gave His one and only Son, that whoever believes in Him shall not perish, but have eternal life" (John 3:16). By this cross, Jesus won heaven for all who believe.

THE CROSS OF RECEPTION: This man died to sin. He was a dying saint. He died with sin taken from him. This criminal believed, and as a result, his sins were canceled by Jesus. He had no time for good works or going to church—only faith in Jesus Christ. What a day! Morning in sin; noon in grace; night in glory. His home in heaven will be shared by all who have faith in Jesus Christ.

Many of us today are so body-conscious in life and death that much of what we do in life and death is centered around this physical part of us. Yes, many are laid out in their finest attire to look as good as possible even at death. However, the spirit is who we really are. Everyone is a triad. We are spirit, soul, and body. The soul is the seat of our feelings and emotions. This body is just an outer shell in which we live. The spirit is that part of us that will live throughout eternity. FOREVER!

That is what separates us from the animal kingdom that God created. They have a body and a soul. We are not just body and soul. We are also a spirit! The spirit is that part of us that can know God. It can talk with God and connect with God. It comes alive when we receive Jesus Christ as our personal Savior. Our spirit is what is important. We should not spend all of our time taking care of the part of us that will surely return to dust.

This chapter began with a question and it is only proper to bring it to a close with some questions. Where do you see yourself in relationship to Calvary's cross?

Do you see yourself at the cross? That is where sin is dealt with. You will never enter Heaven if you haven't been there.

Do you see yourself on the cross? That is where self and pride and ego are dealt with. God the Father sees us not just at the cross but on the cross with Christ as part of His body if we know Him.

Do you see yourself under the cross? That is where commitment, service, and sacrifice are dealt with.

The cross of our Lord Jesus is right at the very heart of Christianity, and also at the very heart of the opposition to Christianity. "For the message of the cross is foolishness to those who are perishing, but to us who are being saved it is the power of God" (1 Corinthians 1:18).

You see, it was at the cross, and on the cross, that Christ defeated Satan. "Having canceled the written code, with its regulations, that was against us and that stood opposed to us; He took it away, nailing it to the cross. And having disarmed the powers and authorities, He made a public spectacle of them, triumphing over them by the cross" (Colossians 2:14–15).

The Old Testament law, the law of Moses, was to expose our sinfulness and wickedness. Jesus Christ came not only to fulfill the law but to give us "freedom" from the law (Galatians 5:1). All believers in Jesus Christ are "sons of God" (Galatians 3:26). In their conversation the night before He was crucified on the cross, Jesus said to the disciples "keep My commandments, cling to the words I have spoken."

Must Jesus bear the cross alone and all the world go free?

Grace, not law. Spirit, not flesh. Faith, not sight. These biblical cornerstones undergird the messages you find throughout the Scripture. They unshackle believers and open the mind of the unsaved. Together, they comprise the core of salvation and sanctification.

The believer is no longer under the bondage of the law. Instead, we are under the delightful yoke of God's grace. We live daily in the sphere of His unconditional love, mercy, and goodness without regard to our merit or performance. Because of the cross, God's grace is freely extended to us. He is not angry with us. He has cleared our sin slate forever. Our guilt is gone. There is nothing we can do to make God love us any more or any less!

The law is a set of rules, a list of do's and don'ts that were meant only to expose our sin, not save us. We have been set free from the law by grace. We don't have to try to please God. We already are pleasing to Him. God wants obedience out of love, not duty, and to Him, not a creed. Grace gives you a second, third, and infinite number of chances because failure is never final with the God of all grace.

The Holy Spirit is our indwelling Helper. We don't have to depend on our own resources or draw from our finite supply. Walking in the Spirit means that you are led, sustained, and strengthened by God. You began the Christian life through the work of the Holy Spirit, and you continue it by His life (Galatians 3:3).

Faith in God will see you through any obstacle. You cannot live an abundant life looking at your circumstances. They will deflate and discourage you. But when you trust God and rely on Him, you place the circumstances into His hands. It is not a matter of how much faith, but in whom you trust. If your faith is in God, expecting Him to act, then you are poised for spiritual greatness.

The Bible says, "For we know that our old self was crucified with Him so that the body of sin might be rendered powerless, that we should no longer be slaves to sin—because anyone who has died has been freed from sin" (Romans 6:6–7). Many Christians resist the demands that are entailed in such total identification with Christ. They would rather seek glory in earthly things. Must Jesus bear the cross alone and all the world go free? NO! There is a cross for everyone. There is a cross for you and there is a cross for me.

If you are a believer, Jesus Christ is alive in you NOW! He lives to conform you to His image and intercedes for you tirelessly with perfect wisdom. Today, in the resurrected Christ, you have all the help and hope you will ever need to overpower Satan and his angels in this war of the spirits.

You will truly understand the cross when you can honestly say, "I have been crucified with Christ and I no longer live, but Christ lives in me. The life I live in the body, I live by faith in the Son of God, who loved me and gave Himself for me" (Galatians 2:20). [1]

---

1 Sermons by Dr. O. S. Hawkins, First Baptist Church, Fort Lauderdale, FL, were helpful to the writer in composing this chapter.

GOOD WORKS

CHAPTER TWENTY–THREE

GOOD DEEDS AND THE JUDGMENT

In this chapter we will look at the good works, the good deeds and the judgment of the believer (Christian), not the lost person (nonbeliever). For the lost person there is nothing encouraging to say regarding the judgment. The fear of the judgment by the non-Christian is legitimate because it will be bad. VERY BAD!

Words cannot describe the guilt, the shock, and the terrifying feeling that will engulf a person who has rejected Jesus Christ as his personal Savior. When that individual stands before the Lord to be judged, Jesus will require him to give an account of all his deeds, whether good or bad. Accordingly, Jesus will decide how much pain and agony that person will suffer throughout eternity. No excuse will be acceptable. It is all over for him. There is no second chance!

So, to receive rewards, let's make it clear that we are speaking specifically to believers who will face Christ in judgment for the good works and the good deeds they did while on earth.

Good works and good deeds are God's will and God's purpose for all Christians. However, we must not confuse good works and good deeds with being saved. We work for Christ, we serve Him, and we serve others not to receive our salvation because we are already saved by grace through faith. The Bible says, "For it is by grace you have been saved, through faith—and this not from yourselves, it is the gift

179

of God—not by works, so that no one can boast" (Ephesians 2:8–9). These two verses are very clear. NO ONE CAN BE SAVED BY DOING GOOD WORKS!

What are good works, good deeds?

Good works are showing kindness to someone, reading and studying the Bible, praying, and reaching out to those in distress. The Bible says, "For we are God's workmanship, created in Christ Jesus to do good works, which God prepared in advance for us to do" (Ephesians 2:10).

Good deeds should involve everything, the devotion of our time, our talents, our experience and our finances to spreading the good news about Jesus Christ.

One primary objective of the Bible is to equip us to do the work God has called us to do. Good works and good deeds are to be our lifestyles. In the home or workplace, the Christian is instructed to do good works and good deeds in the name of the Lord Jesus Christ.

The Bible says, "All Scripture is God-breathed and is useful for teaching, rebuking, correcting and training in righteousness, so that the man of God may be thoroughly equipped for every good work" (1 Timothy 3:16–17).

As believers in Jesus Christ we are to be living, walking examples of good works and good deeds. We are to be sensitive to the needs and the hurts of other people, ready to step in and help in any way that we can.

Not only is it our Christian responsibility to do good deeds, but we also need to learn how to stimulate others to love and serve the Lord. The Bible says, "And let us consider how we may spur one another on toward love and good deeds" (Hebrews 10:24).

In John 5:22–23 Jesus explains to us why He will be the final judge. Since Jesus and the Father are one, to honor one is to honor both. God is the ultimate judge, but God the Father has chosen to place all decisions for judgment in the hands of His Son.

Therefore, when we are judged as believers we will stand before the Lord Jesus Christ. How encouraging it is to know that our judge will be Jesus, the One who loves us all unconditionally and the One who died on the cross for our sins. We know He is going to be absolutely fair and accurate. Jesus Christ is the essence of holiness. For Him not to be absolutely fair would be a violation of His character.

There are three criteria by which Jesus is going to judge individuals:

FIRST, He is going to judge every person according to the amount of truth they have heard and understood. The Christian life is a continuing process of learning, growing and understanding.

SECOND, our judgment will be based on how we used or responded to the opportunities He gave us.

THIRD, our judgment will be based on our gifts and our talents.

One purpose of the judgment is to evaluate how we have lived the life Christ gave us and then to reward us for the good that we have done. We lose rewards that we would have received had we obeyed God in those areas.

When the time of rewards arrives, what is God going to reward us with? There are two aspects of this reward:

FIRST, as we have obeyed God here on earth living obediently for Him, to that proportion He will give us responsibility in Heaven to serve Him. You see, our reward is the opportunity to work with God without tiring and without becoming hungry or thirsty. These are things that we have to deal with here on earth.

SECOND, when we live our lives in obedience to God, we reflect something of His character, revealing the righteousness of God in our lives.

As we carry out good deeds, God will reward us for every one of them. He will reward us not only by increasing our responsibility; but, also, He will give to us the capacity to glorify Him in heaven throughout all eternity to the proportion of our obedience while here on earth.

The Bible teaches in Revelation 4:9–11 that God alone deserves the honor, the praise and the glory for every good thing that has happened. But we will receive reward for our good works and good deeds and we will enjoy that reward for all of eternity.

The Bible tells us to say "NO" to ungodliness and worldly passions. We are to follow the teachings of our Lord and Savior, Jesus Christ, "who gave Himself for us to redeem us from all wickedness and to purify for Himself a people that are His very own, eager to do what is good" (Titus 2:14).

All of us have the need to feel worthy and significant. Ever since the fall of the Garden of Eden men and women have been doing everything imaginable trying to feel worthy. That is the way God made us. But ultimately He intended for us to get that sense of self worth from Him, not from succeeding in life's many challenges or from other people's approval.

If there is only one event in history that should give us all the self significance we need as persons, it is the cross. Jesus loved us enough to die for us even before we were born knowing that we would sin against Him. How much more significance do we need than that?

The judgment will be the moment in our life when we will reach the pinnacle of our significance as persons. Does this not say something about our significance that God the Father records every single thing we do or think?

Moment by moment the Holy Spirit is encouraging us to do the correct thing and we will be rewarded accordingly on judgment day. No one cares about us more than God the Father. He is continuously evaluating us. He is preparing to reward us. He is on our side. He gave us the capacity to glorify God and exalt Him not only here on earth but for all eternity.

Life is serious business because we must account for every single moment that we spend on this earth. But the most exciting part of the judgment is who the judge is. He is our friend, but He cannot be unless we invite Him into our lives. Obedience to God will certainly lead us to receiving many rewards in Heaven.

If God has abundantly blessed you resulting in your

becoming materially rich or wealthy, the Bible has a clear message for you to follow: "Command those who are rich in this present world not to be arrogant nor to put their hope in wealth, which is so uncertain, but to put their hope in God, who richly provides us with everything for our enjoyment. Command them to do good, to be rich in good deeds, and to be generous and willing to share. In this way they will lay up treasure for themselves as a firm foundation for the coming age, so that they may take hold of the life that is truly life" (1 Timothy 6:17–19).

There is nothing in the Bible that condemns money or having lots of it. Being rich and wealthy is not a sin. Sin enters only when we begin to worship money. Money is wonderful when we give God all the glory for providing the wealth and enjoyment and sharing it with those in need as instructed in the Bible. It allows us the opportunity to serve the Lord generously by doing many good works and many good deeds and, simultaneously, store up eternal treasure and reward for ourselves in heaven. What a wonderful, fair and just God we serve.

Our works and deeds must be so evident that other people will see them and praise God, not us. The Bible clearly says, "In the same way, let your light shine before men, that they may see your good deeds and praise your Father in heaven" (Matthew 5:16). That's not to say people should not praise you. On the job, for example, you work hard and you deserve praise. However, you give the praise and the glory to God.

As Christians, we must realize that works and deeds are what the Judgment is all about. When we stand in Judgment before Jesus Christ as a believer our salvation is not in question, the ONLY thing to be considered is our works and our deeds.

When we think about the awesome moment of standing before Jesus Christ one's mind cannot possibly conceive of being in the presence of absolute holiness. And we know that we shall stand in the presence of absolute, complete, and perfect love.

Yes, each of us should evaluate our lives and ask ourselves the following questions:

1. Could my life be characterized by obedience, though I fail at times?
2. Are my deeds good deeds?
3. Is my primary interest in life myself and myself only?
4. Can people see anything of Christ within me?
5. Is Christ glorified in any way through my life?
6. Will someone be helped because of my testimony, my life, my works?
7. Am I giving my best for what God has called me to do?
8. Am I looking forward to standing before His presence to be rewarded or do I fear it?

Many times the word judgment brings thoughts of condemnation. However, the believer's judgment will not be a time of reproof. It will be a time of reward and reckoning as we give an account of our service to God.

Christians who do good works and good deeds frustrate Satan and his evil spirits. Why? Because he knows we are safe and secure when we follow the Holy Spirit of Jesus Christ.

How we handle our Christian lifestyle does make a difference. It makes an eternal difference. **It doesn't matter if you do or do not believe in the Judgment, you WILL be there.** The Bible says, "For we must all appear before the judgment seat of Christ, that each one may receive what is due him for the things done while in the body, whether good or bad" (2 Corinthians 5:10).

One sure way to achieve the ultimate in success while on this earth and to maximize our reward in Heaven is to find the will of God for our lives and DO IT![1]

---

1 Sermons by Ben Haden, Changed Lives, and Dr. Charles F. Stanley, In Touch Ministries, were helpful to the writer in composing this chapter.

JESUS CHRIST OUR RULING JUDGE
CHAPTER TWENTY–FOUR

There is no escaping God's judgment. There are no exceptions! There is a fixed time in which every one of us will be judged individually.

The Bible says that Jesus Christ will judge us. Why? It is the very nature of God to be just. Therefore, God must balance out all things in the life of the BELIEVER as well as the NON-BELIEVER.

Throughout the Bible God shows to us both by example and by Scripture that there will be a judgment. Let's take a walk through the Bible and discover the evidence of God's judgment. As we take this journey, let's ponder our own situation and consider how we will "measure up" when we stand before Jesus Christ to be judged. Where and how we will spend eternity will be exclusively decided by Him at that time.

In Acts, Chapter 5, the Bible teaches, "You know what has happened throughout Judea, beginning in Galilee after the baptism that John preached—how God anointed Jesus of Nazareth with the Holy Spirit and power, and how He went around doing good and healing all who were under the power of the devil, because God was with Him.

"We are witnesses of everything He did in the country of the Jews and in Jerusalem. They killed Him by hanging Him on a tree, but God raised Him from the dead on the third day and caused Him to be seen. He was not seen by all the people, but by witnesses whom God had already chosen—by us who ate and drank with Him after He rose from the dead. He commanded us to preach to the people and to testify that He is the one whom God appointed as judge of the living and the dead. All the prophets testify about Him that everyone who believes in Him receives forgiveness of sins through His name" (Acts 10:37–43).

All through the Bible God indicates to us both by example and by Scripture that there is going to be a judgment

Most people do not like to think in terms of a judgment. If you have judgment then you are going to have a penalty, and you must have a judge. A lawless society is unfit to live in. Law, accountability, judgment, judges, rewards, and penalty are all a part of life. They are also a part of the kingdom of God. God has made each of us a steward and our life is one of stewardship. No matter what our job may be, if it is doing what God called us to do it is honorable work in the eyes of God.

The Bible says that Jesus Christ has been appointed by God the Father as the judge of all humanity: "Moreover, the Father judges no one, but has entrusted all judgment to the Son, that all may honor the Son just as they honor the Father. He who does not honor the Son does not honor the Father, who sent Him. And He has given Him authority to judge because He is the Son of Man" (John 5:22–23, 27).

Jesus said that God the Father had given Him the responsibility of being the judge: "When the Son of Man comes in His glory, and all the angels with Him, He will sit on His throne in heavenly glory. All the nations will be gathered before Him, and He will separate the people one from another as a shepherd separates the sheep from the goats. He will put the sheep on His right and the goats on His left.

"Then the King will say to those on His right 'Come, you who are blessed by my Father; take your inheritance, the kingdom prepared for you since the creation of the world.'"

"Then He will say to those on His left, 'Depart from Me, you who are cursed, into the eternal fire prepared for the devil and his angels'" (Matthew 25:31–34, 41).

The Bible says that Jesus Christ has been appointed by God the Father as the judge of all humanity: "For He has set a day when He will judge the world with justice by the man He has appointed. He has given proof of this to all men by raising Him from the dead" (Acts 17:31). This passage clearly declares that Jesus knew that He would be our judge.

Most people do not like to think in terms of a judgment

There will be two judgments because there will be two resurrections. "Do not be amazed at this, for a time is coming when all who are in their graves will hear His voice and come out—those who have done evil will rise to be condemned" (John 5:28–29).

First, there will be a judgment when Jesus Christ comes for His church (the Rapture). Also, at that time, there will be a resurrection of saints.

Second, in the final judgment there will be a resurrection of all the bodies of the wicked. All BELIEVERS will sit with Christ when He judges the wicked of the world. This is known as the great white throne judgment. The Bible says, "Do you not know that the saints will judge the world?" (1 Corinthians 6:2).

Jesus Christ is going to judge every person: "Just as man is destined to die once, and after that to face judgment" (Hebrews 10:27). Additionally, the Bible reveals to us: "For we must all appear before the judgment seat of Christ, that each one may receive what is due him for the things done while in the body, whether good or bad" (2 Corinthians 5:10).

We may not receive our due on earth. There are greed,

corruption, inequality and injustice on earth. Our work may go unrewarded by man. But God sees and will extend His special rewards in heaven. Whatever we miss on earth will be as dust when Christ acknowledges our faithful service to Him and others.

In the book of Revelation, the Bible says: "And I saw the dead, great and small, standing before the throne, and books were opened. Another book was opened, which is the book of life. The dead were judged according to what they had done as recorded in the books" (Revelation 20:12).

As stated earlier, there is no escaping God's judgment. THERE ARE NO EXCEPTIONS! There is a fixed moment in time in which every one of us will be judged individually. And JESUS CHRIST IS OUR RULING JUDGE!

In the judgment seat of Jesus Christ two things will happen. One is revelation and the second is reward. "He commanded us to preach to the people and to testify that He is the one whom God appointed as judge of the living and the dead" (Acts 10:42).

Revelation means disclosure. Christ knows everything there is to know about us. ALL the things we did while we lived on earth, good and bad, will be unveiled for us to see. We will see ourselves for what we really are. And many of us will surely be ashamed and embarrassed.

The Bible says, "Therefore judge nothing before the appointed time; wait till the Lord comes. He will bring to light what is hidden in darkness and will expose the motives of men's hearts . . ." (1 Corinthians 4:5).

When we stand before the judgment seat of Christ, as born again Christians, we will be rewarded and praised. We will not receive punishment. "And now, dear children, continue in Him, so that when He appears we may be confident and unashamed before Him at His coming" (1 John 2:28).

The evil things will be revealed for what they are and having been pardoned by the blood of Jesus. There will be a moment when each one of us will weep in the presence of Jesus Christ as we see all the evil we have done. When we see that He has pardoned us for all our sins then our love and adoration of Him will be intensified. That is the revelation, the unveiling of everything.

Jesus Christ is going to judge every single person

Following the revelation will be the granting of rewards. Throughout the Bible there is evidence and teaching concerning rewards.

For example, in the first book of the New Testament, the Bible says, "Blessed are those who are persecuted because of righteousness, for theirs is the kingdom of heaven. Blessed are you when people insult you, persecute you and falsely say all kinds of evil against you because of Me. Rejoice and be glad, because great is your reward in heaven, for in the same way they persecuted the prophets who were before you" (Matthew 5:10–12).

And, in the last book of the New Testament, the Bible says, "Behold, I am coming soon! My reward is with Me, and I will give to everyone according to what he has done" (Revelation 22:12).

So, what about these rewards, what instructions does the Bible give us? "By the grace God has given me, I laid a foundation as an expert builder, and someone else is building on it. But each one should be careful how he builds" (1 Corinthians 3:10). We are to be careful of the kind of life we build upon this relationship with Christ. When we were saved (spiritually born again), we received a new eternal foundation, which is the rock of ages (Jesus Christ). From the very moment that we were saved we started building on that foundation—every thought, every motive, every deed is a part of it.

"If any man builds on this foundation using gold, silver, costly stones, wood, hay or straw, his work will be shown for what it is, because the Day will bring it to light. It will be revealed with fire, and the fire will test the quality of each man's work. If what he has built survives, he will receive his reward. If it is burned up, he will suffer loss; he himself will be saved, but only as one escaping through the flames" (1 Corinthians 3:12–15).

Please keep in mind here that in these verses of Scripture, God is speaking of the judgment seat of Christ. They are directed to the BELIEVERS, the born again Christians. Some of us have sinned and neglected things in our life that God commanded us to do.

Whatever we may choose to do in our life that dishonors the temple of the Holy Spirit is like building a house with wood, hay and stubble. All the wood, hay and stubble in our life indicates loss of reward. Do you think that when we get to heaven, we can somehow or in some way make up for that loss? NO WAY! What we lose at the judgment is lost forever.

Concerning heaven, some people may say, "Well, all that really matters is that I get in." That is a most foolish thought. The book of Proverbs says a wise man looks ahead and plans for the future.

How many of us have trusted Jesus Christ as our personal Savior and yielded ourselves to Him and by the power of the Holy Spirit are living for Jesus Christ? Eternal rewards are lost every day that we live in rebellion toward God and in disobedience to Him.

Forgiveness has taken care of the penalty of our sins, but it hasn't taken care of the loss of reward which would have been ours had we obeyed God. Every day of our lives decides our responsibility and our capacity and our privileges in heaven. As you can see, it is not going to be the same for everyone.

Living a Christian life is very serious business

At this point, some of you may be asking "what about the judgment of NON-BELIEVERS?"

Well, those who reject Jesus Christ as Savior, who fail

to receive His offer of forgiveness of sin, will live forever in hell. They will spend eternity in darkness, torment, pain, agony, and The Bible says, "Enter through the narrow gate. For wide is the gate and broad is the road that leads to destruction, and many enter through it. But small is the gate and narrow the road that leads to life, and only a few find it. Not everyone who says to Me, 'Lord, Lord,' will enter the kingdom of heaven, but only he who does the will of My Father who is in heaven" (Matthew 7:13–14, and 21). Now, let's look at what will be the basis of God's judgment for everybody, LOST OR SAVED! In the day of judgment He will consider the following:

- The light of truth that we've known

- The opportunities that we've had

- And what we've done with the above.

Jesus is not going to weigh your good and evil, and if your good outweighs your evil, you will go to heaven; and if your evil outweighs your good, you will go to hell. That is not the way the Lord operates. He operates on one condition only, have you or have you not received Jesus Christ as your personal Savior? If you have not, it is all over. It is just a matter of how much you're going to suffer. If you have received Him, it is a matter of how much reward you will receive.

Living a Christian life is very serious business. We must never joke about Jesus or the cross or the blood. We must never use His name in some profane fashion because He says for every idle word and every deed man shall give an account. Jesus Christ is everything He says He is.[1]

Realizing that Jesus Christ will be our ruling judge, one has to be concerned about the moral decay in Amer-

1 Sermons by Dr. Charles F. Stanley, In Touch Ministries, were valuable to the writer in composing this chapter.

ica. It is amazing how much America has drifted away from the Christian principles that our Founding Fathers worked so hard to include in our Constitution and other primary documents.

The majority of the Founding Fathers wanted God to be the center of the government. That was one of their most fundamental principles. Christian principles were to be the basis of the nation.

The Founding Fathers believed there had to be a standard of behavior, a standard by which you measure right and wrong. A standard to differentiate GOOD from EVIL. They chose the Christian standard of behavior.

What we see in America today is the dark and murky night of pagan immorality. Why? Because we have taken these basic precepts away, the rights and wrongs that we get from the Bible.

Yes, Satan is busily at work today. He and his evil spirits have been successful in eroding the basic foundation that made America great.

However, there is still hope. God is Creator of the universe and Jesus Christ will someday rule that universe totally. Yes, those who know Jesus as Lord and Savior will ultimately be victorious in this battle of GOOD vs. EVIL: A War of the Spirits.

AMERICA
CHAPTER TWENTY–FIVE
A HISTORICAL
REVIEW

Was America founded as a Christian nation? Did our Founding Fathers believe in God and acknowledge Him in our primary documents? Many today would say absolutely not, particularly those in the media, in our universities and editors of magazines and newspapers. They would say the Founding Fathers never intended for any religious principles at all to be part of public society, public life, public affairs. Others are a little more moderate and they say, "Well, they may have, but it's hard for us to know today. It's really difficult to know." Well, this is not true! We can know by their very writings. We can also know by their very acts. One thing we appreciate about our Founding Fathers is that they were prolific writers. They did with writing what we do with VCRs and cassettes and tapes. They recorded it all. The writings of George Washington alone are some 39 volumes. Very small print. Tiny print. And it's that way for most of the Founding Fathers.

Yes, there was a time when our Supreme Court, our government, our universities all agreed that America was founded on Christian principles. In fact, the Supreme Court in 1892 cited 87 examples from American history to prove that America was founded on Christian principles.

The case that came before the Supreme Court in 1892 was called *The Church of the Holy Trinity vs. The United States.* The issue in this case was the hiring of a minister and some had challenged the fact that a Christian minister was being hired in America. However, the Court thought that was ludicrous—that anything Christian should be challenged in America. They went into an explanation of why that it was absolutely absurd to challenge Christian principles in America.

One thing we appreciate about our Founding Fathers is that they were prolific writers

The court emphatically declared, "Our laws and our institutions must necessarily be based on and must include the teachings of the Redeemer of mankind." The Court continued, "It's impossible for it to be otherwise. In this sense, and to this extent, our civilization and our institutions are emphatically Christian."

What would have led the Court to such an emphatic declaration? That our laws, our institutions, our society was emphatically Christian and that it must include the teachings of the Redeemer of mankind?

The Court said, "the reason we say this is because it's historically true. From the discovery of the continent to this present hour there is a single voice everywhere making the same affirmation. We find everywhere a clear recognition of this truth."

And the Court proceeded to go into a history lesson. It went through 87 incidents of American history, starting from the discovery of the continent—the time of Columbus—and going all the way through their current day in 1892. After having gone through 87 precedents, the Court said, "We could go like this for a long time. Eighty-seven is sufficient to say that Christ must be the center."

Now, if we attended school prior to World War II, we would have known of these 87 precedents. We would have found most of them in our textbooks. But anyone that has attended high school since World War II has probably never seen even one of the incidents that the U. S. Supreme Court cited as the emphatic basis for their declaration that we are a Christian nation and that Christian principles are to remain the basis of this society.

The 1892 Supreme Court referred to the Declaration of Independence as yet another instance where Christian principles were to be the basis of the nation. They noted the fact that in the Declaration of Independence four times the Founding Fathers called on God, four times they invoked God, four times they placed God in the midst of the national birth certificate.

There are also other evidences or acts by the Founding Fathers that show they wanted Christian principles to be part of government. The Court of 1892 said, "Look at the governments our Founding Fathers themselves created."

The day the Founding Fathers signed the Declaration of Independence they underwent an immediate transformation. The day before they signed that document, every one of those men had been a British citizen, living in one of the 13 British colonies. But when they separated from Great Britain, they wiped out every civil government. Benjamin Rush, a signer of the Declaration from Pennsylvania, said, "In one day we dissolved every civil government."

So the first task facing the Founding Fathers who gave us the original document was to return to their own home states and create their new state constitutions to replace what they had just abolished. They were creating their first ever governments. The Supreme Court pointed to what our Founding Fathers placed in their first government documents as indication of what they thought was good for the nation.

For example, Thomas McKean and George Read went back to Delaware and wrote the Delaware Constitution. Look what these signers of the Declaration placed in their own state constitution. It says, "Everyone appointed to public office must say, 'I do profess faith in God the Father, and in the Lord Jesus Christ, His only Son, and in the Holy Ghost, One God and blessed forevermore, and I do acknowledge the Holy Scriptures of the Old and New Testament to be given by Divine inspiration.'"

Keep in mind that in 1892 we had 44 states in the Union, and according to the Supreme Court, every state had similar requirements in its constitution. A state constitution sampling follows:

Vermont: "And each member of the legislature, before he takes his seat, will make and subscribe the following declaration: I do believe in one God, the Creator and governor of the universe; the rewarder of the good, the punisher of the wicked . . ."

North Carolina: "No person who denies the being of God or the truth of the Christian religion or the divine authority of either the Old or the New Testaments are capable of holding any office or place of trust in the civil government of this state."

New Hampshire: "Morality and piety, rightly grounded on evangelical principles, gives the best and greatest security of the government. Therefore the legislature is empowered to adopt measures for the support and maintenance of public Christian teachers of piety, religion and morality."

Kentucky: "No person who denies the being of God or a future state of rewards and punishments shall hold any office in the civil department of this state."

Every state constitution also required that you must acknowledge a belief in future rewards and punishments. Not only must you believe in God, you must also believe that you will answer to God for everything you do while in office. That is the language the Founding Fathers gave.

The Founding Fathers were very clearly religious but they were not denominational. There was not a single constitution that said you have to be of a certain denomination to hold office. Oh, they did say "you must believe in God. You must believe in inspiration of the Scriptures." But those were the basic orthodox Christian principles to which they adhered and this is what the U. S. Supreme Court pointed out.

There was further proof given by the Supreme Court in 1892 that America was indeed founded as a Christian nation. The evidence was in a court case they cited from

1799. The decision in this court case informs us of the intentions our Founding Fathers had when they wrote the First Amendment.

The Court says, "By our form of government the Christian religion is the established religion, but all sects and denominations of Christians are placed on the same equal footing." In brief, the Founding Fathers established that Christian principles were to be practiced and to be instituted in government. But no one denomination—like the Baptists or the Catholics—could have total say or total rule in government.

The Founding Fathers were very clearly religious but they were not denominational

The Founding Fathers had an opportunity to establish with their very own hands their first governments. And it is the documents they gave in their first governments that convinced the Supreme Court that the Founding Fathers did want this to be a nation built on Christian principles.

We have bounced back and forth from GOOD to EVIL throughout this volume. Here we have a good example of good. Obviously, those who attended the Constitutional Convention were touched by the power and presence of the Holy Spirit. Yes, it was God Who motivated the Founding Fathers to create a biblically sound Constitution for the United States of America.

The Bible says, "Now the Lord is the Spirit, and where the Spirit of the Lord is, there is freedom" (2 Corinthians 3:17). This is not just an eloquent platitude; it is practical reality. Therefore, our future as a nation hinges upon our moral foundation, upon our relationship with God.

AMERICA
CHAPTER TWENTY–SIX
ITS EARLY
LEADERS

As we continue our history lesson, our analysis of good versus evil, we will examine statements made by important individuals, those early leaders who were part of the Constitutional Convention. Not all of the Founding Fathers were particularly religious. However, there is evidence that the Founding Fathers wanted God, the Bible, prayer, and Christian morality to be a part of our government.

Even if we select those that are conceded to be the least religious of the Founding Fathers, perhaps Jefferson and Franklin, we find that they were strong advocates for religious principles in government.

For example, consider Benjamin Franklin. He was part of the Constitutional Convention. The records of that Convention were given to us by many Founding Fathers who were all writers. Perhaps the best records came from James Madison. He kept meticulous notes on what occurred in the Convention.

James Madison records a very famous speech given by Benjamin Franklin. This is surely the most famous speech of Franklin's political career. It came on Thursday, June 28, 1787. The Convention was really at a crossroads. It was falling apart. They had argued; they had fought; they had bickered. They could not agree on anything. The New York delegation had left and gone home in disgust saying, "We have better things to do than fight with you."

It was seeing the Convention crumble that led Franklin to make this speech. He was indeed the patriarch of this Convention, the wise "old man." Being 81 years old and in very poor health, they literally had to carry him to and from the Convention floor.

Franklin rose and reminded the delegates of something they used to do in that very room. Here they were up against difficult problems they were not able to resolve and he said, "Do you remember what we used to do here 13 years ago?" This was the same room in which they held the first session of Congress, and Franklin was a member of that Congress. Records of that Congress show they prayed faithfully every morning, every day, and sometimes in multi-hour prayer sessions.

Franklin remembered that and said, "Have you noted that we have not yet started this Convention asking God for help? We have gone for days, for weeks [and] we have not even solicited His aid. And really, we had become fairly presumptuous because we'd seen God's direct intervention so often in the American Revolution that we had just assumed that He was on our side."

It was Franklin that brought these delegates back to their senses. He said, "In the beginning of the contest with Great Britain, when we were sensible of danger, we had daily prayer in this room for Divine protection. Our prayers, sir, were heard, and they were graciously answered.

"All of us engaged in the struggle must have observed frequent incidences of a superintending Providence in our favor. And have we now forgotten this powerful Friend? Or do we imagine we no longer need His assistance? I've lived, sir, a long time, and the longer I live the more convincing proofs I see of this truth: that God governs in the affairs of man.

"If a sparrow cannot fall to the ground without His notice, is it probable that an empire can rise without His aid? We've been assured in the sacred writings that except the Lord build the house, they labor in vain that build it. I firmly believe this and I also believe that without His concurring aid, we shall succeed in this political building no better than the builders of Babel."

Then Franklin made the motion, "I therefore beg leave to move that henceforth prayers imploring the assistance of heaven and its blessing on our deliberations be held in this assembly every morning before we proceed to business."

Franklin is admittedly one of the least religious of the Founding Fathers. However, here he is calling the entire group back to prayer at the Constitutional Convention. He is telling them this was a near fatal mistake. He is pleading with them to ask God for assistance. They are also being reminded of how God answered their prayers in the past.

This speech led to the establishment of chaplains in the House and Senate. They knew this was so important that it must never again be forgotten. Chaplains in the House and Senate were not allowed to be members of Congress. That might distract them from their duty. Their only purpose was to encourage Congressmen to get the Congress of the United States before God every morning before they conducted business.

For three days the Constitutional Convention en masse as a single body went from church to church listening to sermons

Jonathan Dayton writes about what happened after Franklin's speech. There were many who wrote about it, but Dayton noted that for the next three days the Constitutional Convention en masse began fasting and praying and visiting every church they could find in Philadelphia.

The entire Constitutional Convention en masse went from church to church, sat down inside, brought the minister out and said, "Preach to us. We need to have our minds renewed. We need to have our thinking turned around."

For three days the Constitutional Convention en masse

as a single body went from church to church listening to sermons. When they reconvened, Jonathan Dayton said, "It was the first time in six weeks that every unfriendly feeling had been expelled. It was the first time in six weeks that we weren't fighting and arguing and bickering. We actually got along."

For five and a half weeks they could get nothing accomplished. Then for three days they seriously set their mind toward seeking God. After that, the Constitutional Convention delegates said, "This was the turning point. That speech by Franklin calling us back to prayer was the turning point."

It is amazing what happens when we fix our eyes on Jesus. He will guide us, direct us, and always lead us to the right decision. The Convention delegates found this to be true. As a result of them turning to God, they produced a document that has lasted for over 200 years. All Americans should indeed be thankful for Benjamin Franklin. Although not overly religious, he did recognize the Convention delegates could not succeed without God.

James Madison wrote the Constitution. He said, "It would be impossible to govern the nation without God and the Bible." However, it was George Washington who said, "It would be impossible to govern without God and the Ten Commandments."

Interestingly, after taking his oath of office, he bent over and kissed the Bible. Yes, the very first act performed by George Washington as the first President of this country was to bend over and kiss the Bible. He then led the entire Senate and House to church for a two-hour worship service for which the members of Legislature had voted.

George Washington believed very strongly that religious principles must be a part of public affairs. As President of the Convention that gave us the Constitution, he was one of the better known Founding Fathers. George Washington later became known as the "Father of Our Country."

Washington voiced his opinions clearly in his final political speech, which is known as his "Farewell Address." George Washington served his country for 45 years. After serving two terms as President, he was leaving office when he gave this historical speech.

The "Farewell Address" is 12 succinct, clear warnings to the nation on what we must do to stay on track. Four of those warnings were clearly religious. He said in one of the warnings, "There's only two supports for political prosperity in America. That's religion and morality. Therefore, don't let anyone claim to be a true American patriot if they ever try to separate religion and morality from politics. All of the habits and dispositions which lead to political prosperity, religion and morality are indispensable supports."

George Washington believed very strongly that religious principles must be a part of public affairs

Washington's "Farewell Address" was found in our school textbooks for over a century. Students studied it for history class, for speech class. It was considered the most significant political speech ever delivered by a U. S. President. However, the "Farewell Address" disappeared from most textbooks about three decades ago.

John Quincy Adams was another Founding Father who had much to say about the importance of religious principles in public affairs. He served the nation in many ways. John Quincy Adams was Secretary of State. He was an ambassador to three different nations. He was a U. S. Senator, and he was President of the United States.

Adams was a highly sought-after speaker during the Fourth of July celebration each year. One of his notable speeches was delivered on July 4, 1837. He was very elderly then. The speech is called "An Oration delivered before the inhabitants of the town of Newberryport at their request on the 61st Anniversary of the Declaration of Independence."

John Quincy Adams said, "Why is it that next to the birthday of the Savior of the world our most joyous and most venerated festival occurs on this day? Why is it that in America the Fourth of July is celebrated second only to Christmas? Is it not that in the chain of human events the birthday of the nation is indissolubly linked with the birthday of the Savior that it forms a leading event in the progress of the Gospel dispensation? Is it not that the Declaration of Independence first organized the social compact on the foundation of the Redeemer's mission on earth? That it laid the cornerstone of human government on the first precepts of Christianity?"

And he continued for 61 pages. Adams pointed out that America became the first Christian government in the history of the world. He wanted future generations to know that Christian principles were the basis of our government.

Now, maybe you are thinking, "Well, Benjamin Franklin, George Washington, and John Quincy Adams made a lot of speeches, but did they ever put their beliefs into law?" The answer is yes. They wrote the "Northwest Ordinance." This was a law our Founding Fathers passed, mandating that religion and morality be taught in all public schools.

The first House passed the law on July 17, 1789. The first Senate passed the law on August 4, 1789. President George Washington signed the Northwest Ordinance into law on August 7, 1789.

What is the significance of the Northwest Ordinance? Article III of the law said that no new territory could become a state in the United States unless the schools in that territory were teaching religion and morality as well as knowledge. Here is a law passed by the Founding Fathers that said, "We won't let you in the United States unless your schools are teaching biblical principles."

This law applied for decades after the Founding Fathers. States such as: Ohio (1803), Mississippi (1817), Michigan (1837), Kansas (1858), Nebraska (1875), plus many others came into statehood under this law. Those original state constitutions said, "Forever in the schools of this state religion and morality will be taught as well as knowledge." America's early leaders believed so strongly in biblical principles that they passed federal laws to insure we would always have these principles in our schools.

Noah Webster was a Founding Father. However, as an early leader and university professor, he best expressed his beliefs through the writing of textbooks and teaching. He was a strong believer that anyone serving in public office must be of strong moral character, both private and public. They must also have a sound religious background.

Noah Webster said, "It is alleged by men of loose principles and defective views of the subject that religion and morality are not necessary or important qualifications for political stations. But the Scriptures teach a different doctrine. The Scriptures direct that rulers should be men who rule in the fear of God, able men with much fear of God, men of truth who hate covetousness. When a citizen gives his vote to a man of known immorality, he abuses his civic responsibilities."

Noah Webster was a true believer in Jesus Christ. His teaching was simple. Elect people of good moral character who practice good Christian principles. If you do, the Holy Spirit of God will lead America to prosperity and greatness. If you do not, the evil spirit of Satan will gain a stronghold in the affairs of America and trouble will follow.

The Bible says, "When the righteous are in authority, the people rejoice; But when a wicked man rules, the people moan" (Proverbs 29:2 NKJV).

AMERICA

SEPARATION OF CHURCH AND STATE

"Separation of Church and State." That is a phrase we have all heard many times. It is an important issue in differentiating between good and evil. We were told for years that it was in the First Amendment. Do you know that the words "separation of church and state" are not in the First Amendment? That phrase does not exist in any founding document.

Before we tackle this thorny phrase, let's look at what our early universities had to say about Christianity. How did they view the role of government in the affairs of citizens? Many of the Founding Fathers attended these great universities. What philosophy did they have?

The entrance requirements for Harvard, Yale, and Princeton Universities were reviewed by the Supreme Court in 1892. The Court cited these requirements as proof that America was founded as a Christian nation.

Harvard was founded in 1636 and was among the first universities in America. Harvard had requirements to attend school then just as it has now. The requirements to attend Harvard in 1636 are very revealing. It says, "We would love to have you at Harvard. We want every student to be plainly instructed and consider well that the main end of your life and studies is to know God and Jesus Christ and therefore to lay Christ on the bottom as the only foundation of all sound knowledge and learning. Everyone shall so exercise himself in reading the Scriptures twice a day that he shall be ready to give an account of his proficiency therein."

That was the first stated purpose at Harvard. If you wanted to attend Harvard that was fine. But you had to know that your number one purpose for being there was to know God and to know Jesus Christ. Another requirement of Harvard very simply said, "And seeing the Lord only gives wisdom. Let everyone seriously sit himself by prayer to seek it of Him."

Yale University was founded later, in 1701. It had requirements that every student was to comply with. Yale said, "If you've come to school here, it's because you want a religious education. You know that this is a school for the liberal and the religious education of suitable youth."

Yale said, "Seeing that God is the Giver of all wisdom, every student, in addition to his private or secret prayer, must be present morning and evening at public prayer." If you went to Yale you had to be serious about prayer. Yale considered prayer to be a part of American education.

Princeton University is of particular interest. Princeton was founded in 1746, and it had a significant impact on the establishment of America as a nation. Why is this? Well, there were approximately 200 Founding Fathers, and nearly one-third of them had attended Princeton University. They were surely influenced by the teaching of that institution.

John Witherspoon was a signer of the Declaration of Independence. He was also the President of Princeton University. He had personally trained one-third of the Founding Fathers. This is why he became known as the "father of the Founding Fathers."

The founding statement of Princeton University says, "Cursed is all learning that's contrary to the cross of Christ." This very powerful statement is short, but it speaks volumes. This statement is from the university from which one-third of the Founding Fathers received their degrees and their diplomas.

John Witherspoon wrote about how to identify a true American patriot in his writings at Princeton. He gave students three ways to identify an American patriot. He said, "What follows from this? That he is the best friend to American liberty who, number one, is most active and sincere in promoting true and undefiled religion. Number two, whoever sets himself with the greatest firmness to bear down on profanity and immorality of any kind. Number three, whoever is an avowed enemy of God, I don't hesitate to call him an enemy to his country." Witherspoon continued, "Everything we founded this on, all that we fought for have been godly principles. Whoever opposes God therefore opposes the very basis of America."

Now, with this background, let's examine the phrase "separation of church and state."

The First Amendment simply says, "Congress shall make no law respecting an establishment of religion or prohibiting the free exercise thereof." It is very obvious, the phrase "separation of church and state" does not appear in the First Amendment. But yet we have been told that for decades.

Well, if the phrase does not appear in the First Amendment, where do we find the phrase? **The phrase appeared in a private letter that was written by Thomas Jefferson 11 years after the First Amendment.**

In 1801 the Danbury Baptist Association of Danbury, Connecticut, heard a rumor that the Congregationalist denomination was about to be made the national denomination in America. It greatly distressed them and it should have. They wrote a letter to the President of the United States, Thomas Jefferson.

Jefferson wrote back to them on January 1, 1802. In his letter he said, "You don't have to worry about this. The First Amendment has erected a wall of separation between church and state." That is the source of the phrase!

What we have not seen in decades is the remainder of that letter. The Supreme Court currently quotes this phrase but not the letter. Jefferson went on to explain that they would never need to fear the establishment of a single denomination. He said, "On the other hand, you'll never need to fear that that wall will remove Christian principles. It won't. The First Amendment means that the government will not get involved with the church unless the church does something that is a direct violation of a basic Christian principle."

He gave many examples, such as, "If someone in the name of Christianity were to advocate human sacrifice, the government would get involved. If they were to advocate bigamy or polygamy or licentious, promiscuous sex, we would get involved, the government would get involved." But he said, "In all other religious activities, the First Amendment keeps the government from getting involved in church affairs."

The phrase "separation of church and state" does not appear in the First Amendment

Jefferson clearly explained that the wall of separation was a one-directional wall. It kept the government from running the church. However, it never separated Christian principles from government. A national denomination was not established at the time so Jefferson's letter fell into disuse until some years later.

The Supreme Court resurrected Jefferson's letter in the 1878 case, *Reynolds vs. the United States.* The Reynolds' group was advocating bigamy and polygamy. They filed a suit against the U. S. Government saying, "Our religion says that we can practice bigamy and polygamy." They said, "The First Amendment of the Constitution says that we are to have our free exercise of religion. Based on the First Amendment you can't stop us from exercising our religion."

They said, "Second of all, Jefferson said that there is to be a wall of separation, that the government is not to get involved in church affairs. This is a church affair, you are not to get involved."

The 1878 Supreme Court then printed Jefferson's letter in its entirety. The Court said, "You know, you're right.

Jefferson did say that we're not to get involved in church affairs." But they said, "But notice what else Jefferson said. Jefferson also said that Christian principles were not to be separated." And they said, "Bigamy and polygamy is not a Christian practice, therefore it is not protected by the First Amendment."

The Supreme Court used Jefferson's letter for the next three decades to make sure that non-Christian practice was not allowed in America. This is the letter we hear so much about but we just don't hear the full letter!

There are many evidences that the Founding Fathers intended for basic Christian principles to be part of society, and that separation of church and state did not mean removing Christian principles from society.

There were court cases that went for a century-and-a-half that showed that we were never to remove Christian principles from society. For example, there was a U. S. Supreme Court case in 1844 that is relevant, particularly when you consider the cases we see today. Let us look.

In 1844 there was a school in Philadelphia that said, "We are going to teach our students morality, but we are not going to teach Christian principles at this school. We will not teach the Bible here at this school but we will teach morality." This case made the Court because this school was receiving government funds.

The Court's response was clear and to the point. They said, "Now wait a minute. If you don't want to teach the Bible and Christianity, that's fine. You've just got to go be a private school. But if you're going to receive the government funds, if you're going to be a government public school, you've got to teach the Bible and Christianity in your school."

Two years later, in 1846, the Court very clearly explained why Christian principles were to be the basis of society. The Court says, "Christianity has references to the principles of right and wrong. It's the foundation of those morals and manners on which our society is formed. It's our basis. You remove this and it will fall."

In 1952 the Supreme Court continued to stay in that

very same vein. In a case called *Zorach vs. Clauson* the Court said, "When the state encourages religious instruction or cooperates with religious authorities by adjusting the schedule of public school events to meet denominational or sectarian needs, it follows the best of our traditions. We find no constitutional requirement which makes it necessary for government to be hostile to religion and to throw its weight against efforts to widen the effective scope of religious influence."

The Supreme Court concluded by saying, "That would be preferring those who believed in no religion over those who do. That can't happen in America. We can't have policies that favor those who believe in no religion over those who do." This was in 1952. Yet our current policies do just that.

Our policies now say, "No, we cannot have prayer in a public arena because that would offend those who do not like prayer. So now we prefer those who believe in no religion over those who do. It is a very simple problem: you will either have prayer or you won't have prayer. One group will win, the other group will lose. Today, the group that believes in no religion is winning. In 1952, just a few decades ago, we said this will never happen in America.

Does separation of church and state really mean that a person cannot take their religious values and principles and activities into public affairs? Under current definition it does. But that is the wrong definition. That completely violates the intent of the Founding Fathers. It violates all Supreme Count decisions prior to 1962. All writings of the Founding Fathers are violated. It even violates the intent of Thomas Jefferson who gave us the phrase, "separation of church and state." Everything historically that exists proves the current application we have of "separation of church and state" is totally wrong.

Even though the makeup of the Supreme Court has changed, there is reason to believe that not all justices are blind. Chief Justice William Rehnquist said recently in one of his briefs, "The 'wall of separation between church and state' is a metaphor based on bad history, a metaphor which has proved useless as a guide to judging. It should be frankly and explicitly abandoned."

At the same time that Justice Rehnquist handed down his opinion, Justice Byron White offered his concurrence, saying, "I appreciate Justice Rehnquist's explication of history of the Religion Clauses of the First Amendment."

The Bible says, "Stand fast therefore in the liberty by which Christ has made us free, and do not be entangled again with a yoke of bondage" (Galatians 5:1). America's Christian forefathers originally settled this country and later established our nation primarily to be able to exercise this liberty of serving God according to His word.

Just as the Galatians had been in grave danger of losing their freedom in Christ to the Judaizers, we today are in even greater danger of losing our religious liberties to the secularizers. Our humanist-denominated educational and judicial systems have been able to establish anti-biblical humanism as our unofficial state religion, with legalistic encumbrances to our exercise of true freedom in Christ.

During the past three decades, Satan and his evil spirits has made immeasurable progress toward eliminating God, the Bible, and Christian principles from the lives of many Americans. How urgently we need today to "stand fast therefore in the liberty by which Christ has made us free."

AMERICA
THE
CURRENT
ERA

In the opinion of this writer, the current era began in 1962. This is the year the Supreme Court abruptly changed directions. In the landmark case *Engel v. Vitale,* the Court removed prayer from our public schools. This decision by the Court was totally opposite from the intent provided by our Founding Fathers in the Constitution. Yes, this ruling would change America dramatically over the coming years. A new era was born.

Yes, 1962 was a victorious year for Satan and his angels. Christians had become complacent and were not attentive to what was happening in the Supreme Court. They had taken their eyes off Jesus and were focusing on the material things of the world. Satan had been waiting for such an opportunity. Ever since that fateful day, he has been using the American judicial system to attack and destroy Christian principles throughout the country.

Another landmark case, *Abington v. Schempp,* occurred in 1963. In this case the Supreme Court declared that Bible reading could be "psychologically harmful" to children and would no longer be permitted in public schools.

In the 1980 case of *Stone v. Gramm,* the Court removed the Ten Commandments from our public schools. Thanks to these and other rulings, our schools have become "demoralized." All of these Court cases can be scored as victories for Satan and his evil spirits.

Because of these court decisions, we have taken religion out of our schools by removing the Bible and prayers. We have taken morality out of our schools by removing the Ten Commandments.

In the landmark case *Engel v. Vitale,* the Court removed prayer from our public schools

We have also gotten rid of knowledge. After the *Engel v. Vitale* decision of 1962, which removed prayer from the schools, SAT scores plummeted downward for eighteen straight years. Student scores fell by more than eighty points between 1962 and 1980.

Today, as high as 80 percent of all crimes in America are committed by school-age young people. For the most part, these are children who have never been to church; most have not been taught morality or a code of ethics in their homes or schools. They have no concept of right and wrong, good or evil. They do things today as a matter of routine that earlier generations would have considered intolerable, immoral, and unnatural.

Why? Because we have lost sight of the Christian principles our Founding Fathers took for granted. We have taken the engines of democracy off the tracks that the founders laid down so carefully, and we have replaced the teaching of the Bible with secularism.

As we have already seen in previous chapters, the Founding Fathers never intended for the United States to be considered a "secular" nation. They did not want the people of this country, nor their government, ever to become hostile to religion. Instead, our government was to accommodate religious and moral values and to encourage a reverence for God. As Justice Joseph Story wrote in his *Commentaries of the Constitution of the United States:* "Christianity aught to receive encouragement from the state." The intention of the Constitution and the First Amendment, said Story, was to encourage Christianity "so far as was not incompatible with the private rights of conscience and the freedom of religious worship."

The great patriot Patrick Henry said, "It cannot be emphasized too strongly or too often that this great nation was founded, not by religionists, but by Christians; not on religions, but on the Gospel of Jesus Christ." Samuel Adams, the great orator of the Revolution, claimed that the victory of the patriots helped to ensure that God would be supreme in the New World.

But today the ungodly are doing their best to destroy all of that, and the club they are using to beat back the idea of religious liberty is the "wall of separation between church and state," usually in the hands of the American Civil Liberties Union (ACLU). Like Hitler's big lie, this false doctrine has been used to brainwash the American people and to attempt to drive Christians and the Christian faith into oblivion.

In the 1980 case of *Stone v. Gramm,* the Court removed the Ten Commandments from our public schools

Under the benign sounding name of civil libertarians, the ACLU has been behind some of the most destructive and defamatory ant-religious litigation in history. Founded as the Bureau for Conscientious Objectors in the middle of World War I, the organization was the brainchild of Roger Baldwin, a pacifist, atheist, and anarchist. Originally the group was part of the pacifist organization American Union Against Militarism. However, in October 1918, it became independent under the name of National Civil Liberties Bureau.

From the start, members of this group were involved in anti-American activities. In August 1918, FBI agents raided the Bureau and discovered subversive materials. Three months later, Baldwin began serving a one-year term for sedition. After his release from prison the organization changed its name to the American Civil Liberties Union.

Today, the aims, values, and objectives have hardly changed since those days. The ACLU currently claims more than 250,000 dues-paying members, seventy staff lawyers, and as many as five thousand volunteer attorneys. Supreme Court Justice Ruth Bader Ginsburg served as an attorney for the ACLU.

The ACLU has an annual budget in excess of fourteen million dollars and is capable of handling as many as six thousand separate cases at any given time. Needless to say, this organization is one of the most formidable adversaries of conservative Christian values on earth.

In his book, *Character & Destiny* (Zondervan: 1994), Dr. James Kennedy says, **"Each year, like clockwork, the ACLU sues cities and other organizations that wish to display Nativity scenes or Hanukkah symbols at Christmas.** They have been successful in stopping carolers from singing 'Silent Night' and 'Away in a Manger' in public places. They have fought to deny tax-exempt status to churches while maintaining it for themselves and even occultic groups. They have been consistent opponents of prayer in schools, at graduations, and at any public event. They have tried to force the armed forces to get rid of all chaplains and to remove the words 'In God We Trust' from American coins. Simply stated, the ACLU is one of the most prominent organizations in this nation, and they are sworn enemies of God and those who love Him." (Emphasis added)

What are the results of these successful liberal actions by the ACLU, this dismantling of basic Christian principles in America? The results have surely been disastrous. The horrendous crime rate in our country—sickening numbers of murders, rapes, and other assaults—soaring numbers of abortions—an epidemic of domestic abuse and violence— these are more than social problems. They are spiritual in nature. They are Satanic spirits of the worst kind!

Since the 1962 Court decision to remove prayer in our

schools, Satan and the evil spirits have permeated our culture with all sorts of sexual immorality. Despicable sexual behavior is now rampant all across America. On a worldwide basis, sexual immorality is at a disturbingly low point in the history of man. The human race has become almost animalistic in nature.

Animalistic? Yes! Are we talking about Madonna and her new highly publicized book, *SEX*? No! We are talking about MAN. About man having sex with monkeys! African green monkeys. Monkeys that carried the deadly HIV virus. As you may already know, scientists have determined the AIDS virus originated in the African green monkey and was transmitted to man through sexual intercourse.[1]

This pathetic immoral sexual act between man and monkey, and subsequent sex acts between man and man (homosexuals), has resulted in a worldwide epidemic of the deadly AIDS disease. There is no cure for AIDS now, and a cure is not expected in the foreseeable future.

The Bible clearly teaches us about the consequences of homosexual behavior. It says, "Do not be deceived: Neither the sexually immoral . . . nor male prostitutes nor homosexual offenders . . . will inherit the kingdom of God" (1 Corinthians 6:9–10).

We became aware of the AIDS virus in the early 1980's. It was originally considered a sexually transmitted disease in homosexuals and infected drug addicts that shared needles. Billions of dollars have already been spent, and billions more will be spent, on research in hopes of finding a cure for AIDS.

Countless billions more are lost through the loss of productivity by those infected with this horrible disease. The cost of medical treatment for those infected with AIDS is absolutely astronomical and will continue to rise.

With the widespread immoral sexual conduct in our

---

1 Gene Antonio. *The AIDS Cover-Up.* (San Francisco: Ignatius Press, 1987), p. 1.

society today, the AIDS virus has spread far beyond the homosexual community. Millions of heterosexuals are now infected, and millions more are silent carriers of the deadly virus. And, of course, many innocent children and adults die each year from AIDS as a result of contaminated blood transfusions. Hemophiliac children are very susceptible to the AIDS virus through contaminated blood transfusions.

AIDS is a much bigger problem than most people realize. Why? Because our government has lied to us since the very beginning. We were told it was only a problem in the homosexual community, that the HIV virus could not be transmitted through blood transfusions, etc. And, of course, if a condom is used, there is nothing to worry about. During the current era in America, the lack of biblical principles has produced a bold society in which sexually promiscuous women are commonplace. These "liberated" women are independent and openly express their idea of the "good life," which is: good food, good music, and good sex.

And they will keep changing sexual partners until they find the "right" man. With these women, sexual pleasure is "IN," moral conduct is "OUT." They live for the excitement of the moment. The rules have changed. Before these new "freedoms" were discovered, men were the aggressors. That is not the case today. Women play the aggressive role now.

What does the Bible say about those who follow this worldly lifestyle? It says, "They are darkened in their understanding and separated from the life of God . . . Having lost all sensitivity, they have given themselves over to sensuality so as to indulge in every kind of impurity with a continual lust for more" (Ephesians 4:18–19).

We have taken morality out of our schools by removing the Ten Commandments

With moral standards almost a thing of the past, hardcore pornography has come out of the closet as an adjunct to the home video entertainment industry. More than 2,400 new adult titles are being introduced each year and the profitable industry appears to be gaining legitimacy within our society.

Adult films have grown into a $3 billion-a-year business. The films are not hard to find if you know where to look. "Videotaped pornography is one of Hollywood's fastest-growing products."[2]

During the current era, Satan's influence within the secular segment of our society is obvious. However, his influence is being felt by young Christians as well. A recent survey of 3,795 young people from Christian churches of 13 different denominations revealed 86 percent of them had made a personal commitment to Jesus Christ.

Yet, when these young people were asked if they believed the devil or Satan is only a symbol of evil and not a living being, shockingly, 31 percent said they believed that was true; 49 percent "disagreed;" and 20 percent said they "didn't know." Satan is alive, seeking new victims every day.

To the question, "Do you think it is true that no one can really prove which religion is absolutely true?" Sadly, only 40 percent of these young people believed that was true; 34 percent "disagreed;" and 26 percent said they "didn't know."

When asked "Did you watch MTV at least once a week during the past three months?" 45 percent said "Yes," 55 percent said, "No." Also, to the question, "During the past three months did you lie to a parent, teacher, or other older person?" Surprisingly, 66 percent of them said, "Yes," only 34 percent said they had not.[3]

The survey also showed that many of our Christian young people either do not know what the Bible teaches about moral absolutes or think they do not have to live according to those teachings. The survey showed that our

---

2 Jack B Simpson, *Sounding the ALARM: Moral Decay in the U.S.A.*

3 From a survey quoted on the John Ankerberg Show in November 1994.

young people do not know the evidence or reasons for what they believe.

Alarmingly, the survey also showed how rock music has influenced and persuaded our young Christian people to embrace non-biblical ideas about Satan and the occult.

The removal of Christian principles from our schools in 1962 has had an adverse effect on the American lifestyle. The Bible has also lost its prominence in many American families during the current era. This has produced a secular generation that is easily influenced by Satan.

During the past thirty years, America has witnessed a steady rise in Satanism and a steady decline in Christianity. Spiritual warfare is escalating with each passing day. It is GOOD vs. EVIL: A War of the Spirits. It appears, at least for the moment, that EVIL is progressing very nicely.

However, GOOD will prevail in the end. The Bible says, "There is now no condemnation awaiting those who belong to Jesus Christ. For the power of the life-giving Spirit has freed me from the vicious circle of sin and death" (Romans 8:1 TLB).

AMERICA
THE
CURRENT DAY
BABYLON

As we have seen in earlier chapters, the patriots who founded this country were people of strong character and moral vision. Great Americans throughout our history have been Christians who strove to make this a moral country. They all assumed that the nation's freedom depended upon its character. In short, they believed that to live free, the people had to live morally.

However, over the past thirty years or so, our culture has changed dramatically. Today there are many who say that Christians *are* the problem. They say Christians have no right to express their views in public. This trend has accelerated during the past two years (which represent the first two years of Bill (Hillary) Clinton as President(s) of the United States of America).

This is a strange phenomenon when you consider that both Bill and Hillary claim to be Christians. She is a Methodist and he is a Baptist. However, one must wonder if they believe the Bible to be the inerrant Word of God. Why? Because many of their secular actions are in direct violation of what is taught in the Bible.

For example, after being sworn into office, one of the first acts by President Bill Clinton was to endorse the homosexual agenda. By executive order, President Clinton declared that homosexual individuals must be allowed to serve in the military. The Bible says homosexuality is a sin. It tells us clearly that homosexuals will not be found in the kingdom of God. The Bible also says, "If a man lies with a man as one lies with a woman, both of them have done what is detestable" (Leviticus 20:13).

One could say, "well, that is the Old Testament Bible. The Clintons follow the New Testament Bible." What does the New Testament Bible say about homosexuality? It says, "Do not be deceived; Neither the sexually immoral . . . nor male prostitutes nor homosexual offenders . . . will inherit the kingdom of God" (1 Corinthians 6:9–10).

During their first two years in the White House, Bill and Hillary have demonstrated that they are very comfortable associating with those of secular beliefs. They love to visit with and to be entertained by the Hollywood stars. They like musicians of all sorts, including rock music artists.

The point is this: they claim to be Christians, however, they act like pagan secularists! Bill and Hillary Clinton should read the following Scripture carefully, "I know your deeds, that you are neither cold nor hot. I wish you were either one or the other! So, because you are lukewarm—neither hot nor cold—I am about to spit you out of my mouth. You say, 'I am rich; I have acquired wealth and do not need a thing.' But you do not realize that you are wretched, pitiful, poor, blind and naked" (Revelation 3:15–17). In short, Jesus Christ says, "you are either for Me, or you are against Me." There is no "in between" with Christ like there is with earthly politicians.

And, on the abortion issue, the Clintons are avid supporters of pro-choice. This group of people believes that women alone should have the right to choose abortion. In some cases, the abortion is paid for by the government (by the taxpayers). Another of President Bill Clinton's acts by executive order was to order government financial support to those "poor" women in need of an abortion.

What does the Bible say about life in the womb? It says, "Before I formed you in the womb I knew you, before you were born I set you apart . . ." (Jeremiah 1:5). The Bible tells us that life begins at conception. Therefore, anyone who kills an unborn baby has committed murder. And we all know what the Bible has to say about murder!

Hillary has a problem understanding the Bible. Look at what she says in a recent interview with *Newsweek:*

Question: "Do you have a favorite Bible passage?"

Answer: "At this point I am spending a lot of time thinking about the Sermon on the Mount, and particularly the Beatitudes, but really Matthew 5, 6, and 7. Those three chapters I think are just filled with challenge and it's very hard to read and for me to fully understand (she is a Yale University graduate). Or the whole Book of James—because I, being a Methodist, am big on deeds as well as words."[1]

Question: "The United Methodist Church is very strong on inclusive language for God as both He and She. Are you?"

Answer: "I'm sort of agnostic when it comes to inclusive language. I've always thought that language was so inadequate to express the mystery and power of God. **I mean, use He, use She—none of us are capable of really describing who God is."**[2]

Question: "What about God as Mother as well as Father?"

Answer: **"I think God is both . . ."**[3]

In Arkansas, Hillary taught Methodist Sunday school. She also attended church regularly.[4]

During the course of the exclusive Newsweek interview, Hillary said, "One of the differences I have with some of the denominations is the idea that one's Christianity is sealed at the moment that you accept Christ as your Savior and become in whatever ways are open to you a practicing Christian."[5]

This is a very revealing interview. Hillary is studying Matthew 5, 6, and 7. However, she does not know whether

---

1 *Newsweek*, October 31, 1994, p. 25.

2 Ibid.

3 Ibid.

4 Ibid., p. 24.

5 Ibid.

God is Father or Mother! Jesus repeatedly refers to God as Father throughout Matthew 5, 6, and 7. How can Hillary teach Sunday school if she cannot understand that God is Father? The answer is simple. She can't. (Review the chapter "What is the Lord's Name?") Her statements in this interview that question eternal salvation upon acceptance of Christ as Savior is troubling indeed!

Hillary's preference for the more liberal, social activist United Methodist denomination is well known. She does not like Baptist churches. They are too dogmatic, too fundamentalist, she says. Because of this, on Mother's Day, May 10, 1982, Bill took Hillary to visit the Glide Memorial church in San Francisco. This, she glowingly told reporters outside on the steps, was "the best Mother's Day present anyone ever gave me."[6]

What kind of church is Glide Memorial? Well, the church once hosted a national hooker's convention. The congregation is strongly pro-gay and has repudiated most basic Christian doctrines. **The pastor of Glide Memorial has said he "is tired of hearing about Jesus."**[7]

The way things are going, Hillary's typical Methodist church may not be too far behind Glide Memorial in adopting New Age absurdities. In Louisville, Kentucky, last year, a Methodist General Conference endorsed a new "Book of Worship" for America's 8.9 million United Methodists. The most startling new prayer, unearthed from the 11th century writings of St. Anselm, is addressed to Jesus: ". . . In truth, Lord, you are my Mother."[8]

Hillary seems to feel right at home in a church which addresses Christ as Mother. She also feels comfortable with other spiritual leaders. In early May 1993, in Billings, Montana, Hillary arranged for an Indian "spiritual healer" and

---

6 *Christian News*, January 18, 1993, p. 8; March 1, 1993, p. 21; October 12, 1993, pp. 9, 15.

7 Ibid.

8 "A More Maternal God," *Time*, May 25, 1993.

shaman to bless and purify her. Hillary even allowed photographers to record the event for posterity.[9]

Hillary is spiritual and religious. Words like "God" and "heal," "transform," and "spirit" roll easily off her lips. But is her God the Jesus of the Christian Bible? Is her spirit the Holy Spirit sent by the Father to those believers in Christ who are born again? Is she out to heal the environment of Mother Earth, or to heal broken and lost souls, as the apostles of the early church labored to do?

The question, really, is this: Is Hillary Rodham Clinton a true Christian or is she a modern-day false apostle, a "worker of deceit" as the Bible says? Do we have a woman of God in the White House—or a New Age goddess?

At their inauguration, rock bands thrilled the Clinton's and their liberal Hollywood friends with the old Beatles tune, "Say You Want a Revolution" and Fleetwood Mac's catchy "Don't Stop Thinking About Tomorrow." This was a throwback to the magic of the 1960's, the hippie generation—the revolutionary generation of Bill and Hillary Clinton.

In his book, *Big Sister is Watching You*, Texe Marrs says, "In the '60's, the Hindu gurus preached of the Great Mother Goddess who would soon come to recreate and renew the planet. Now, in the '90's, according to Hillary, the Goddess has arrived. The time for renewal—for reinventing—is here."

Let us examine the character and the moral background of certain people the Clintons have appointed to powerful positions within our government. As this "awesome" circle of power was created, Hillary was indeed very influential in choosing the individuals that were appointed by Bill.

During the 1992 campaign, Clinton promised "a Cabinet that looks like America."[10] Let us look at that "Cabinet." Do you really believe it "looks like America?" A look at their lifestyles before their "Cabinet" appointments will help us find the answer to the question.

---

9 *Intercessors for America* (newsletter), July 1993.

10 *Sun-Sentinel*, October 24, 1994. p. 3A.

GOOD vs. EVIL

A sampling of Bill's (and Hillary's) appointments follows:

ROBERTA ACHTENBERG. Position: Assistant Secretary of Housing and Urban Development. Roberta ("My friends just call me Bob.") Achtenberg is a successful starlet in her own way. She has starred in a very special movie—a cinematic extravaganza graphically depicting the excesses of "Gay Pride." Indeed, "Bob" Achtenberg seems to be the first pornographic "film star" to ever win appointment to a major government post—that of assistant secretary of HUD.

Roberta Achtenberg's starring role was her knockout "performance" in a 1992 video of a San Francisco Gay Pride parade. **That sickening video captures a scene in which Ms. Achtenberg passionately embraces and kisses her lesbian lover—a San Francisco woman judge.**

This bizarre lesbian activist is also demanding that queers be appointed Boy Scout troop masters. Achtenberg was also angered that the Boy Scouts include a reference to God in their oath. That, she fumed, is un-American![11]

DR. JOYCELYN ELDERS. Position: Surgeon General of the United States. Why did Bill and Hillary Clinton choose such an obnoxious, power-hungry bureaucrat for such an important position? The immediate answer is fairly simple: Joycelyn Elders perfectly mirrors the Clinton's ultraradical views favoring sexual promiscuity, lesbianism, homosexuality, aggressive promotion and taxpayer funding of abortions; and lax policies on the sale, possession, and use of illegal drugs.

Surgeon General Elders addressed the Association of Reproductive Health Professionals Conference on January 31, 1993. **She said, "We've taught our children in driver's education what to do in the front seat, and now we've got to teach them what to do in the back seat."**

11 Texe Marrs. *Big Sister is Watching You*. (Austin, TX: Living Truth Publishers, 1993), p. 79.

228

To say that Joycelyn Elders is a wild woman consumed by thoughts of sex is not an understatement. She is absolutely fascinated with the subject. As far as Elders is concerned, condoms are the answer to everything. Sexual promiscuity isn't a problem, Dr. Joycelyn Elders insists; it's okay for even the youngest of kids to "do it." The problem, she says, is being protected by a condom when you do it.

The majority of Americans would be shocked to even imagine a mandatory public school program which has adult teachers instructing 3- and 4-year-olds on how to put on and wear a condom! But Dr. Elders is not embarrassed one bit that most Americans find her ideas on sex education for the youngest of kids abhorrent and perverted. "Give me the choice of trying to educate a 3-year-old or trying to educate an 18-year-old, and I'll take the 3-year-old every time," she has stated.[12] Elders has earned the title "Condom Queen."

Joycelyn Elders caused an uproar in 1993 when she suggested legalizing drugs was an idea that should be considered. Just two weeks later, Elders' 28-year-old son was arrested for selling cocaine to undercover agents.

However, the title Condom Queen and her outspoken position on such issues as drug legalization and teenage sex finally cost Dr. Joycelyn Elders her job as surgeon general. Due to much public pressure, particularly from conservatives, President Clinton fired her on December 9, 1994.

Joycelyn Elders is no longer surgeon general but she is still outspoken. In a recent interview with *Playboy* magazine she said: Clarence Thomas is "an Uncle Tom," Jesse Helms "a typical white, Southern, male bigot" and Newt Gingrich might be among a minority of people who don't masturbate.[13]

MAYA ANGELOU. Position: Inaugural Poet. Well over a billion people around the globe viewed the presidential inauguration. What a pulpit for the New Age religion phi-

12 *The Wall Street Journal*, July 22, 1993, p. A14.

13 *Sun-Sentinel* (Associated Press), December 10, 1994.

losophy! Surely, Bill and Hillary did a number on Christianity and on the American people that deceitful day, January 20, 1993, when Maya Angelou, former stripper, prostitute, racial agitator, socialist, anti-American flag demonstrator, and unqualified Wake Forest professor, rose to her feet and read her unholy pagan propaganda piece in poetry.

Maya Angelou wowed an international TV audience with dreamy, spiritually-oriented lyrics which had human beings talking to rocks, trees, forests, and rivers. The poem also stated something to the effect that the Earth and its people "are one."[14] It was very touching and sensitive—that is, if you are one of those witchcraft, environmentalist, New Age types into crystals, the worship of the Mother Earth goddess, and Hindu pantheism.

During the 1992 campaign, Clinton promised "a Cabinet that looks like America"

With the Bill Clinton and Al Gore inauguration, the people of America quite obviously left the realms of presidential dignity and good taste and entered some kind of bizarre twilight zone of demonic weirdness. How else can you explain the preposterous events that occurred?

During the week of the inaugural festivities, the nation was treated to a gay, lesbian and homosexual band trooping down Pennsylvania Avenue. All in all, this was a weird extravaganza: a week of witchery, sodomizing, New Age quackery, and Satanic symphonies. Satan was very pleased!

Then there were the gala parties and balls which the dynamic quadruplet—Bill, Hillary, Al, and Tipper—attended. The performers included Bill's favorite rock band, Fleetwood Mac, with self-proclaimed witch, Stevie Nicks, on the vocals. And naturally, there were the Elvis impersonators, Barbra

14 Barbara Reynolds, "Maya Angelou: Silent No More," *USA Today*, January 18, 1993, p. 13A.

Streisand, and all the other glitzy Hollywood stars. Immersed in ecstasy, the dynamic quartet literally drank and danced the nights away. Television coverage of these gala events was extensive. They were truly having a ball.

RUTH BADER GINSBURG. Position: U. S. Supreme Court Justice. "Ruth Bader Ginsburg: A Mainstream Justice," blared the *USA Today* headline.[15] "Clinton Selects Ginsburg, a Moderate, for the Supreme Court," wrote Robert Rankin in a nationally syndicated story for the Knight-Ridder News Service."[16] "Ruth Ginsburg Has a Record of Judicial Restraint," said *Newsweek* magazine."[17]

Who were these liberal news reporters trying to kid? Ruth Bader Ginsburg mainstream? . . . a moderate? **In reality, Ginsburg is possibly the most radical liberal who has ever been appointed to the U. S. Supreme Court in the history of America.** However, what other kind of judge would you expect Bill and Hillary (and the "circle of power") to pick?

Let us take a close look at her scarlet record and you decide if the biased news media is simply trying to put one over on "we, the people." R. E. McMaster, in *The Reaper* newsletter writes: "Clinton picked Judge Ruth Bader Ginsburg for his first Supreme Court vacancy. She is a one-time crusader for women's rights . . . Ginsburg was a liberal during her years as a practicing attorney which included seven years as general counsel for the American Civil Liberties Union. She is Jewish, from Harvard, and spent time at the Aspen Institute."[18]

The left-wing ACLU was covered in an earlier chapter. The Aspen Institute is notorious for its black reputation as a New Age and pro-New World Order think tank.

---

15 *USA Today*, July 29, 1993, p. 1.

16 *Austin American-Statesman*, June 15, 1993, p. 1.

17 *Newsweek*, June 28, 1993, p. 29.

18 R. E. McMaster, *The Reaper*, May 19, 1993, p. 14.

DONNA SHALALA. Position: Secretary of Health and Human Services (HHS). "Donna Shalala, you know you're a lesbian, and we know you're a lesbian. So why don't you just come out of the closet and admit it? These are words of homosexual firebrand Larry Kramer, co-founder of the gay activist group, ACT-UP, who "outed" Donna Shalala over national television on April 25, 1993.[19]

Designated an official "Friend of Hillary" (FOH) by *Newsweek* **magazine, Shalala is a real liberal.**[20] In fact, she is so proud of the label that she has openly bragged about it. Shalala has also earned a notorious, but well-deserved, reputation as one of the meanest and most diabolically militant Christian haters in America today.

Shalala has been called the "High Priestess of Political Correctness," a title richly earned due to her anti-Christian persecution of so-called "politically" and "religiously incorrect" students at the University of Wisconsin where Shalala held the leadership position as chancellor.[21]

As chancellor, Donna Shalala made it one of her prime goals to drive true Christian believers off the campus. In a Nazi-type campaign to intimidate and shut Christians up, she originated what she called her "hate speech" code. Joined by other liberal ideologues on the university's board of regents, Shalala drafted rules that banned the use of any language, epithets, or symbols which "demean" a person or group because of race, religion, gender, ancestry, age, disability, or sexual preference.[22]

New Agers, pedophiles, sexually kinky types (the leather and chains, sadist crowd), Satanists, occultists, homosex-

---

19 C-Span, April 25, 1993.

20 *Newsweek*, July 19, 1993, p. 6.

21 Connie Zhu, "Queen Shalala Mounts HHS Throne," *Christian American*, March 1993, p. 12.

22 Ibid. Also see "Shalala Faces Questions on 'Politically Correct' Issue," by Julia Malone (Cox News Service), *Austin American-Statesman*, January 10, 1993, p. A7.

uals and lesbians, multiculturals, and other one worlders, as well as strangely nontraditional staff, faculty, students, and hangers-on, were delighted.

Shalala's new University of Wisconsin hate crimes ordinance meant that Christians on campus, espousing their detestable, "Jesus is the only way to salvation" philosophy, could finally be silenced once and for all. To claim that your religion is better or more true that someone else's—now that is pure hate, they reasoned. Their goal for America is a multicultural society devoid of Christianity.

JANET RENO. Position: Attorney General. Janet Reno's record as the state attorney and chief prosecutor for Miami and Dade County, Florida, is so incredibly deficient that it boggles the imagination.

Even the *Miami Herald*, a newspaper whose liberal editors adore Janet Reno and the Clintons, was forced to admit that her performance as a prosecutor was atrocious. "She has a losing record in the highest profile cases," the newspaper reported, adding: "Her office has been accused of lacking investigative zeal, often letting cases languish for years."[23]

It is common knowledge to those of us who live in South Florida that Miami became the drug-running, Mafia capital of the world during Reno's years as state attorney. Further proof of Janet Reno's incompetence comes from Thurman Brown, a former federal investigator stationed in South Florida: "Miami's Brickell Avenue is now lined with glittering new banks full of drug money," says Brown.[24]

Janet Reno (unmarried, childless, and 6'2") has been called "a queer choice for attorney general." Florida attorney Jack Thompson says the new attorney general is a hardened lesbian in the worst conceivable way. Janet Reno,

23 *Miami Herald*, February 10, 1993.
24 "Hope for America in Honest AG," *Spotlight*, March 1, 1993.

according to Thompson, is a closet lesbian who is so wickedly, sexually corrupt that she has frequently used call girls for sex and, as Dade County, Florida, attorney, she sexually harassed female county employees.[25]

Amazing as it may seem, when President Bill Clinton (or was it Hillary?) nominated Janet Reno as the nation's first female attorney general, he boasted that, "She is a front-line crime fighter and a caring public servant."[26]

Only six individuals are analyzed above. Many more could have been added to the list. Such as: Madeleine Albright, U. S. Ambassador to the United Nations; Jane Alexander, Chairperson, National Endowment for the Arts; Carol Bellamy, Director of the Peace Corps; Carol Browner, Head of the Environmental Protection Agency; Hazel O'Leary, Secretary of Energy; Margaret Richardson, IRS Commissioner; Alice Rivlin, Deputy Director, Office of Management and Budget; Laura D'Andrea Tyson, Chairman of the Council of Economic Advisors; and Sheila Widnall, Secretary of the Air Force.

However, the revelation is clear, Bill and Hillary have surrounded themselves with a group of powerful, greedy, sexually liberal (some admittedly lesbian), and secular women. Some of them hold religious beliefs that are EVIL. Materialism and sensuality dominate this "circle of power."

Vice President Al Gore and his wife Tipper are Southern Baptists from Tennessee. They claim to be Christians. Does this secular "circle of power" assembled by the Clintons bother them? Apparently not! As already stated, they surely enjoyed the secular activities during inauguration week. There were no reports that they rushed off to the nearest Baptist church for prayer and thanksgiving praise to Lord Jesus. And reporters did not catch them strolling

---

25 *American Freedom Movement Newsletter*, April 1993, p. 7. Also see the following sources: "Janet Reno A Lesbian?," *Wisconsin Report*, March 4, 1993, p. 3; and "Hillary Selects Lesbian as Attorney General," by Larry Patterson, *Criminal Politics*, February 1993.

26 As reported by the Associated Press and Republic Wire Services.

down Pennsylvania Avenue singing "Amazing Grace" or "Onward Christian Soldiers" either!

This is a big reversal for the Gores. What happened? Well, in the summer of 1992, the political fortunes of Al and Tipper Gore shifted dramatically. It was announced that Al Gore would be Bill Clinton's running mate. New social and political conditions prevailed. To appease the crazy, spaced-out liberals within the Democrat Party, Al and Tipper were prepared to make a 180 degree reversal in their positions on such issues as filth and decadence in rock music and on the immorality of abortion.

Al Gore immediately began to depict himself as a lifetime supporter of the radical, pro-choice, abortion-on-demand position. **He enthusiastically embraced the entire pro-abortion leadership and pledged his undying devotion to their cause.** Unwanted babies had to go. Women's privacy was at stake.

Tipper Gore, too, experienced a born-again experience as a new, radical liberal. Asked at campaign stops about her previous Christian position on rock music lyrics, Tipper flip-flopped. She totally denied that she had ever favored restrictions! What's more, she publicly scoffed at the notion that her book, *Raising PG Kids In An X-Rated World,* was a "Christian" book (although the book became an immediate best-seller throughout the Christian community).

This never was a moral or religious issue at all, Tipper assured the press. It was a feminist issue! You see, she gingerly explained, she had become upset because there were so many anti-women lyrics in rock music. That's all.

To prove once and for all to the doubting Thomases of the closed-minded, liberal community that she had really been one of them all along, Tipper and Al next began to dutifully take their teenage son, hand-in-hand, to heavy metal rock concerts.

On one occasion, the Gore family showed up at a Grateful Dead rock concert. A smiling and chatty Tipper Gore touchingly told amused reporters that the Grateful Dead was her and Al's favorite rock group.

As Al and Tipper well know, the Grateful Dead is unquestionably one of America's sickest and most despicable Satanic rock groups. In fact, one of their best known tunes is entitled "Friend of the Devil." For over a quarter of a century, the "Dead," as they are called by their adoring fans, have been preaching and pitching their depressing messages of dope, death, and the devil to thousands of groupies. Now, Al and Tipper proudly identify themselves with those groupies.[27]

Al even bought a psychedelic Grateful Dead tie. He has been pictured in rock magazines wearing the tie. None of this should surprise us. The hypocrisy of the Clintons and the Gores is now legend. **In US magazine, Satanic rock band star Jon Bon Jovi raved about what a great president America has: "Bill Clinton's the first president who's not old enough to be my father, who understands rock 'n' roll, who smoked dope . . . and avoided the draft. He did the things that I can relate to. He called me up last week. I spoke to him. That's pretty hip."**[28]

For the reader who would like to see a more detailed background on the Clintons, the video "The Clinton Chronicles" is highly recommended. An extensive look into the secular background of Bill and Hillary is vividly portrayed in this 83 minute video.[29]

If any of the allegations in this video are true (and the evidence presented is overwhelming), then Bill and Hillary are secularists of the worst kind. Bill is shown as a big-time dope-using womanizer, and a protector of drug dealers.

Hillary is depicted as a power-hungry lawyer who will do "whatever is necessary" to achieve her goal of becoming the most powerful woman in America. As a lawyer for the

27 *Rolling Stone,* September 2, 1991, pp. 42–46, 76–77.

28 *The Reaper,* May 19, 1993, p. 12.

29 "The Clinton Chronicles" © 1994, Citizens For Honest Government, P.O. Box 220, Winchester, CA 92596.

"Rose" law firm in Little Rock, Arkansas, she is accused of many corrupt activities. Some are very serious. And, of course, the "Whitewater" case is covered in detail.[30]

Bill Dannemeyer, a former United States Congressman (1979–1992), says, "We have in the White House today a womanizing draft-dodger who is a pathological liar. It is a very dangerous thing for America, a very dangerous thing for the world."[31] Dannemeyer would like to see President Bill Clinton impeached.

However, Vice President Al Gore says, "We have the highest ethical standards in the White House. You can be sure of that."[32] (Say what?!)

Dark clouds are appearing over the White House. For several months last year, the Whitewater saga dominated the headlines, and then it seemed to go away. Well, it is back. **And the news is not good for the Clinton White House:** Prosecutors are targeting Bruce Lindsey, currently the deputy White House counsel, and they may seek an indictment against him on federal banking charges.[33]

This is no small matter, and it signals that the Whitewater affair is once again heating up. Kenneth Starr, the Whitewater independent counsel, and three assistants strode into the White House during the month of April and interviewed the president and Hillary. Each session lasted two hours. Separately, Starr's staff is continuing to question **Webster Hubbell, the Clinton confidant and former associate attorney general who has pleaded guilty to tax and fraud charges.**[34]

Lindsey's troubles became clear during the week of May 8, 1995. Word leaked from the White House that Lindsey had been officially notified that he was a "target" of the

---

30 Ibid.

31 Ibid.

32 Ibid.

33 *Sun-Sentinel* (The Associated Press), May 9, 1995, p. 5A.

34 *The Washington Times*, May 8, 1995.

Whitewater inquiry. Prosecutors are focusing on his dealings with the Perry County Bank in rural Arkansas. That
bank served as the depository of Clinton's campaign funds
in 1990.

In a major development, the former president of the
bank, Neal Ainley, admitted he helped the Clinton campaign
conceal the withdrawal of $52,500 cash from the cam-
paign's account. Ainley pleaded guilty to two misdemeanor
charges and agreed to cooperate with the continuing investigation. Ainley has told prosecutors that Lindsey and others directed him not to report the cash withdrawals to the
Treasury Department, as required by law.[35]

If Lindsey is forced to resign, he would join a growing
list of Clinton confidants who have endured untimely depar-
tures from the administration. All were friends of long
standing who came to Washington with great expectations,
then left, objects of disgrace and dark accusation.

In yet another Whitewater case, Arkansas Governor Jim
Tucker was indicted on June 7, 1995, by a Whitewater grand
jury on charges of lying to obtain $300,000 in Small Busi-
ness Administration loans for his personal use. If convicted,
Tucker could face up to 12 years in prison and $750,000 in
fines, and would have to resign.[36]

Tucker, a Democrat who succeeded Bill Clinton as governor, was charged along with William Marks, his partner
in a Florida cable TV venture. Tucker's attorney, was charged,
along with the other two, with conspiring to hide the cable
venture's true value from the Internal Revenue Service.[37]

Tucker is the most prominent figure yet to be charged
in the Whitewater investigation, which began as an investigation of President Clinton's business dealings in Arkansas.
This dark cloud over the White House does not seem to
bother Clinton. He continues to praise these close friends

---

35 *U.S. News & World Report*, May 15, 1995, p. 40.

36 *The Wall Street Journal*, June 8, 1995, p. 1.

37 *Sun-Sentinel* (Thje Associated Press), June 8, 1995, p. 3A.

even though they have broken the law. Clinton is reported as saying "Jim Guy Tucker is an outstanding public servant."[38]

Has the Day of Babylon arrived? "Babylon" is described in the Bible as both a religious and a political system. All mankind is united under a new world religion, the World Church ("mystery" Babylon). The Bible says, "This title was written on her forehead: MYSTERY BABYLON THE GREAT, THE MOTHER OF PROSTITUTES AND OF THE ABOMINATIONS OF THE EARTH. I saw that the woman was drunk with the blood of the saints, the blood of those who bore testimony of Jesus" (Revelation 17:5–6). Ancient Babylon believed in religion without God. America, with its trend toward secularism, resembles that of Ancient Babylon. Revelation Chapter 18 tells us that after religious Babylon is destroyed, commercial Babylon will be destroyed as well.

The moral of this passage of Scripture is not to trust in material things, but to have faith in Jesus Christ as personal Savior. The things of this world will pass away, but spiritual truth as found in God's Word will endure forever.

Will the Clinton Era bring an end to Christian freedom in America? Well, if the recent midterm elections, held on November 8, 1994, are any indication, the answer is NO. Exit polls showed an overwhelming majority of American voters are fed up with the liberal lifestyles and secular behavior of those who represent them in Washington.

The Bible says, "For the time will come when men will not put up with sound doctrine. Instead, to suit their own desires, they will gather around them a great number of teachers to say what their itching ears want to hear. They will turn their ears away from the truth and turn aside to myths" (2 Timothy 4: 3–4).

Prior to the midterm elections, America had drifted too far to the left. Voters were concerned about the political agenda and about the moral decay of their political lead-

---

38 Ibid.

ers. In short: something is wrong when a government that does not adequately deliver the mail delivers condoms to our children. And it appears that the voters wanted to send a strong message of disapproval to Bill and Hillary Clinton and their "circle of power" secular cronies.

The historic GOP sweep, which gave Republicans control of both the Senate and the House, is nothing less than a repudiation of the president's party and his politics. Not one GOP congressional incumbent was defeated.

Newt Gingrich, R–Ga., the new Speaker of the House, promised to push for a constitutional amendment that will permit school prayer. Let us pray for his success.

Unfortunately, truth in politics is almost impossible to uncover—and because of this, it is even more important for Americans to discover what the Bible says. If ever there was a time when we needed to ask God for wisdom and to sincerely seek the understanding of His Word, it is NOW.

TERROR IN OKLAHOMA
CHAPTER THIRTY

The illusion that Beirut-style terrorism could not occur in the United States of America has come to an abrupt end. On April 19, 1995, a homemade bomb devastated the Alfred P. Murrah Federal Building in Oklahoma City, Oklahoma. There were at least 168 people killed in this heinous act. Almost two dozen of those killed were children who attended a daycare center located in the building. This is not Jerusalem. This is not the Gaza Strip. This is not Sarajevo. This is not Baghdad. It is nowhere in the Middle East or Europe. It is Oklahoma—the heartland of America!

This was truly an act of EVIL. We have seen the power of Satan revealed right before our eyes. During the Memorial Service in Oklahoma City, Dr. Billy Graham spoke about the power of Satan as described in the Bible. He also pointed out that many Christians do not realize that Satan works through depraved people to cause destruction of all sorts. The Bible repeatedly warns us about the vast power of Satan. Any person who murders innocent children—or any person—has to be under the influence of Satan.

If there can be a darkest part of the Oklahoma City tragedy, it lies in the wreckage of the America's Kids daycare center. The random and senseless destruction of a government building shows a nation how vulnerable it is; the random destruction of innocent children shows how deep the pain can go. "I think it is the death of the children that has everybody the most upset," said Oklahoma Governor Frank Keating. "Everybody I talk to mentions the kids."[1]

Less than 90 minutes after the massive explosion, Oklahoma Patrolman Charlie Hanger stopped a young man for driving north on I–35 without a license plate. It seemed like a routine arrest—the kind of thing Charlie Hanger had done many times in 15 years as a trooper. This time, however, the offender turned out to be prime suspect, Timothy McVeigh. There are other suspects but they are still at large at the time of this writing.

There is much speculation among politicians and ordinary citizens about what strain of evil in American society could have produced the terrorists responsible for the atrocity. But there was also a positive lesson to be learned, and it would be a shame if it were lost in the debate about the dark side of our culture. That lesson was clear to those in Oklahoma City after the explosion: Ordinary people have not lost their instinct for performing extraordinary acts of goodness.

Individuals initially by the hundreds and later by the thousands responded in a vast collective expression of decency that needed no prompting from leaders in government. They poured out of hospitals, fire stations, police departments, office buildings, and private homes to help. Volunteers from fire departments and rescue squads from all across America arrived to help rescue survivors.

It is, of course, necessary to have a standard of good when battling evil. President Clinton accurately condemned those who killed innocent men, women and children in the Oklahoma City bombing as "evil cowards." In doing so, he invoked a word—*evil*—that has suffered in recent years from lack of use.

When Ronald Reagan applied the word to the Soviet Union—"evil empire," he called it—sophisticated commentators were shocked that a word they regarded as crude

---

1 *Newsweek*, May 1, 1995, p. 48.

was employed by a national leader. But what other explanation satisfactorily describes such a despicable act or a soul-destroying government that causes men and women to sob in grief and others to declare their lives drained of meaning and joy?

Acknowledging the existence of evil—not just evil people but evil itself—is a prerequisite to understanding and controlling it. Denying that evil exists, and that it is a proper metaphor for the worst kind of behavior, ensures that evil will prosper.

The dictionary is of some help. It defines evil as "morally reprehensible; sinful, wicked; arising from actual or imputed bad character or conduct."[2] This presumes a standard of good conduct against which evil may be measured. It also indicates that evil begins in a heart and works outward and is not created by one's circumstances. Such a notion contradicts most modern teaching and philosophy.

The Bible repeatedly warns us about the vast power of Satan

Evil is as old—older, really—than the second chapter of Genesis, where God instructs Adam, "You are free to eat from any tree in the garden; but you must not eat from the tree of the knowledge of good and evil, for when you eat of it you will surely die." If evil existed at the time of creation, this suggests that evil and its author (Satan) came before. Is this what *New York Times* columnist Bob Herbert was getting at when he wrote of the Oklahoma City tragedy: "From what universe beyond the one that most of us inhabit does this kind of evil arise?"[3]

Will this horrible terrorist act in Oklahoma City teach us anything, or will we allow the shock to subside and even-

2 *Random House College Dictionary,* Revised Edition. Copyright 1984 by Random House, Inc., p. 458.

3 Cal Thomas, *Los Angeles Times,* April 28, 1995.

tually be able to look back on it with detached and emotionless hindsight? Many people have short memories in America today.

Those who would do such evil things show the capacity of humanity uncontrolled by the restraining influences of an inner power and a culture that believes evil must not only be resisted but opposed. While we have always had with us those who would kill the innocent, rarely have we thrown a party and celebrated the killers and the profit potential of their acts. Even now there must be lawyers jockeying for the position of defense counsel and thinking about exclusive rights to books and movies. The O. J. Simpson trial has shown us how easily we can forget about the innocent dead and focus instead on the side issues and non-issues as we pay homage to the cult of celebrity.

Once God defined the norms of our society, but we decided we could do a better job. To speak of evil requires a knowledge of its opposite, good, and good's author (God). Otherwise, evil is simply a label we apply to actions a majority likes the least at a given moment. This floating "standard" is not permanent, but for the moment only, and it can be changed or shaded when public opinion requires something new.

A nation that rejects a universal standard eventually experiences an Oklahoma City tragedy. If hate groups are proliferating, if evil seems ever more the norm and not the exception, perhaps it is time to re-examine the old values and seek the One who defines good. Only the Bible reveals true values and God tells us throughout His Word what is truly good.

In the wake of the Oklahoma City bombing, it is important for Christians to remember who our enemy is. The Bible says, "For our struggle is not against flesh and blood, but against the rulers, against the authorities, against the powers of this dark world and against the spiritual forces of evil in the heavenly realms" (Ephesians 6:12). Terrorists who claim to be Christians do not represent the people of that faith. In other words, they are fraudulent Christians.

They do not have a true personal relationship with the Jesus Christ that I know.

Genuine Christians who know Jesus Christ as Lord and Savior can see that Satan and his evil spirits are responsible for the tragedy experienced at Oklahoma City. Timothy McVeigh and his companions—if they are found to be guilty—were only puppets of Satan at the time of their actions.

The villainy in Oklahoma City did not happen in a vacuum. It is part of an international, political, and social environment where terror and war seem to be the preferred tools for change.

Sadly, what is happening around us is not coincidental. The handwriting is on the world's walls. There are worse things to come. Satan will intensify his global effort to terrorize decent citizens, Christians in particular.

A homegrown, all-American conspiracy—if that is proved to be the source of the violence—has more in common with business as usual in Bosnia, Beirut, or Algiers than the heritage left by the Founding Fathers in Philadelphia.

For the past year, Pentagon staff officers have been required to read an article titled "The Coming Anarchy" published by *The Atlantic* magazine in February 1994. It is an unsettling futuristic account of a 21st Century beset by growing turmoil and violence. It is required reading in Israel's Defense Ministry as well.[4]

Some people believe the Oklahoma City bombing was retaliation against the government raid on the Branch Davidian compound near Waco, Texas. April 19, 1995, was the second anniversary of the Waco disaster in which 85 people were killed.

What happened at Waco? There are two versions of the truth.

In two videos, Indianapolis activist Linda Thompson argues that the 1993 attack on the Branch Davidian com-

---

4 Roberto Fabricio, *World Observer*, April 30, 1995.

pound in Waco, Texas, was an act of government-sponsored terrorism.

THE CONSPIRACY THEORY—FRINGE GROUPS BE-
LIEVE THE RAID WAS GOVERNMENT TERRORISM.

The Bureau of Alcohol, Tobacco, and Firearms raided the Branch Davidian compound mainly because it suspected the group had a machine gun on which it had failed to pay a $200 tax.

ATF agents fired automatic weapons at Branch Davidians who were not shooting back.

The fire that engulfed the Branch Davidian compound was deliberately started by government tanks.

The FBI trapped Branch Davidians inside a burning bunker by destroying part of the house over a trapdoor.

Government tanks deliberately destroyed evidence by pushing it into the fire.

THE GOVERNMENT VERSION—OFFICIALS CONCEDE
MISTAKES WERE MADE BUT DENY THERE WAS A PLOT.

The Branch Davidians had stockpiled more than 200 firearms, including dozens of illegal machine guns, grenades and grenade components.

ATF agents were attacked from nearly every area of the compound with "insurmountable, unrelenting" semi-automatic and automatic weapons fire.

David Koresh, leader of the Branch Davidians, preached that as the "Lamb of God" he could have sex with teenage girls and women in the compound.

Koresh used children as a shield against FBI efforts to resolve the 51-day standoff, and he threatened to fire on FBI positions and blow up government vehicles.

The Branch Davidians set fire to three separate areas within their compound. No government tanks were equipped with any sort of flame-throwing device.

The tanks were used to lob tear gas into parts of the compound in an effort to flush out the Davidians. Later, they were used to open avenues of escape.

Agents risked their lives to save the Branch Davidians. One jumped off the roof and ran into the burning building to save one woman's life.

While the fire burned, negotiators repeatedly broadcast messages urging the Davidians to leave. Only nine heeded the warnings and left.[5]

Which of the above versions are really true? Your guess is as good as mine. This has been a controversial issue since the incident occurred over two years ago. And it will continue to be debated for many years. We will probably never know the real truth.

We do know that the Branch Davidians were a religious cult. David Koresh *claimed* to be Jesus Christ—the Lamb of God. Fraudulent Christians such as David Koresh have become all too common in society today. It is difficult for many in the world today to differentiate between those of us who are true believers in Jesus Christ and those who only use His precious name to legitimize their evil activities. Fraudulent Christianity is on the rise not only in the United States, but around the world as well. Any earthly person who claims to be Jesus Christ is a FRAUD.

Terrorists who claim to be Christians do not represent the people of that faith

The Bible warns us to be on the lookout for false Christians. It tells us that many will come in the name of Christ but in reality are impostors. The Bible also tells us to "test the spirits." False Christians use the Scripture to promote their personal agendas—which may include acts of violence. They may quote the Scripture correctly but have no knowledge of its meaning.

The Michigan Militia has gained national attention

---

5 *U.S. News & World Report*, May 8, 1995.

since the bombing of the federal building in Oklahoma City because Timothy McVeigh has connections there. Many of the militia groups around the country are religious cults. They claim to be Christians but are actually agents of Satan. Beware of those individuals who quote Scripture and use it as justification for violent acts. The Bible does not teach us to kill people. It teaches us to love people. Jesus' main commandment is that we love one another. Those in the militia who oppose taxes should heed what Jesus said: "Give to Caesar what is Caesar's, and give to God what is God's" (Matthew 22:21).

Many of the self-styled militia organizations in the United States call government an enemy and preach violence against it. There is nothing patriotic about hating your country. However, this is how Satan works. He instills hate into someone and then encourages them to commit violent acts. Many times this is done under the banner of Christianity. Satan is a master of deception and terror.

MILITIAS AND THE MILLENNIUM

The banners being raised by American militias have a particular fabric in Utah, often woven with strands of prophetic patriotism and patriarchy stretching back to the earliest days of the Mormon Church. Mormon theology and history are catalysts for militant ultra-conservatives.

Church founder Joseph Smith formed the 5,000-member Nauvoo Legion in Illinois in 1840 in part because he considered the state and federal governments too corrupt to protect him and his followers.

Today, in enclaves from Morgan to Kanab, there are — among dozens of other groups — the Culpepper Minutemen, the Mormon Battalion and the Sovereign Freemen. Like many of their counterparts in the West, these groups were forged out of a distrust of government and fear that the Constitution is eroding. But in many cases, Mormon millennialism is the catalyst.

They literally believe they are in the last days "and interpret perceived attacks on their rights from both a political and theological perspective," says Beck Johns, a Weber State University communications professor who has studied fundamentalist Mormons in Utah.[6]

"They are very cognizant of time, and believe things happen in an order and that somehow there is an end," she says. "And for these types of extremists, the end is always close."[7]

Authorities cannot pinpoint how many such groups are operating in Utah, although they say there are enough to cause concern. "The Mormon religion is fertile ground for those kinds of anti-government-we-can-take-care-of-ourselves beliefs," says Jimmy Gober, a retired 25-year veteran of the federal Bureau of Alcohol, Tobacco, and Firearms. "There are groups all over Utah waiting for Armageddon."[8]

In Sanpete County, for instance, Gober once found himself in a basement where the homeowner had stashed 137 SKS rifles—a cheap, Chinese-made semi-automatic carbine patterned after the AK-47. In northern Utah, he says, some groups "parceled out" an entire boxcar of SKS ammunition, likely intent on burying it. All of it, he says, was legal.[9]

"Some of these groups are seeing evidence and signs of the last days in all that is happening around us," Gober says. "They're coming around to the idea that government is the anti-Christ."[10]

"Militant Mormon ultra-conservatives have theological underpinnings to their political beliefs that others— most often Protestants—don't have," historian D. Michael Quinn says. Conspiracy theories come easily to believers in the Book of Mormon, which warns of "secret combinations" involving judges, military leaders and regular folk who become linked with bandits and common criminals. "It is an historical event, and the book warns its 19th Cen-

---

6 *Sun-Sentinel* (The Associated Press), May 6, 1995, p. 7D.

7 Ibid.

8 Ibid.

9 Ibid.

10 Ibid.

tury readers to beware of future secret combinations,"
Quinn says. "There is a very clear doctrinal basis to be on
the lookout for conspiracy. The paranoia once directed at
the communist conspiracy is now directed at the federal
government."[11]

Another strand of Mormon belief—particularly strong
during the 19th Century—is in the ideal of a literal kingdom of God on Earth that supplants a strictly secular government with a theocracy. That is not to say that people
who hold those beliefs necessarily join militias or band
together in paramilitary sects. But many scholars and law
enforcement officers recognize a certain overlapping of doctrine among the Constitutionalists, tax protesters or avowed
freemen who proclaim their sovereignty from government
rule.

The Utah State Guard, a state militia, was forced to dis-
band and reorganize in 1987 after it was infiltrated by the
Aryan Nations and other extremists. What began as a cadre
of retired soldiers to lead a militia in the event of a civil
emergency degenerated into a renegade commando unit
whose members provided combat training to white supremacists. They put together a hit list of state enemies. Similar
circumstances forced Cleon Skousen, the patriarch of the
constitutionalist movement in Utah, to change the name of
his Freemen Institute to National Center for Constitutional
Studies.

Many believe it is no coincidence that ex-Green Beret
James "Bo" Gritz—a one-time Mormon convert and 1992
Populist Presidential candidate—received 28,602 votes in
Utah, more than any other state. He is a retired Army
Colonel, a survivalist, reputed white supremacist and a
tough-talking constitutionalist with government conspir-
acy theories. He also believes the CIA could have been
behind the bombing in Oklahoma City.[12]

11 Ibid.
12 *Phoenix Gazette*, April 27, 1995.

Gritz was one of several individuals featured on "The American Agenda" on Wednesday, May 3, 1995. This is a part of ABC World News Tonight with Peter Jennings. It was titled "Guns and Bible." Peter Jennings reported, "we have all learned a great deal since the Oklahoma bombing about the scope of the various paramilitary groups which exist in 40 states. We have learned more about the depth of their antagonism toward their government. And in many cases we are learning they have a common fundamental belief that God is on their side."[13]

The ABC report continues, saying, "the Michigan Militia is preparing for battle against the forces of evil. Many militia members consider themselves God's front line in a war against a godless federal government. From Michigan to Texas, militia members are saying 'things are not what they should be in this nation. We are in danger of losing everything we've got and it can only be a return to the Christ-centered society that these things can be returned.'"[14]

Ralph Turner and other militia leaders believe America was founded as a Christian nation. They fear that the federal government is violating what they consider to be God-given rights. For the Texas Constitutional Militia, it is mainly the right to carry weapons. Other militia members rally around a broad range of explosive social issues. Some are anti-abortion. Some resist taxes. Some are opposed to gay rights, and some are white supremacist.

Together these independent militias make up a national paramilitary subculture. And, although they publicly denounce the kind of violence that occurred in Oklahoma, they insist on their right to defend themselves. These people say they are inspired by Jesus Christ. They say, "He was militant, he drove the money changers out of the Temple. He instructed his disciples to carry weapons for self-defense.

13 ABC World News Tonight with Peter Jennings, May 3, 1995.
14 Ibid.

He has instructed us through all his teachings to resist evil."[15] The evil they see is within the U. S. Government which they believe is abandoning its Christian origins to become part of a one world government. One that will persecute Christians and usher in an evil leader called the anti-Christ—or the beast. All of this, they say, is predicted in the Bible.

Bo Gritz, considered a hero by the militia movement, quotes liberally from the Bible. On the ABC News program, he said: "In Revelation 13, it tells all about what is going to happen, I believe, in our generation. And it says that the beast will have power over all kindreds, tongues, and nations. Does that sound like a global government?" The apocalyptic vision Gritz and others preach was fueled by the siege of the Branch Davidian compound two years ago. Many militia members identify with the Davidians, who they say died at the hands of the government for simply exercising their right to follow their faith, and to bear arms. [16]

Ralph Turner said the government actions at the Branch Davidian compound strengthened his resolve and that of others. Turner said: "In order to protect the God-given rights from totally being taken away by an out-of-control government, I am willing to lay down my life."[17] Turner and his militia placed a memorial at the Waco compound on April 19, 1995, the day of the Oklahoma City bombing, promising to be armed and ready the next time they think federal agents are threatening the rights of American citizens.

Gordan Nelson directs the National Institute for the Study of American Religion in California. He says, "They have used this kind of biblical fundamental Christianity as a basis, a justification, for their political program. Rather than reading Scripture and trying to understand and inter-

---

15 Ibid.

16 Ibid.

17 Ibid.

pret it, they are trying to impose meaning upon Scripture which simply is not there."[18]

Dehumanization of the enemy is traditional among violent sects. And if the opponents are accepted as children of Satan, killing becomes that much easier. The very basis of their faith makes such killing not only legitimate but also mandatory. In the United States there are many shadowy groups lurking—covert militias, survivalists, religious and political cults—with agendas of destruction and a newfound taste for exotic weapons. "You don't hear much about them," says Hugh Stephens of the University of Houston, "but these people are anti-government and fearful. They are running around with arms and training for the millennium."[19]

The mixture of religion and anti-government feeling, often laced with racism, can brew trouble within civilian militias. They often lack a rigid command-and-control structure or well-defined mission. The real problem, of course, is these people may be religious but they do not truly know Jesus Christ as personal Savior. As revealed throughout this book, any religion that does not truly proclaim Jesus Christ as Lord is a false religion. And they are not following His lead. The Bible tells us that many will claim to know Jesus on the day of judgment. However, His reply to the frauds will be "depart from Me into eternal punishment, I do not know you."

TERRORISM IN TOKYO

The people of Japan well know the shock and fear that Americans are experiencing as a result of the bombing in Oklahoma City. Another poison chemical attack was barely averted in the heart of Tokyo on May 5, 1995. Police began looking for clues in yet another suspected terrorist attack.

---

18 Ibid.

19 *Time*, April 3, 1995, p. 41.

Experts said that two flaming bags of chemicals found at a busy train station in the heart of Tokyo could have killed thousands of people.

Two burning bags—one containing sodium cyanide and the other diluted sulfuric acid—were doused in a men's room at a Tokyo station before the fumes could combine to make the deadly hydrocyanic gas. More than a dozen train and subway lines converge at the station, in the bustling Shinjuku district where millions of people go for its department stores, restaurants, and nightclubs.

The incident—the fourth in just over a month since the deadly nerve gas sarin was released on Tokyo's subways—might easily have swelled into a catastrophe, experts said. Japanese media reported that the ingredients found in the restroom, if properly combined could have produced enough hydrocyanic gas to kill as many as 14,000 people.[20]

The Kyodo News Service said that because the ingredients cannot be purchased easily in Japan, the incident was probably more than simply a copycat crime. "This gas isn't as poisonous as sarin, but it is still extremely deadly," said Kanagawa University professor Keiichi Tsuneishi, an expert on poison gases. When inhaled, hydrocyanic gas can kill within seconds![21]

Japan has been on edge since the March 20, 1995, subway gassing, which killed 12 people and sickened another 5,500, and a subsequent wave of violence. Japan's top police official, who was responsible for the investigation into that attack, was shot and nearly killed 10 days later. Hundreds of people have been sent to hospitals after attacks with poison gas in at least three incidents since.[22]

Police have made no arrests in any of the gassings but, starting two days after the March 20th subway attack, they have been raiding facilities of the Aum Shinrikyo religious

---

20 *Sun-Sentinel* (The Associated Press), May 7, 1995, p. 23A.

21 Ibid.

22 Ibid.

cult. They have found tons of chemicals—sodium cyanide, sodium fluoride, isopropyl alcohol, phosphorus trichloride, acetonitrile, sulfuric acid—some benign, but others deadly, and still others that if mixed together might create something deadlier still. Enough to kill 10 million people, guessed one newspaper. Authorities suspect these chemicals were used to produce sarin, the nerve gas used in the attack, as well as the chemicals left in Shinjuku. They are also searching for the cult's leader, Shoko Asahara.[23]

Shoko Asahara is a self-appointed messiah. He established his Aum Shinrikyo (Supreme Truth) religion in 1987. Not much later, he began conferring on himself such titles as "Today's Christ" and "the Savior of This Century." His community branched out rapidly in Japan. Soon it had established some beachheads overseas—including the United States and Germany but most notably Russia. Asahara once preached before a crowd of 15,000 in a Moscow sports stadium.

As his fortune grew, Asahara seems to have grown more reclusive and obsessed with danger. The religion is nominally Buddhist but really a hodgepodge of ascetic disciplines and New Age occultism. It focuses on supposed threats from the United States which he portrayed as a creature of Freemasons and Jews bent on destroying Japan. The conspiracy's weapons: sex and junk food. The guru's sermons predicted the end of the world sometime between 1997 and 2000, and began citing the specific peril of poison-gas attacks.[24]

The price of fanaticism is very high. Now that extremists are willing to use homemade weapons of mass destruction, they have crossed a threshold that experts have feared for two decades. The poison-gas attacks in Tokyo show how easily terrorists can strike.

For the rest of the world, the deadly Tokyo attack was

---

23 *Time*, April 3, 1995, p. 27.

24 *Time*, April 3, 1995, p. 31.

yet another shocking reminder of just how vulnerable most societies are to terrorism. The weapon was not an exotic nuclear device but a relatively unsophisticated mixture of chemical agents, most of them readily available. And the alleged perpetrator was not a distant hostile government closely watched by intelligence agencies but a shadowy, global and unpredictable religious band—much like David Koresh's Branch Davidians. The Tokyo subway poisoning should be viewed as a "wake-up call" for governments around the world.

Are doomsday cults only the beginning? Imagine the devastation in Waco if David Koresh had stockpiled a nerve agent like sarin. Suppose the Swiss Order of the Solar Temple had used anthrax instead of bullets to commit mass suicide last fall. Unthinkable? Some cult experts believe such scenarios are a terrifying possibility. "This is only the beginning as the year 2000 approaches," says Hal Mansfield, a Colorado expert on alternative religions. "We are in for a helluva ride with these millennial groups. Whatever technology is out there, they are going to use it."[25]

The number of terrorist groups driven by religious rather than political zealotry is on the rise. Virtually unknown before the 1970's, such groups now number over a dozen—from Christian white supremacists and messianic Jews to Islamic fundamentalists and radical Sikhs— says Bruce Hoffman, director of the Centre for the Study of Terrorism and Political Violence at the University of St. Andrews. Religious zealots, he adds are not out to score political blows but to wipe out entire classes of enemies.

Millennial cults may be particularly prone to violence because of their belief that a catastrophic war or natural disaster will land them in paradise. "Every cult has this sense of urgency," says Marcia Rudin of the International Cult Education Program in New York. "But when you add

---

25 *Newsweek*, April 3, 1995, p. 40.

in millennialism, it really increases the danger that something drastic can happen."[26]

Some groups have already flirted with the use of chemical and biological weapons. "Religion provides justification and context," says Hoffman. "If God's telling you to do it, anything goes."[27]

The United States has been especially fertile ground for millennial ideas—and mad prophets like Charles Manson and Jim Jones. American cult experts see parallels between David Koresh and Aum Shinrikyo leader Shoko Asahara, who has about 100 followers in New York. Both leaders shared an authoritarian style and a tendency to isolate disciples and subject them to ever-greater tests of their devotion and endurance. "It's a very effective tool for manipulating minds," says Rick Ross, who works as a "deprogrammer" for parents who lose children to cults. "Both Koresh and Asahara began creating the dark environment that they foretold; they fulfilled their own prophecies."[28] They will not be the last prophets to see doom approaching—or to take others with them.

Even though the country is riddled with cults and so-called religions, many Japanese asked themselves what had happened in their society that could cause thousands of people to follow a 40-year-old man who believes he can fly and predicts Armageddon in 1997. They also wonder, in the wake of the Kobe earthquake and a stubborn economic recession, whether the comfortable lives they had been leading were now threatened by forces beyond their control.[29]

The Kobe, Japan, earthquake occurred at 5:46 on the morning of January 17, 1995. This horrifying killer quake registered 7.2 on the seismic scale and lasted 20 seconds—20 seconds of pure terror. This devastating quake left over

---

26 Ibid.

27 Ibid.

28 Ibid.

29 U.S. News & World Report, April 3, 1995, p. 35.

5,000 dead and over 26,000 injured. More than 52,000 buildings were destroyed or badly damaged from the force that equaled 240 kilotons of TNT. Yes, it took only 20 seconds to shatter Kobe and the myth that Japan was ready for natural disaster. Repairing the vast damage will take years.[30]

Could it be that God is sending Japan and the rest of the world a message? In the opinion of this writer, the answer is YES! The three main events discussed in this chapter all occurred within a three-month time frame. From January 17, 1995, to April 19, 1995, we experienced the Kobe earthquake, the poison-gas attack in Tokyo, and the Oklahoma City bombing.

Look at the worldwide devastating events of recent years: frequent earthquakes, massive flooding, killer hurricanes, increasing acts of terrorism. The news media seems to be constantly reporting a major catastrophic event somewhere in the world. **God will not tolerate the blatantly sinful acts that are occurring within our world culture forever.** It is time for all peoples to carefully examine the book of Revelation. If the world continues to ignore God and His prophecies described in the Bible, the devastation will only get worse.

To those who know Jesus Christ as their personal Savior, there is no need for fear. He will see you through any situation that may arise. Your citizenship is in Heaven. God will collect your passport at the appropriate time.

To those who have rejected Christ, now is the time to reconsider before it is too late. It does not matter how much you suffer while on earth. Hell is a lot worse. And without Christ, hell is where you will spend eternity. The choice is yours. Will it he heaven or will it be hell? Please ask Christ to forgive all your past sins. Acknowledge that He died on the cross and rose again, and that you now want Him to come and live within your heart. It is that simple. If you prayed that prayer sincerely, you now have the assurance of salvation. You are a member of the Body of Christ, part of His eternal Kingdom.

---

30 *Newsweek*, January 30, 1995, p. 24.

GOD'S WISDOM VS. MAN'S INTELLECT
CHAPTER THIRTY–ONE

Christianity is on a collision course with intellect. We see in America today a culture that questions the wisdom of God. The intelligence of man says America no longer needs God, the Bible, or prayer in public schools, and we cannot use the name Jesus, or Christ, or Savior, even if we are permitted to say a prayer in public.

Look at the secular lifestyle of many people in America today and you will see that man considers himself smarter than God. These are intellectual people, some in powerful positions, who subscribe to the New Age philosophy—the One World Order. Many have degrees from prestigious universities. The halls of Congress are filled with these people. President Bill Clinton is a Rhodes Scholar.

As we have seen in earlier chapters, our forefathers drafted a sound Constitution based on Christian principles and the wisdom of God. They prayed, read the Bible, and sought God's wisdom as they created this most important document. However, it was the intelligence of man in 1962 that said we no longer need these Christian principles.

In subsequent years, all traces of God, prayer, Bible, Jesus Christ, The Ten Commandments, or anything that concerned Christianity was methodically eliminated from our public institutions. Eliminating God from our schools has cost America dearly. It has produced a steady rise in immoral behavior throughout our society. The educational mechanism has become fertile ground for Satan and his evil spirits. Many of our teachers today are seasoned secularists. And children are negatively influenced by those teachers.

How has man's intellect affected our school system? It is indeed a sad situation in American today. Students and teachers in schools are prohibited from professing allegiance to their God. They may not pray, they may not bring a Bible even if it is concealed. It is unconstitutional for a board of education to use or refer to the word "God" in any of its official writings. It is unconstitutional for a kindergarten class to ask during a school assembly whose birthday is celebrated at Christmas.

The Supreme Court ruled in 1962 that organized prayer in public schools violated the Constitution

Furthermore, it is unconstitutional for a school graduation ceremony to contain an opening or closing prayer. In the Alaska public schools, students were told that they could not use the word "Christmas" in school because it had the word "Christ" in it. They were told that they could not have the word in their notebooks, and they could not exchange Christmas cards or Christmas presents.

In many places, teachers have taken the spirit of these anti-Christian laws into their own hands and humiliated and punished students who somehow let it be known that they harbor religious sentiments. A kindergarten teacher in Michigan stopped a five-year-old from bowing her head and saying a silent prayer before lunch, telling the child that praying is against the law.

In Selkirk, New York, a third-grade teacher stopped a child from reading the Bible in her free reading time. The child was threatened and, in tears, she was told never to bring the forbidden book to school again. A small boy in Texas was forbidden to read the story of Noah's Ark in school. In California, children singing Christmas songs were told to hum or be silent if the words Lord, or Savior, or King appeared in their songs. The idea that religion might enter the classroom was apparently horrifying to these teachers. What a sad and tragic day for America!

But the tide may be turning for America. The midterm election results have sent a message to the lawmakers in Washington. The message is similar to one spoken by a great American patriarch, "Is life so dear or peace so sweet as to be purchased at the price of chains and slavery?" Patrick Henry asked. "Forbid it, Almighty God . . . Give me liberty or give me death!" This reminds me of my favorite Scripture, "For to me, to live is Christ and to die is gain" (Philippians 1:21).

Many of the newly elected congressmen favor prayer in public schools. That, coupled with those already in office, gives a constitutional amendment some hope. Rep. Newt Gingrich, R–Ga., House Speaker, has called for a hearing and a House vote on an amendment to permit organized school prayer. Clinton's support is not required to amend the Constitution.

President Clinton is not for prayer in public schools, he would prefer a moment of silence. However, he did not say that he would oppose a proposed constitutional amendment allowing school prayer. "Civil liberties groups reacted in horror, and some critics suggested his position was shaped by the Republican landslide in Congress."[1]

The Supreme Court ruled in 1962 that organized prayer in public schools violated the Constitution. Many Catholic, Protestant and Jewish groups have supported the 1962 ruling and subsequent Supreme Court church-state decisions that flowed from it.

Before the 1962 ruling, many schools across the nation featured prayers to start each day. Some recited the distinctly Christian "Lord's Prayer," and others made use of

---

1 The Associated Press, November 18, 1994.

state-written prayers. Would a new amendment undo the rest of the 1962 ruling? There is no definitive answer to that key question. Backers are hesitant to discuss all ramifications. Liberal critics say turning the clock back to before 1962 is what the amendment is all about.

A likely model of what the House will vote on in 1995 is the proposed constitutional amendment introduced in the 1994 Congress by Rep. Ernest J. Istook Jr., R-Okla. It states: "Nothing in this Constitution shall be construed to prohibit individual or group prayer in public schools or other public institutions. No person shall be required by the United States or by any state to participate in prayer. Neither the United States nor any state shall compose the words of any prayer to be said in public schools."[2]

Our federal courts have totally lost touch with the majority of Americans. A federal appeals court ruled recently that school graduation prayers are unconstitutional even if a majority of students vote to pray. A panel of the 9th U. S. Circuit Court of Appeals voted 2–1 to bar the annual religious observance in an Idaho school district. It is this type of arrogant behavior by the courts that has American voters angry. They are now ready to voice their opinions where it counts the most—at the polls. Yes, the voters are saying "it is time to throw the liberal rascals out."

It will be interesting to watch the prayer debates unfold during 1995. The liberal secularists are already speaking out. The government has no business telling children how to pray, Vice President Al Gore said recently, "I oppose any proposal and the president opposes any proposal to have government . . . taking over the responsibility of teaching our children how to worship God. They should get that at home, in churches or synagogues"[3] Of course, as we have seen, Al Gore has a problem identifying God. Al worships

---

2 The Associated Press, November 19, 1994.

3 Ibid.

nature and that is not what the Bible teaches. And, Al Gore is known as a true intellect.

Leaders of the International Network of Lesbian and Gay Officials say their success was especially encouraging. Concerning openly homosexual officeholders, "We have a net gain, despite a conservative streak to the right,"[4] said Seattle City Council member Sherry Harris. When it comes to the GOP, Harris added, "we have to challenge them to do the right thing, to change their party platform. We have lesbian and gay Republicans. We're saying that we won't go away. You'll have to deal with us."[5] And, yes, there are many intellectuals within this organization.

We see in America today a culture that questions the wisdom of God

However, Man's intellect is worthless when compared to God's wisdom. Man is not smarter than God and never will be! Man's intelligence has given us a secular society filled with homosexuality, the AIDS virus, pornography on display, prostitution, abortions-on-demand, a plentiful supply of drugs and a justice system that protects their "rights." And these "rights" produced an alarming rise in crime of all sorts.

In short, man's "shallow" intelligence has resulted in a society permeated with thugs, thieves, whores, pimps, drugs, and child molesters. The Bible says, "have nothing to do with them." Read 2 Timothy 3:1–9 for more details.

What does the Bible say about God's wisdom and man's intellect? It says, "I will destroy the wisdom of the wise; the intelligence of the intelligent I will frustrate. Where is the wise man? Where is the scholar? Where is the philosopher

---

4 *Sun-Sentinel*, November 20, 1994, p. 9A.

5 Ibid.

of this age? Has not God made foolish the wisdom of the world?" (1 Corinthians 1:19–20).

The word Christian is used too loosely by many in our society today. Many claim to be Christians but show no signs of Christ in their lifestyles. We see too many public figures and politicians today that fall into this category. The Bible teaches us to test the spirits and be on the lookout for false teaching and false Christians. Those who claim to be Christians but live a life of sin that is contrary to biblical teachings should be viewed as agents of Satan and his evil spirits. The Christian that is filled with the Holy Spirit will be obvious because he will show a love for Jesus Christ. He will follow the Christian principles as outlined in the Bible.

Today, too many people in America make self the center of attention. As a result, this predominantly secular, humanistic philosophy is becoming more evident throughout our culture and our education system! However, if we are to restore biblical family values in society and reclaim America for Christ Jesus, we must return God to the center of our activities.

Indeed, the war of the spirits will continue. However, the midterm election results may produce an answer to the prayers of many Christians. God may be giving America an opportunity to return to its Christian foundation. The Bible says, "The prayer of a righteous man is powerful and effective" (James 5:16).

CHAPTER THIRTY–TWO
CONCLUDING COMMENT

As this book, *GOOD vs. EVIL: A War of the Spirits,* comes to a close, it is the writer's hope that the reader will better understand the evil spirits that permeate the heavenly realms. These evil spirits must be dealt with on a daily basis and the way in which we handle them will surely have eternal consequences. Satan's plan for our lives is one of destruction. God's plan for our lives is one of peace. The writing is intended to be both informative and inspirational.

This entire volume is devoted to spiritual warfare. The world has experienced spiritual warfare since Adam and Eve sinned in the Garden of Eden. This ongoing war between God (GOOD) and Satan (EVIL) will continue until Jesus returns to earth. Then Satan will be defeated and Jesus will become the ultimate Victor.

Everyone is involved in this spiritual war. Why? We become involved at birth because we are all born into sin. We automatically fall into Satan's kingdom at the age of accountability. There is not one square inch of the universe in which there is peace between Christ and Satan. Not one person can stand back, refusing to become involved. Jesus said: "He that is not with Me is against Me." If you say that you are "not involved," you are in fact involved in Satan's camp. The only way one can move from Satan's kingdom into God's kingdom is by accepting Jesus Christ as personal Savior. This free gift of eternal Salvation is ours for the asking. If you have not already received Christ, please do so NOW! Tomorrow may be too late.

Factual knowledge concerning the heavenly realms, the unseen spirit world, is surely necessary if we are to become effective against Satan and his evil spirits. Only God can provide us with true wisdom and sound knowledge. How do we gain this wisdom and knowledge? By reading the Bible.

WHO CONTROLS THE WORLD TODAY?

There is no need to guess at the matter, for the Bible clearly shows that an intelligent, unseen person has been controlling both men and nations. It says, "the whole world is under the control of the evil one" (1 John 5:19). And the Bible clearly identifies him, saying, "The devil, or Satan, is leading the whole world astray" (Revelation 12:9).

The Bible also says, "The god of this age has blinded the minds of unbelievers, so that they cannot see the light of the gospel of the glory of Christ, Who is the image of God" (2 Corinthians 4:4). Satan is their god of choice. Freedom from Satan occurs when one is filled with the Holy Spirit.

RESIST EVIL SPIRITS

These unseen evil world rulers are determined to mislead all mankind, turning them away from the worship of God. One way evil spirits do this is by promoting the idea of survival after death, even though God's Word clearly shows that the dead are not conscious (read Genesis 2:17; 3:19; Ezekiel 18:4; Psalm 146:3–4; Ecclesiastes 9:5, 10).

Thus, an evil spirit, imitating the voice of one who has died, may talk with one's living relatives or friends, either through a spirit medium or by a "voice" from the invisible realm. The "voice" pretends to be the departed one, yet it is actually a demon!

So if you ever hear such a "voice," do not be deceived. Reject whatever it says, and echo Jesus' words: "Away from me, Satan!" (Read Matthew 4:10; James 4:7). Do not allow curiosity about the spirit realm to cause you to become involved with evil spirits.

Such involvement is call spiritism, and God warns His worshipers against it in all its forms. Those who practice spiritism will be cast into "the fiery lake of burning sulfur." The Bible condemns anyone "who practices divination or sorcery, interprets omens, engages in witchcraft, or casts spells, or who is a medium or spiritist or who consults the dead" (please read Deuteronomy 18:10–12; Galatians 5:19–21; Revelation 21:8).

Since spiritism brings people under the influence of Satan and his demons, we must resist all its practices regardless of how much fun or how exciting they seem to be. These practices include crystal-ball gazing, use of Ouija boards, ESP, palmistry, and astrology. Satan masquerades as a god, however, this does not make him a god. Jesus describes Satan as "a liar, and the father of lies" (John 8:44).

Also, evil spirits capitalize on the sinful bent of humans by promoting literature, movies, and television programs that feature immoral and unnatural sexual behavior. Satan knows that wrong thoughts if not expelled from the mind will cause an indelible impression and lead people to behave immorally—like the demons themselves (read Jude 6; 1 Thessalonians 4:3–8). Avoid such Satanic mediums.

SUGGESTED ACTIONS TO BE TAKEN

The failed promises of the 1960's ideologues must be replaced with the time-tested Christian values that made America free and prosperous. If you think that families do matter, that fidelity does count, and that fighting for one's country is noble, then consider doing the following:

● Live your life in such a way that those around you will see your love for Jesus Christ. This is a powerful testimony.

● Pray for our government leaders. Ask God to open their eyes to the immorality surrounding them. Pray specifically for your locally elected officials.

● Witness to non-Christians when you have an opportunity. Give them God's plan of Salvation. Share Scripture with them such as John 3:3, 16 and John 14:6.

● Get involved with a Bible-believing church. Become involved in local politics. Encourage local Bible-believing Christians to run for political office.

● Teach your children how to pray. They are America's future. Explain America's Christian heritage to them.

● Analyze the material that is being taught in your local schools. You may discover Satanic teaching in the curricula, if so, voice your objections to this type of material.

● Call your congressman and let him know your views on important moral issues on which he will vote.

● Boycott the advertisers who sponsor repulsive programs that promote immoral behavior. Write a letter expressing your action to the Consumer Relations Department of the company which you are boycotting.

● Write to the local radio or TV station manager and voice your displeasure with programs that "legitimize" immoral behavior and unnatural sexual scenes.

● Vote. Vote for those candidates who have demonstrated a love for Jesus Christ. America needs politicians who are willing to defend biblical principles. Your vote is indeed important. Look at the recent midterm elections: some were decided by a mere handful of votes.

CLOSING THOUGHTS

Clearly, we are living in troubled times. We are in a nationwide crisis of character. We are indeed a nation in search of its soul. Many people in America have turned their backs upon God. They are surely in the process of destroying themselves. You see, it is impossible to maintain civilization with 12-year-olds having babies, 15-year-olds killing each other, 17-year-olds dying of AIDS or 18-year-olds getting diplomas they cannot read.

Even some churches make Satan their god today. They have fallen for one of the devil's schemes—giving him a lot more credit and power than he deserves or possesses. In light of all the dangers around us, can we honestly expect significant moral and intellectual renewal? The immediate and absolute answer is YES.

The world is crying out for answers in the face of bewildering and seemingly unsolvable problems. **This writing has repeatedly confirmed that the Bible has genuine answers.** What Moses brought down from Mt. Sinai were not the Ten Suggestions. They are commandments. Are, not were! The sheer brilliance of the Ten Commandments is that they codify in a handful of words acceptable human behavior, not just for then or now, but for all time.

Language evolves. Power shifts from one nation to another. Messages are transmitted with the speed of light. Man erases one frontier after another. And yet we and our behavior and the commandments governing that behavior remain the same.

Every reader of this book is challenged to engage in serious prayer before Almighty God. Ask Him how you can help restore morality in America. Before praying, it is recommended that you read the sixth chapter of Matthew. Pay close attention to verse six.

There is hope because our hope is in Jesus Christ, the Prince of Peace, who holds tomorrow in the palm of His hand. You must seek God's face. Ask Him how you can help reclaim America for Christ. As a Christian, God has given you a special gift—a talent that only you can perform.

The sooner the people of America return to this basic fundamental truth, the brighter our future and destiny will be. The Bible says, "Righteousness exalts a nation, but sin is a disgrace to any people" (Proverbs 14:34) and "Blessed is the nation whose God is the Lord" (Psalm 33:12).

As Bible-believing Christians, we must not passively stand by and watch our nation be destroyed by Satan and his evil spirits. We have the awesome power of the Holy Spirit at our disposal. We can reclaim America for Jesus Christ. Let us get started TODAY!

"Turn to Me and be saved, all you ends of the earth; for I am God, and there is no other" (Isaiah 45:22).

SOURCES OF INFORMATION

Many sources of information were utilized in the preparation of this volume.

Periodicals and Newspapers

Numerous quotes, other than those from the Bible, were used from publications such as:

- Time Magazine
- Newsweek
- U. S. News & World Report
- Business Week
- The Wall Street Journal
- The Sun-Sentinel
- The Miami Herald
- The New York Times
- The Washington Post
- The Chicago Tribune

Influential Individuals

Numerous books and messages by the following Christian leaders were referenced and found to be of immense value in the preparation of this volume:

O. S. Hawkins, First Baptist Church, Dallas, TX

Charles F. Stanley, First Baptist Church, Atlanta, GA

Kay Arthur, Precept Ministries, Chattanooga, TN

Ben Haden, Changed Lives, Chattanooga, TN

Dave Breese, The King is Coming, Colton, CA

John Ankerberg, The John Ankerberg Show, Chattanooga, TN

D. James Kennedy, Coral Ridge Ministries, Ft. Lauderdale, FL

John MacArthur, Grace to You, Sun Valley, CA

BIBLIOGRAPHY

In addition to articles from several periodicals that are cited in the text, the following sources were consulted during the writing of *Good vs. Evil, A War of the Spirits.* Some are cited in the text by title and author's name to indicate a direct reference. These sources are highly recommended to anyone interested in learning more about this ongoing war of the spirits:

Anders, Max E. *30 Days to Understanding the Bible.* (Brentwood, TN: Wolgemuth & Hyatt, Publishers, Inc., 1988).

Ankerberg, John, John Weldon, and Eric Holmberg. *Rock Music's Powerful Messages.* (Chattanooga, TN: Ankerberg Theological Research Institute, 1991).

Ankerberg, John, and John Weldon. *The Facts on the Occult.* (Eugene, OR: Harvest House, 1991).

Ankerberg, John, K. Craig Branch, and John Weldon. *A Parent's Handbook.* (Chattanooga, TN: Ankerberg Theological Research Institute, 1992).

Antonio, Gene. *The AIDS Cover-Up.* (San Francisco, CA: Ignatius Press, 1987).

Arthur, Kay. *Lord, Is It Warfare? Teach Me to Stand.* (Portland, OR: Multnomah, 1991).

Backus, William D. *The Hidden Rift With God.* (Minneapolis, MN: Bethany House Publishers, 1989).

Backus, William, and Marie Chapian. *Telling Yourself The Truth.* (Minneapolis, MN: Bethany House Publishers, 1980).

Barton, David. *The Myth Of Separation.* (Aledo, TX: WallBuilder Press, 1992).

Cohen, Gary D., and Salam Kirban. *Revelation Visualized.* (Chattanooga, TN: A M G Publishers, 1990).

271

Graham, Billy. *How to Be Born Again.* (Dallas, TX: Word, 1989).

Graham, Billy. *Peace With God.* (Dallas, TX: Word, 1984).

Graham, Billy. *The Holy Spirit.* (Dallas, TX: Word, 1988).

Ham, Kenneth. *The Lie: Evolution.* (El Cajon, CA: Master Books, 1987).

Hawkins, O. S. *Unmasked!...Recognizing and Dealing with Impostors in the Church.* (Chicago, IL: Moody Press, 1989).

Hawkins, O. S. *Jonah: Meeting the God of the Second Chance.* (Neptune, NJ: Loizeaux Brothers, 1990).

Hawkins, O. S. *Revive Us Again.* (Nashville, TN: Broadman Press, 1990).

Hawkins, O. S. *Getting Down to Brass Tachs.* (Neptune, NJ: Loizeaux Press, 1993).

Hawkins, O. S. *Drawing the Net.* (Nashville, TN: Broadman Press, 1993).

Hunt, Dave. *Global Peace and the Rise of Antichrist.* (Eugene, OR: Harvest House Publishers, 1990).

James, Edgar C. *Armageddon and the New World Order.* (Chicago, IL: Moody Press, 1991).

Jeremiah, David. *Escape the Coming Night.* (Dallas, TX: Word, 1990).

Johnston, Jerry. *It's Killing Our Kids.* (Dallas, TX: Word, 1991).

Johnston, Jerry. *The Edge of Evil: The Rise of Satanism in North America.* (Dallas, TX: Word, 1989).

Kennedy, D. James. *Character & Destiny.* (Grand Rapids, MI: Zondervan, 1994).

Kennedy, D. James. *Why I Believe.* (Dallas, TX: Word, 1980).

LaHaye, Tim. *Revelation–Illustrated and Made Plain.* (Grand Rapids, MI: Lamplighter Books, 1975).

Lindsey, Hal. *There's A New World Coming.* (Eugene, OR: Harvest House Publishers, 1984).

Lucado, Max. *The Applause of Heaven.* (Dallas, TX: Word, 1990).

Lucado, Max. *Six Hours One Friday.* (Portland, OR: Multnomah Books, Questar Publishing, 1989).

Lyons, Arthur. *The Second Coming: Satanism in America.* (New York, NY: Dodd, Mead, 1970).

Lyons, Arthur. *Satan Wants You: The Cult of Devil Worship in America.* (New York, NY: Mysterious Press, 1988).

MacArthur, John. *The Gospel According To Jesus.* (Grand Rapids, MI: Zondervan, 1994).

MacArthur, John. *Our Sufficiency In Christ.* (Dallas, TX: Word, 1991).

MacArthur, John. *The Vanishing Conscience.* (Dallas, TX: Word, 1994).

MacArthur, John F. *Drawing Near.* (Wheaton, IL: Crossway Books, 1993).

Marrs, Texe. *Big Sister is Watching You.* (Austin, TX: Living Truth Publishers, 1993).

McRae, William. *Dynamics of Spiritual Gifts.* (Grand Rapids, MI: Zondervan, 1976).

Morris, Henry M. *Creation and the Second Coming.* (El Cajon, CA: Master Books, 1991).

Packer, J. I. *Keep in Step with the Spirit.* (Old Tappan, NJ: Revell, 1984).

Peretti, Frank. *This Present Darkness.* (Westchester, IL: Crossway Books, 1986).

Peretti, Frank. *Piercing The Darkness.* (Westchester, IL: Crossway Books, 1989).

Perkins, Bill. *Fatal Attractions: Overcoming Our Secret Addictions.* (Eugene, OR: Harvest House, 1991).

Pew, William. *Second Chance.* (Troy, MI: Maranatha Foundation, Inc., 1991).

Robertson, Pat. *The New Millennium.* (Dallas, TX: Word, 1990).

Schultze, Quentin. *Televangelism and American Culture.* (Grand Rapids, MI: Baker Book House, 1991).

Schwarz, Ted, and Duane Empey. *Satanism: Is Your Family Safe?* (Grand Rapids, MI: Zondervan, 1988).

Simpson, Jack B. *Sounding the ALARM: Moral Decay in the U.S.A.* (Fort Lauderdale, FL: Acrovest, 1992).

Sproul, R. C. *The Mystery of the Holy Spirit.* (Wheaton, IL: Tyndale, 1990).

Stanley, Charles. *Eternal Security.* (Nashville, TN: Oliver Nelson, 1990).

Stanley, Charles. *How to Listen to God.* (Nashville, TN: Oliver Nelson, 1985).

Stanley, Charles. *Temptation.* (Nashville, TN: Oliver Nelson, 1988).

Terry, Maury. *The Ultimate Evil: An Investigation into America's Most Dangerous Satanic Cult.* (Garden City, NY: Dolphin/Doubleday, 1987).

Vitz, Paul C. *Psychology as Religion.* (Grand Rapids, MI: William B. Erdmans, 1994).

Walsh, Sheila. *Holding On To Heaven With Hell On Your Back.* (Nashville, TN: Thomas Nelson Publishers, 1990).

Warnke, Rose Hall. *The Great Pretender.* (Lancaster, PA: Starburst Publishers, 1985).

About the Author

Jack B. Simpson is married and the father of four grown children. He and his wife, Winona, live in Fort Lauderdale, FL. His academic background was attained at Western Kentucky University and Indiana University. He is a graduate of Norton School of Medical Technology, Louisville, KY. Jack is currently president of Acrovest Corporation which engages in business consulting and corporate finance.

Jack's various activities and accomplishments can be found in such publications as: *Who's Who in Finance and Business; Community Leaders of America; Personalities of the South; The International Who's Who of Intellectuals; Who's Who in the Midwest;* and, *Who's Who in the World.*

Inspired by his best friend and mentor, Dr. O. S. Hawkins, Jack has utilized his experience as a research scientist to compose this powerful book that exposes and analyzes the spiritual war that is raging within the heavenly realm. Many will find it provocative and controversial, however, it is based on biblical fact. He has referenced an abundance of Scripture which substantiate his views relating to the Satanic activity that has permeated our society today.

As a Christian layman, Simpson says, "Some write from the intellect; I very much write from the heart." His deep concern regarding the moral decay that polarizes America today is obvious throughout the volume. In a time when there is a massive gray of what is right and wrong, Jack gives the reader the only prescription and point of reference that will cure today's moral dilemma—the Bible. Using history, philosophy, ethics, and logic, he explains why the Bible's answers are true and life-transforming in this incredible book. Anyone who longs to see the restoration of our traditional and moral values will find *GOOD vs. EVIL: A War of the Spirits* inspirational and informative.

About the Cover Artist

Christopher Parrish lives in Santa Rosa, California. He majored in Fine Art and Visual Design at the University of Oregon. He paints with air and sable brush, employing these techniques in his cover work for Vision Books as well as in his large scale paintings. His work will soon be on display in galleries in Sonoma County and the Bay Area.